D1360200

Books by Sylvia Engdahl

Enchantress from the Stars

The Far Side of Evil

Journey Between Worlds

The Planet-Girded Suns

This Star Shall Abide

Beyond the Tomorrow Mountains

Universe Ahead: Stories of the Future
COMPILED BY SYLVIA ENGDAHL AND RICK ROBERSON

Anywhere, Anywhen

Anywhere, Anywhen

STORIES OF TOMORROW

edited by Sylvia Engdahl

ATHENEUM · new york 1976

Library of Congress
Cataloging in Publication Data

Main entry under title: Anywhere, anywhen:
stories of tomorrow.
CONTENTS: Pierik, R. The left-handed boy.—
Farley, C. The DILLOPs are coming.—Murphy,
S. R. The Astoria incident. [etc.]
    1. Science fiction, American. [1. Science fic-
tion. 2. Short stories] I. Engdahl, Sylvia Louise.
PZ5.A6   [Fic]   76-5485
ISBN 0-689-30537-0

Published simultaneously in Canada by
McClelland & Stewart, Ltd.
Manufactured in the United States of America by
The Book Press, Brattleboro, Vermont
Designed by Nora Sheehan
First Edition

Contents

THIS IS A BOOK OF STORIES ABOUT the future—or at least, about things that *might* happen in the future. Usually, all such stories are called "science fiction." But that is often a misleading label, not only because some science fiction has nothing about science in it, but because different readers have different ideas of what science fiction is. Even experts in the field of SF do not agree in their definitions of it. It's not surprising that the term has various meanings to people outside that field.

I myself would prefer not to call this book "science fiction." I feel that to do so may give the impression that it is a book meant for a special group of readers with special background, and it is not. On the other hand, an SF label may be useful to people who enjoy fiction about the future and are looking for more. I think that in the end, each reader will have to make his or her own decision about whether or not this is a science fiction anthology.

I hope, however, that no one will assume that the authors who've written stories for the book are abandoning their regular fields of writing to enter another field. Personally, I do not believe that the future is something that should be set apart and mentioned only in literature of one particular type, directed to one specific audience. To me, past, present and future are all parts of an unbroken thread, the thread of human experience. Almost everybody is interested in the future. All of the authors represented here are interested in it, although most of them have not happened to write about it before. When I asked them to contribute to this volume, I did not ask them to adopt the traditions of the SF genre; instead, I asked for stories that readers of their other work would enjoy. In one sense these stories are about future or imaginary worlds, yet in another sense, no story is really about the world in which its action takes place. Authors write not about worlds, but about people. The people in a story are more important than where—or when—they live.

Of course, the ways people live in the future will not be like the ways they live now, and the differences will be greater than the obvious ones like development of interplanetary travel and new inventions. The differences between the ways they live on Earth and the ways they live on other worlds must be greater still. If authors could actually foresee the future, they would see much that would seem strange. Often, science fiction is made to seem as strange as possible for that reason; some readers feel that to show tomorrow's ways as similar to today's is unrealistic. But for many other readers, strangeness serves to separate SF from real life. I believe that stories to be read today should seem "real" today, even when they are about people of tomorrow. Strange accounts of strange, imaginary ways are not pictures of real life, after all. Differences between present and future imagined merely for the sake of strangeness are no closer to tomorrow's reality than similarities that aren't apt to exist.

Furthermore, some similarities *will* exist. Many things will change, but certain things never change. Customs vary from place to place and from era to era, yet human feelings stay the same. The importance of human beings remains the same, even on different worlds, and even, perhaps, among human races different from the human race of planet Earth.

The stories in this book are not meant to be "true" in the sense of being predictions. Portions of what's shown are quite likely to be real someday: travel to and from distant worlds, for instance. The specific events and specific lifestyles are much less probable. It would be surprising if they were to become part of future history—and in fact, in some cases, it would be discouraging, because several authors have written about things they would not want to have happen. These things, and others, will almost certainly never happen just as they're described here. My own story concerns a development I don't think will occur at all.

Nevertheless, I think that this story and the rest do have truth in them. No author can predict what the future is going to bring. Realizing that, we who've contributed to this book have chosen not to speculate too much about the details of what we don't know, and to focus instead on what we do know, what we believe has lasting significance: the unchanging truths about how people feel and what they value. Truth of this kind applies, and will always apply, *anywhere* and *anywhen*.

Sylvia Engdahl

Robert Pierik:

The Left-Handed Boy

I KNEW THAT SOMETHING WAS WRONG when Instructor Andiers contacted me on Visafon for the second time in a week. The first time, he'd called to say that my son had been spending most of his valuable time daydreaming; now, Mr. Andiers was telling me that Nyong had failed to meet the standards of Computscript. Naturally, I was embarrassed, but I had to agree that non-standard writing was inexcusable, and I admitted to myself that every school age child should be capable of learning Computscript correctly, especially a boy on the Fourth Level whose father held the important position of Manager of Interplanetary Finance.

The Left-Handed Boy : 3

My daughter Adanza, who's the delight of her father's days, had learned Computscript by the Second Level. The system of coded writing is simple: letters are all very much alike—so high and so wide and spaced just so. Any schoolboy, I had thought, could master the skill. Then why wasn't my Nyong able to do it? Like any mother, I suppose, I took his part, and perhaps I even became overly protective, for Mr. Andiers seemed to think that I'd made a personal attack upon him.

"Mrs. Thebquoe," he said defensively, "I am considered one of the best teachers at the Academy. There is nothing wrong with my methods." Mr. Andiers began raising his voice and flailing his arms about excitedly like an Artist, so I blanked him out on the Visafon and turned down the decibles. "Your son," the teacher concluded in a haughty tone, "is either unwilling or totally incapable of learning Computscript or anything else!"

"You've gone too far," I said angrily. "Remember that my husband is in a position to have you removed from the Academy. You make it sound as if you think Nyong should be mentally reconditioned."

The teacher backed down and even apologized to me, saying that he hadn't meant to suggest that Nyong needed a Personality Alteration. "And please," he added with a touch of anxiety in his voice, "don't say anything about this to the Manager."

Later that day, when Nyong had been transported home, I looked over his Computscript. As the teacher had led me to expect, my son's writing was quite shoddy; instead of being straight up and down, it slanted—one line to the left, another to the right. And the letter size varied. Some small letters were larger than the large letters were supposed to be; also, the shapes and widths were wrong, and spacing between letters and words changed as many as six times a line. The work appeared more whimsical than methodical.

"Nyong," I said with exasperation, "can't you follow the model you've been shown? Is it so difficult? You should have learned Computscript a long time ago."

He hung his head and didn't say anything for a minute. "I'm sorry, Mother."

"Sorry you can't do it? Or sorry you won't?"

"I—I can't." Tears started down his cheeks. "Something in me wants to do it differently," he sobbed.

"Nyong, you know your mother loves you. But you're behaving just like an Artist!" Even skilled graphologists, I went on to tell him, had difficulty translating the slipshod style of writing before Computscript. Having had my say, I felt content that I'd done my motherly duty, and I fully expected that I'd be seeing a marked improvement in my son's work.

Instructor Andiers called me on the Visafon again the early part of the following week. "Mrs. Thebquoe," he informed me in a voice that showed his chagrin, "Nyong has begun to write with his left hand."

"What? Didn't you try to change—?"

"Of course I tried. Your child," said the teacher with a mixture of anger and frustration, "is being unreasonably stubborn, if not malicious."

"Malicious? Mr. Andiers," I warned, "I told you before—"

"I'm sorry," he said, without sounding as if he had

The Left-Handed Boy : 5

meant it. "But I agree with those ancient Romans who thought that there's something sinister about left-handedness."

"How can you think such a thing about my son? Now I will speak to the Manager about you, Mr. Andiers. You're the one who should have a Personality Alteration!"

"Please," he begged. "Don't tell Mr. Thebquoe. Forgive me. It's just that it has been proven beyond doubt that all of us are ambidextrous and are able to become right-handed."

Since the teacher promised to be more patient with Nyong, I let the matter drop. It was a mother's pride, I suppose, that prevented me from owning up to the fact that he had shown a tendency to use his left hand during the First and Second Levels. I had carefully guarded the secret from my husband, and I saw no reason to upset him with it now. While Phegmor was away at work, I devoted every minute I could spare to helping Nyong overcome his left-handed habit. When praise didn't get the needed results, I used reproof, reminding him that he was his father's only son and that he surely didn't want to disappoint him.

As I was helping him after school one afternoon, his sister barged into the compartment, and as usual tried to interfere. Adanza, I'm afraid, sometimes acts as if she's superior to everyone else; she'd often complained how humiliated it made her feel to have Nyong attending the same Academy.

"I learned to write Computscript by the Second Level," she boasted.

"We know that Adanza," I said coolly. "You don't

have to remind us. Nyong finds Computscript a bit difficult."

"All his studies are too difficult for him," she said cruelly. "Why don't you take him out of the Academy?"

"That'll be enough," I said.

Nyong's lip trembled. "I'm going to b-be a Manager like Father some day."

"Manager?" Adanza laughed mockingly. "You'll be lucky to end up a Helper to a Technician!"

Once my daughter started giving advice, she found it hard to stop. "He needs a Personality Alteration," Adanza said. "If he acted more like everyone else I wouldn't have to be ashamed of him at school."

Nyong seemed to shrink within himself. Tears flooded his eyes, and he looked small and helpless. "B-But I don't want to b-be like the others."

Reason told me that there might be some justification for Adanza's remark, but instinctively I had an aversion to the idea of his personality being changed.

"Get out!" I said angrily to her. "And I don't want you ever to come into your brother's compartment!"

For the next few days I continued to work with Nyong on his Computscript. He began using his right hand like any other normal boy, but he acted moody and depressed; and there was something else. He began to stutter.

The stuttering, I hoped, was merely a temporary condition that Mr. Andiers wouldn't have to know about. So the morning after it began, instead of sending Nyong to school, I thought it might cheer him up to visit his father at work. He had never visited the office before; even the Manager of Interplanetary Fi-

The Left-Handed Boy : 7

nance needs a special pass for his family. Phegmor was pleased by Nyong's enthusiasm when I asked for one.

It had never occurred to me that my son would be interested in interplanetary finance. He pestered the guards to take us on a tour of every vault—those containing computer printouts of credits, those holding precious metals, and those filled with such unusual commodities as antiques, sculptures, and other art works. I was completely worn out by the time we'd seen everything, but Nyong seemed strangely exhilarated. That night he bombarded his father with endless questions.

"Why do you k-keep the sculptures and paintings c-crated, Father?"

"For one thing," said my husband, "they are protected."

"Aren't there t-transparent protective coverings?"

"Yes."

"Then why do you have to c-crate them?"

Phegmor said, "Partly for concealment. You see, they're so valuable someone might try to steal them. Also, the paintings can be readily transported when crated."

"But," Nyong objected, "how can anyone enjoy s-seeing them?"

"We have microfilms and prints of them. Anyway, who in this world but Artists would enjoy such things? They are merely products to be sold or traded on the interplanetary market."

Nyong's face took on a dreamy expression. "I s-saw a painting that was being recrated for shipment to a b-buyer on another planet."

"Oh," said my husband. "How old was it?"

"I don't know," my son said.

"Who was the Artist?"

"I read the name on the p-plate, but I f-forgot."

"Do you remember the number of the painting?" asked Phegmor.

"No, but I can d-describe it," said Nyong excitedly. "It's setting is an old b-barn or stable. A mother and her baby are s-surrounded by people in robes. And there are sheep and oxen s-standing nearby."

"If you could only remember the number."

Nyong seemed puzzled. "Don't you know w-what the paintings look like, Father?"

"What difference does that make?" grumbled Phegmor. "Isn't it enough that I know their value?"

It seemed a good idea to change the subject at the moment, so I mentioned to Phegmor that if he hadn't been so busy we would have gone to lunch with him. He explained that he'd been tied up with some eccentric doctor who wanted to buy a painting for a friend on another planet.

"I can imagine what kind of friends he must have," I said. "Let me guess what he bought. One of those decadent Dutch paintings from the Renaissance period."

"Worse than that. He picked some outlandish work of Garmonteau!"

"If word ever gets out," I commented, "that doctor won't have a patient left."

"That won't happen. He was a sly devil," said my husband. "Didn't let me transport it because it'd be a matter of record. Said he'd arrange for the shipment himself."

"What's his name?" I asked.

"Doctor Markois. I'm told he's one of the best in the city, in spite of his strange friends."

I was wrong in thinking that my son's stuttering would stop, and now there were added problems; his appetite became poor. No matter how appetizing I tried to make his food, he just picked at it. And after school he'd spend hours alone in his living compartment, showing no interest in playing outside with his friends—not that Nyong has many friends from the Academy.

When he started looking pale and thin, I became quite concerned. Nyong, I knew, required the services of a doctor; but I hesitated to call upon Doctor Tragiron from the Academy, not merely because Phegmor and I did not like him but also because Mr. Andiers might have spoken to him about Nyong and suggested a Personality Alteration at the Academy treatment center. Phegmor would be very much upset if word spread that the Manager of Interplanetary Finance had a son who was not happy and normal like other boys. Phegmor had confided to me that he'd stretched the truth a bit about Nyong's record of success at the Academy, and for the real facts to leak out would make my husband a laughingstock.

Nyong, I had to admit to myself, was different from other children, and yet I'd been like him in some ways as a child: I was quiet and kept to myself and certainly did my share of daydreaming. Perhaps, though, I'd been more lighthearted. Nyong was terribly serious. If he went on being so unhappy and misdirected, a PA might be necessary. Still, it would be sad to erase his special nature.

Then I remembered my husband telling me about Doctor Markois. The thought occurred to me that he might be just the one for us. The doctor had asked Phegmor to keep quiet about his purchase of the Garmonteau painting, and now we wanted an efficient medical man who'd keep quiet about our son. I felt that if Markois was as clever as my husband seemed to think, he'd be able to cure Nyong without mental reconditioning. If, though, Nyong were to need a Personality Alteration, Doctor Markois could take care of it without embarrassment to the family.

Doctor Markois, I must say, proved to be an impressive-looking man with dark, piercing eyes and a lion-like mane of hair; he was tall and carried himself with the dignity of a leader, although he dressed casually, almost carelessly. His clothes were somewhat spotted and quite gaudy for a Professional, I thought. Nyong's stuttering, the doctor agreed, was merely a temporary condition; but he was concerned with the weight loss. He prescribed a diet supplement.

It didn't help much. My boy turned very quiet and continued to keep to himself—moping around daydreaming in his compartment. One afternoon when I walked in, I found him staring vacantly at the walls; then, the next day, I caught him tearing up a packet of his father's color-coded computer cards and arranging the pieces into peculiar patterns.

"Are you going to leave that mess on the floor?" I asked.

"What?" He hadn't heard me.

"Pick up that mess."

"M-Must I, Mother?"

"Of course you must," I said irritably. "We can't leave all that paper scattered around your living compartment, can we?"

"If you d-don't mind, I like it there."

"Like it?" Such strange behavior, I must confess, was beginning to alarm me. "Whatever for?" I asked.

"The colors are n-nice."

"Colors?"

Nyong squinted. "My room is all white. It makes it feel c-cold and w-wintry in here all the t-time."

"White is functional," I tried to explain. "It reflects the light."

He squinched up his eyes again. "I w-wish my compartment was a color that's w-warm and s-soft like early autumn."

"Sometimes, Nyong," I said, "you act just like an Artist. Why can't you model yourself after the Technicians or the Managers? Your father sets a fine example for you to follow."

"I know he d-does, Mother. I'll try to b-be more like him." Then he started blinking his eyes rapidly, the way he always does when he's deep in thought.

"What is it?" I asked. "What are you wondering about?"

"Have I ever m-met an Artist?"

"I hope not."

"Who are they, M-Mother?"

"They're impractical dreamers that have to be taken care of like helpless children."

"Why d-do they? Have to be t-taken care of, I mean?"

"Artists have no ability for organization like Managers, no special knowledge like Professionals, and no skills like Technicians."

"B-But aren't p-paintings valuable?"

"Very few Artists make paintings good enough for your father to sell to other planets. So we end up supporting most of them. Artists consider our planet a playground on which they can do what they wish, in spite of the needs of the rest of us."

Nyong didn't ask any more questions but his eyes kept blinking.

Gradually, his appetite increased and the color came back into his cheeks; yet he continued his stuttering. He must have been making an improvement in his school work, though, because I hadn't heard from Mr. Andiers in two weeks. At last, I dared to hope, Nyong had settled down to being like any other normal boy his age. And why shouldn't he? I asked myself. His sister had been a model student from the beginning.

I should have known that things were going too smoothly. When Mr. Andiers got in touch with me again, I was sure that Nyong had started using his left hand once more.

"It's not that," the teacher said curtly. "Now your son has adopted his own style of Computscript."

"Own style? What do you mean?"

"He's putting in odd curves and loops," the teacher muttered. "The machines, of course, are rejecting it."

"Curves and loops?" I said, aghast.

"That's right. Not only is your son's writing rate the slowest at the Academy, his work is the most illegible!"

I had no way of knowing when I requested examples of Nyong's work sent home that Phegmor would

get hold of one of them. He was horrified at the worthless writing with all its individual embellishments.

"Just look at this," Phegmor growled. "All this
scratching and scribbling in the margins."

"It's not scratching and s-scribbling, Father," said
Nyong, hurt at this description. "It's c-called calligraphy. I saw it in an old b-book that the Academy was
d-discarding."

"If it had been discarded, didn't you have sense
enough to leave it alone?" I asked.

"Stay out of this," Phegmor snapped at me.

"Why are you angry at me?" I asked. "What did
I do?"

"It's what you *didn't* do," my husband said accusingly.

"What do you mean?"

"Mr. Andiers from the Academy told me of all the
trouble he's been having with Nyong. You've kept this
from me, haven't you?"

"Yes," I admitted.

"I've put up with Nyong's stuttering and strange behavior, but when he begins to develop the quirks of an
Artist—"

Nyong smiled shyly. "That's right, F-Father. This
writing is decorative art."

"Where's that book?" Phegmor asked.

"In my c-compartment," said Nyong. "Why?"

"It must be destroyed at once!"

"But Father—" Nyong started to cry.

"What if word got back to the office that I had a son
who—?"

"So that's it," I said.

"Nyong, bring the book to me," demanded Phegmor. Our son stormed out unhappily.

"Be patient with him," I pleaded.

"It was my hope," said Phegmor, the anger suddenly gone from him, "that my boy would become a Manager like me some day. Or a Professional at the very least."

"Perhaps he will," I replied without conviction.

Later, I think my husband was trying to make up for the argument when he invited Nyong and me to lunch with him. After eating, the three of us took a walk and, for the first time in a long while, had a chance to talk. But it amused me that Phegmor still carried his compulsion for work with him, for he used the occasion to stop by a recently erected City Treasury building. After he had talked with a head Technician, we went on until Nyong pleaded for us to take time to see a decadent medieval cathedral, which somehow had survived the last Building Renovation. Phegmor grumbled about how much space the old Gothic structure occupied.

Nyong tilted his head toward the lofty cathedral spires. "One . . . three . . . f-five. . . ."

"What are you counting?" I asked.

"Those little c-columns. They multiply as they r-rise. It's like seeing a tree with b-branches."

Phegmor snorted. "It would have been better if a tree *had* been planted."

"Just look at that whole w-wall of colored glass," exclaimed Nyong.

"Most impractical," I pointed out.

Then my son's eyes started blinking rapidly. "It's so

b-beautiful. One part seems to f-flow into the next. And do you know s-something, Mother?"

"What, Nyong?"

"It feels like the cathedral's m-moving or growing."

As we went around the edge of the building, Phegmor said, "You do say the oddest things, son." Then, observing the walls, "Look here, Nyong. Some good examples of Computscript."

Nyong stared at the writing on the walls of the cathedral. Both children and adults, it appeared, had made contributions. "B-But should people be d-doing that?"

"What difference does it make?" asked Phegmor, starting to add a couple of letters of his own. "No one ever pays to visit here any more. And people didn't come when it was free either. Besides—the cathedral's being torn down next week."

My son was difficult to understand. I'd taken him out to be with his father, which I'd thought would surely cheer him up, and now I noticed his eyes filling with tears. It worried me to think of what would become of him. There's no place for such emotion in our rational society.

Nyong's stuttering grew worse and his lack of appetite returned; his face looked as though all blood had drained from it. Although he was willing to go to school—to try to live up to what his father expected of him—I kept him home and made him stay in bed. It didn't take me long to realize that we needed Doctor Markois.

When I led the doctor into my son's compartment,

I was embarrassed to find that Nyong had gotten out of bed and had begun to act irrationally again. Tiny bits of color-coded computer cards lay about the floor.

Doctor Markois observed him for a few minutes without saying anything. Then he asked, "Why did you do that?"

Nyong blinked his eyes rapidly. "I like to see the c-colors."

It made me nervous the way the doctor kept staring at Nyong, as though he were a butterfly to be mounted. "Why didn't you lay out the whole cards?" he asked. "Was it necessary to tear them?"

"I like putting the p-pieces down in different sh-shapes."

I wondered if the doctor was thinking that the scattered pieces of paper reflected the disorder in Nyong's mind. As he examined him, I noticed that Doctor Markois's hands were not as smooth and soft as those of most Professionals.

"When did you and the Manager last take your son out of the city?" he asked.

"When Nyong was four," I answered, "we visited Central Treasury."

The doctor frowned. "No, what I had in mind was a complete change of scene."

"That's quite impossible. You know how hard my husband works. You can't ask him to suddenly abandon his responsibilities, like an Artist."

I thought I detected a faint smile on the doctor's lips. "No, I suppose not. We're all indebted to the Manager for the healthy state of our economy. Nevertheless, if your husband is not available, I suggest you

The Left-Handed Boy : 17

or someone else accompany Nyong out of the city for the sake of his health."

"Doctor Markois, are you worried about my boy's physical or mental condition?"

"Both."

"And you think a change necessary?"

"Yes, unless you'd prefer that Nyong receive the usual treatment called for in cases like his."

"Do you mean a Personality Alteration?"

He nodded.

I tried to swallow my disappointment. This doctor, I had hoped, would surely have seen that although Nyong was an unusual boy with original thoughts and actions, he wasn't abnormal to the point of requiring mental reconditioning. Phegmor, I felt certain, would be concerned, too, but for different reasons from mine. Unless a PA was absolutely necessary, he wouldn't want to risk word getting back to his office about Nyong.

The thought of Doctor Tragiron at the Academy prompted me to say, "Of course, if you find later on that a Personality Alteration is the best thing, I'd like you to go ahead with it."

"Naturally," the doctor said, smiling. "We wouldn't want him to develop the traits of an Artist." At that moment, and I must have been mistaken, I could have sworn that Doctor Markois winked at Nyong.

That week I took my son to the coast, to a remote seaside place that I'd known as a girl. We went outdoors early on our first morning there. It had been years since I'd walked along the beach, and childhood memories stirred within me. It was just turning light, my favorite time. The earth appeared to have taken a moment to pause, jealously holding back the dawn; the ocean seemed to be breathing and sighing, stalling before starting the labor of another day. Appearing from nowhere, sandpipers began their business, scootching along the shore on skinny stilt legs, grubbing for morsels with their long beaks.

Nyong seemed fascinated as he watched a wispy fog spook in from the sea. This was all new to him. He stood motionless on the sand, and I began to wonder if he was enjoying himself. Then suddenly, before I could stop him, he let out a loud cry and, although fully clothed, plunged into the foaming surf and was swallowed up by fog and water.

My first instinct as a mother was to leap in after Nyong, but the awful clap of waves terrified me. Anyway, the offshore fog made it impossible for me to see him. It seemed insane to think that I could rescue Nyong. I'm not much of a swimmer and he had never swum a meter in his life. Find help, that's what I had to do!

Quickly, I surveyed the beach. I could barely make out a lone figure in the distance. My breath came in hot gasps as I ran, sinking and falling in the sand. I tried to push away the thought that it was already too late. Nyong must have tried to kill himself. What else could I think? All evidence pointed to it: his recent erratic behavior, his apparent depression and withdrawal, and his misery at school. Why hadn't I let Doctor Markois perform the PA?

Finally, I reached a shabbily dressed man hunched over something. Viewing him closer, I was dismayed to discover that he was an Artist painting at his easel! I feared that such a social outcast would refuse to help me. Except for us, the beach was deserted. There was no one else to save Nyong.

"Oh, please!" I shouted, trying to conceal the contempt I felt for him. "My son is drowning!"

The Artist immediately turned away from his work. "Where? Show me! Hurry!"

He followed me, shouting encouragement, and we struggled back to the place where Nyong had lunged into the water. To my astonishment he was right there, grinning happily, casually scratching with a stick in the wet sand.

"Nyong, why did you throw yourself into the sea like that?" I demanded, surprised at my anger. "You might have been killed!"

"I'm s-sorry, Mother. I didn't think, I g-guess."

"You guess. That's your trouble," I flared up. "You never think. You just do things from impulse like an Artist!" For a moment I'd forgotten the man and wondered if I'd hurt his feelings.

If the Artist had taken offense, he showed no sign of it. "How did you manage to get ashore?" he asked Nyong.

"I w-walked," replied Nyong, making another stroke with his stick. "The water was only as high as my knees."

Observing Nyong playing in the sand, the man said, "You have quite a talent for art."

I had to keep from laughing because my son had scribbled a few childlike lines that were scarcely distinguishable; perhaps he'd intended to draw a sea bird,

I'm not sure. While the two of them talked, I moved off several meters, for the man's grubby appearance was offensive to me.

I was about to call Nyong away from the dreadful fellow when he asked, "Would you like to see a few of my paintings?"

"C-Could we, Mother?" begged Nyong.

"All right," I agreed reluctantly, and we trudged after the man. He showed us a seascape that was half completed; to the side of the easel, I noted two finished canvases that looked about the same as the one he was working on. But to hear the Artist talk, you'd think he considered each of them a distinct masterpiece!

Rubbing a paint-smeared thumb over his scraggly beard he asked, "Do you think I've captured it?"

"What?" I asked.

"The power of the sea?"

"Oh, yes," I said, humoring him. "The paintings are worth a good deal, I'm sure."

"Would you like to buy one?" he asked, grinning.

"Could we, M-Mother?" Nyong said enthusiastically.

"Certainly not."

"Wouldn't one of them look nice in my c-compartment?"

I shuddered at the thought. I could imagine Pheg-mor's reaction!

Nyong had to be almost dragged away because he'd become completely absorbed in watching the Artist at work. The next day I headed for a different part of the beach, and fortunately we didn't see the man again.

But when the time came for us to return home,

Nyong cried, and I agreed to join him in one last walk along the beach. I even let him persuade me to take off my shoes and loosen my tightly wound plaits; sand squiggled between my toes and an offshore breeze gently lifted my hair. All at once, I had the irresistible urge to run along the sand like a little child, and I realized that I must be feeling the same kind of impulse as Nyong had when he'd plunged into the sea.

We raced to an outcropping of rocks, where we discovered a tidal pool. For several minutes we watched as a sea anemone opened and closed like a flowering plant; then a hermit crab crawled into an abandoned shell where he stayed hidden from us. Nyong picked up a stick and quickly etched something on the sand, but before I could see it he'd wiped it away.

Phegmor and Adanza had hardly missed us. It wasn't long before the routine of our lives went on as before. Nyong's health had been restored, although he still stuttered and spent long hours alone in his compartment. Happily, there were no more complaints from Mr. Andiers, so I felt hopeful that my son had finally settled down to being a serious, well-adjusted student.

Then one morning, Nyong said that he didn't feel well. Doctor Markois came over at once and examined him but found nothing whatsoever wrong with the boy; in fact, the doctor thought Nyong looked better than he'd ever seen him, and it was easy to see why. He had put on weight and his color was good.

"Nyong," Doctor Markois concluded, "is in excellent condition."

"Then why does he say he's ill?" I asked.

The doctor grinned. "What's wrong with any healthy boy who doesn't want to go to school?"

"You mean, he's pretending to be sick?"

"Something like that. Why don't you allow him to stay home a day?" Doctor Markois rumpled Nyong's hair. "Are you still tearing up color-coded cards?"

Smiling shyly, Nyong unrolled a paper and handed it to the doctor. Doctor Markois's eyes widened in surprise or alarm—I don't know which.

"What is it?" I asked. "What did he show you?"

The doctor passed the paper to me. I couldn't believe my eyes. Nyong had drawn a sea anemone in such lifelike detail that it looked as though it would close at the touch of my hand.

"Where did you get the paint?" I asked.

"The m-man on the beach. He gave me a few t-tubes."

That despicable Artist! I tore up the paper at once, for I knew how upset Phegmor would be if he had any idea that his son had wasted his time in such a pursuit.

Because of a two-day Planet Federation holiday, there was no school that weekend and all government offices were supposed to be closed. I thought it would be nice if our family could be together during that time, but Phegmor said that there were far too many official matters that he had to take care of outside regular work hours. Adanza announced that she had to finish a computer assignment for school, although she's already far ahead of her class. Nyong asked if he could go with his father to the office, but I had no intention of giving up my holiday in wandering around inside vaults, and Phegmor, I knew, would be unable to supervise him. So I thought the matter was ended.

Nyong, though, insisted that he could stay in the office near Phegmor. "But son," my husband hedged, "I'll be there the whole day."

"I w-wouldn't mind, Father. I'll l-look at the micro-films and p-prints you told me about."

They returned late that night. I expected that Nyong would be weary after such a long day—which I thought must have become boring to him—but I was wrong. He was so filled with things to say that I thought he'd never stop talking, in spite of his stumbling speech. His comments frightened me. Nyong spoke of works of art that burned brighter than comets, of dimensions not seen in our ordinary worlds.

"Meaningless tricks that Artists play upon canvas," Phegmor scoffed. "It's always been a wonder to me that there are planets willing to pay such outlandish prices for mere nonsense!"

"But some of the p-paintings are so beautiful, Father."

"Beautiful." Phegmor seemd to spit back the word. "If civilizations were left to impractical Artists, our whole efficient system would cease to exist. It's the Technicians and Managers who've made the great contributions."

Nyong looked at him innocently. "Are Artists b-bad?"

"They're social irritants," grumbled Phegmor.

"What does that mean, F-Father?"

"Artists are always dissatisfied. They can't find perfection in their own work, but they expect our civilization to be perfect."

24 : *Anywhere, Anywhen*

"And Artists are different," I added. "They don't fit in."

Nyong blinked. "Why is it b-bad to be different?"

"Can you imagine a society made up of individuals who didn't think alike or act alike? Why, there'd be chaos." Afterward, I wondered to myself if what I'd said to Nyong was really true.

Then Nyong asked, "Isn't an Artist creative?"

"How creative can any individual be?" Phegmor commented. "Not as creative as a group."

The boy seemed puzzled. "A group is more creative?"

Phegmor was amused. "Of course. Why do you suppose our whole interplanetary system is run so efficiently?"

I could tell that it pleased my husband to see that his son was capable of carrying on an intelligent discussion, even though Nyong did speak haltingly. That must have been why Phegmor remained so good-natured, for Nyong had never openly questioned his father's word on anything before.

"What Artist did you like best?" Phegmor asked.

"Garmonteau," answered Nyong without hesitation.

Phegmor laughed mockingly. "Garmonteau's paintings are ugly, but I like the prices I can get for them."

"Do you know his w-work?" my son asked.

"Not personally." Phegmor scowled. "But I understand it's called Cosmic Art."

"W-What's that?"

"Cosmic Art?" sneered Phegmor. "I consider it a ridiculous joke—an insult to the intelligence."

I asked Nyong, "Could you tell what the paintings

were supposed to be?"

"They d-didn't look like anything I'd ever s-seen before."

Now Phegmor roared with laughter. "Cosmic Art doesn't look like anything *anybody* has seen before!"

"Why do you like Garmonteau best?" I asked.

"I c-can't exactly explain. It's mostly a f-feeling. One p-painting made me want to laugh and another made me very s-sad." Even though he hadn't understood them, he claimed that he sometimes knew what the Artist was trying to say. And he liked the colors, one shade right next to another that made him feel either excited or restful.

I'd read an article on the pyschology of Artists, and since Nyong seemed so earnest in his quest for knowledge, I tried to tell him what I remembered. "To a Cosmic Artist, the meaning is in the work itself, in the process of self-expression. He claims it shows his inner nature and spirit."

Phegmor guffawed. "Whatever that is!"

My efforts were rewarded, for my son suddenly broke into a smile. "Thank you, M-Mother. I think I understand better now."

I suppose I should have been more tactful because my husband's pride was hurt by not being able to explain more about Cosmic Art himself. Perhaps he was trying to make up for it later when he brought home some microfilms of Garmonteau's work.

"I may not be as uninformed about this Artist as you think," said Phegmor to Nyong. "Notice the slant of his brush strokes."

"W-What do they show?"

"Garmonteau," Phegmor said triumphantly, "is one of those left-handed Artists!"

If I had thought that Nyong had stayed in his living compartment too much before, I now felt he'd become a regular recluse. What he did in there I don't know. But we allowed his eccentricity, for his progress at the Academy had taken a sudden spurt; in fact, Mr. Andiers's reports were actually becoming complimentary. My daughter showed signs of jealousy, which was unusual because Adanza had been ignoring Nyong since that day I'd forbidden her to enter his compartment.

One evening Phegmor came home in a bad mood because he felt duty bound to attend an art sales display that was featuring, of all things, Garmonteau's work. Garmonteau himself, in fact, was to be present, at the request of the interplanetary buyers.

"I only wish there was a way I could make a brief appearance and then leave," Phegmor sighed.

The idea hit me that if we took our children, there would be a legitimate excuse for leaving early. Adanza didn't care to go, but Nyong, of course, was enthusiastic.

There were dealers from several planets, testifying to the high value placed on Garmonteau's work—in spite of how my husband felt about it. Phegmor's staff was doing a brisk business; within an hour, it appeared as if nearly half the paintings had been sold.

One particular work was attracting an especially large crowd. When we finally got close enough to see the painting, Phegmor and I had to keep from laughing. What an absurd monstrosity!

"It's a landscape," whispered a staff member, out of the hearing of the dealers from other planets.

"No," another staff person disagreed, "it's a sea-scape."

When Garmonteau was asked what he'd intended, he shrugged his shoulders and said, "It's whatever you think it is."

It was obscure, of that I was positive. Garmonteau's use of symbolic meanings in this painting was even more pronounced than in the others; so it was little wonder that the viewers were confused. I overheard one woman say that it appeared as if fish were swimming in a dry desert. Alongside of the fish, as far as I could tell, seemed to be some kind of mythical birds or animals.

We were about to leave when the Artist approached Nyong, the only child present. "What do you think it is, boy?"

"I'm not s-sure," answered my son, his eyes wide with innocence. "Maybe it's a shepherd feeding his f-flock, like in a fable I r-read once."

"But Nyong," I said, "sheep don't eat fish."

My son cast his head down in embarrassment. "I f-forgot. I guess I was w-wrong."

Garmonteau looked at Nyong with interest. "Art has neither right nor wrong. It's created for its own sake."

"No," disagreed Phegmor with an edge to his voice, "it's created to sell like any other negotiable product."

"I beg to contradict you, Manager Thebquoe," said the Artist. "Perhaps on our planet my work has no value except as a commodity, but on some planets I hear my work provides human values."

"How could it?" snorted Phegmor. "It's ugly."

Garmonteau tensed. "No art is good because it has beauty. It has beauty because it is good."

Phegmor laughed mockingly. "It's good when it can bring a good price on the interplanetary market!"

"Come Phegmor," I urged, sensing that there might be heated words in a minute. "Nyong needs to get to bed."

My son continued to make progress at the Academy. Phegmor and I were pleased to discover that he had abilities that we'd never suspected. Then, unexpectedly, Mr. Andiers paid me a visit. I could tell by his manner that something was terribly wrong.

"Your son," he said solemnly, "is scrawling on the margins of his Computscript again."

"Scrawling?"

"Nonsense designs that don't look like anything. Mrs. Thebquoe, your son's wild behavior can't go on." Then the teacher said that he'd already taken the first necessary step in handling the situation: he'd summoned Doctor Tragiron, who had given Nyong extensive tests.

"You did this without consulting me?" I said heatedly.

Mr. Andiers gave me that smug look that infuriates me. "The situation required immediate action."

"What," I asked with mounting concern, "did the doctor decide?"

"He is convinced that the only solution is a Personality Alteration."

The Left-Handed Boy : 29

My mind churned with conflicting thoughts. Should I withdraw Nyong from the Academy? Or should I have Phegmor remove Andiers from the teaching staff? No, it would be best not to stir up a controversy that would only end in hurting our family. Doctor Tragiron had been Phegmor's political enemy for many years. I wondered if the doctor would try to humiliate him by making it known that the Manager of Interplanetary Finance had a boy with a psychological problem.

Although Andiers hadn't come right out and said it, it was obvious that our son would be required to have a Personality Alteration before he'd be allowed to reenter school. What should I say? Years of living with a Manager stood me in good stead. My plan formed as I spoke.

"Well, of course if it's what is best for Nyong, it should be done."

The instructor's jaw went slack. "You're not angry?"

"I'll admit I was when you first suggested it several weeks ago. But I've come to the conclusion that you've been right all along."

"Thank you," purred Mr. Andiers, no doubt feeling completely vindicated.

I went on to say that I'd prefer to have the PA done by a private doctor and asked Mr. Andiers if it would be all right if I kept Nyong out of school till afterward. The teacher, I knew, wanted to avoid any trouble with Phegmor; he didn't give me an argument.

By the time I'd finished talking with Mr. Andiers, I'd completed my plan. If Doctor Markois agreed that a PA was in order, we'd let him perform it instead of the Academy doctor; if Markois didn't think a Personality Alteration was necessary, we'd nevertheless tell the school that it had been done. It was a source of satisfaction to me to realize that either way, Doctor Tragiron would not be able to say that he'd treated Nyong and Mr. Andiers would be satisfied that his recommendation had been complied with.

The Academy, of course, would want proof. But I'd even figured out a way around that. Since purchasing his first Garmonteau painting, Doctor Markois had returned twice to buy other works; and both times, desiring to keep his transactions secret, he had arranged for his own delivery. Phegmor had bent a few corners for the doctor in not requiring regular interplanetary transportation; in addition, he'd allowed Doctor Markois to use a fictitious name to protect his reputation. Therefore, I was sure that Phegmor was now in a position to ask the doctor to return the favor by forging the proper medical documents. My husband had called the doctor a sly devil, but I didn't think he was so clever. If we wanted, we could blackmail him.

There was a slight hitch to my plan. Doctor Markois, I learned, was to be out of the city for the next couple of days. This, though, merely meant that Nyong would miss school a little longer.

During this time, Nyong hardly came out of his compartment; he seemed completely self-absorbed in some occupation—just what, I had no idea. Then one morning when he joined us for breakfast, he didn't seem hungry and he appeared nervous or excited, I couldn't tell which. I was sorry that Doctor Markois had been delayed, for I was beginning to think there might be a real cause for him to see Nyong now.

That night at the evening meal Phegmor said to him, "Your mother tells me you've been keeping to yourself too much."

"I'm s-sorry, Father."

"What have you been doing?"

"It's a s-surprise," said Nyong, with a secret smile.

"If it takes every minute of the day," I remarked, "it must be quite a surprise."

"Do your mother and I get to see it?" asked Phegmor.

"It's not r-ready yet."

Phegmor's curiosity was piqued. "What is it?"

The smile returned. "I told you. It's a s-surprise."

My husband was much more patient than I. "Aren't you even going to give us a hint?" he asked.

Nyong laughed happily. You'd never have known that he needed the help of a Personality Alteration. "It's like s-something you have at w-work."

"I know," said Phegmor. "You've programmed a system of some kind."

"N-No."

"Financial computations?" my husband guessed again.

Nyong was enjoying the game. "N-No."

"Don't guess any more," said my daughter, jealous of the importance being put on Nyong's surprise. "It's probably nothing anyway."

"It is s-so," stuttered Nyong.

"How could it be?" snickered Adanza. "Any boy who has to be taken out of school—"

"That's enough," said Phegmor sternly.

Nyong asked, "May I go to my c-compartment?"

"Eat your dinner first," I said.

I don't know why I hadn't noticed it before: Nyong was holding his fork in his left hand. I suppose I should have mentioned it to him, but he seemed so happy in spite of Adanza's cruel remark that I didn't have the heart to spoil the moment for him. I decided he was excited about the surprise that he was getting ready for us; so though he ate little of the food on his plate, I let him go to his compartment anyway.

Since Doctor Markois still hadn't returned the next day, I kept Nyong out of school again, and he spent the entire time secluded in his compartment. Just before dinner that night, I heard my children arguing. A few minutes later Adanza came pounding in, screaming at the top of her voice.

"Father, you should see what's in Nyong's compartment!"

"Your mother's forbidden you to go in there," Phegmor said sharply. "You disobeyed her, didn't you?"

Adanza set her mouth in a hard line. "But just wait until you see what a dreadful thing he's done. Nyong should be punished."

"You're the one who should be punished," I said.

Phegmor asked, "What did Nyong do?"

I could tell that Adanza was savoring the moment. "Come and I'll show you."

Phegmor and I followed her. Adanza, I felt sure, was merely trying to get attention.

At first Nyong seemed startled to see all of us; then he suddenly smiled. "Have you come to see my s-surprise?"

Adanza pointed her finger and, in a self-satisfied

voice, said: "Look at that!"

Never in my wildest imagination could I have anticipated what Nyong's surprise would be. And yet, logically, if I had pieced together the pattern of his actions, I should have known that something like this would eventually happen. I stared in disbelief at a series of wall paintings rendered in vivid colors, a child's version of a Cosmic Art style, influenced, no doubt, by the work of Garmonteau.

"S-See, Mother," said Nyong proudly. "My compartment's no longer c-cold and w-wintry. Doesn't it feel w-warm and s-soft like early autumn?"

"Oh, Nyong," I said, horrified. "What have you done? Don't you realize what this means?"

Phegmor stood speechless for several minutes, stunned by the mural. "I can't believe it. My own son. An Artist!"

"What are we going to do?" I asked.

"No one must ever know," muttered Phegmor half to himself. "This could ruin my career. Who would believe that I didn't encourage him?"

Tears flooded Nyong's eyes; he seemed hurt and confused. "F-Father, you did encourage m-me. You let me s-see the microfilms. D-Don't you like my surprise?"

"Oh, Nyong!" I cried. "Why did you do it?"

"I couldn't h-help myself, M-Mother. It was like when I p-plunged into the ocean."

Mr. Andiers, I hated to admit, had been right from the start about Nyong. His actions had become so erratic that there was only one thing left to do now: give him a Personality Alteration. I reminded myself that a PA would be the best possible cure for him; it would make Nyong well and happy like other children. It was unreasonable, I know, but I couldn't stop shaking.

Within an hour of his return to the city, Doctor Markois arrived at our home. When we showed him our son's mural, he showed deep concern and said that without proper treatment Nyong's mind would be forever occupied with thoughts of art that would separate him from the life of other people. The doctor pointed out that Nyong had used a silent language, which, when developed later, might reflect the ideas of discontented poets or philosophers who were seldom satisfied with the normal existence that everyone else enjoyed.

Then he examined Nyong's mural for a few minutes without saying a word. Finally, half to himself, the doctor commented, "Notice how your son's use of color suggests space, solidity, and a sensation of light. There's a texture of pure tones that unites the whole surface."

He turned to me and continued, "I assume you do want your son to be happy."

"Oh, yes," I said positively.

"And we certainly don't want him living a life of fantasy either," grumbled Phegmor. "The way he's been acting lately, you'd think he believes there's a world of reality up there in his head."

"Manager Thebquoe, are you and your wife ready to—?"

"Yes, let's get down to business and straighten this boy out."

Phegmor and the doctor worked out the practical considerations for the Personality Alteration. If it was to be kept confidential, they agreed, it couldn't be performed in a treatment center; even Doctor Markois's office was too public a place. In the end, the doctor decided to use his portable equipment and give Nyong the PA in the privacy of his own compartment.

I had not realized that it would take such a long time. Nyong and Doctor Markois were alone in the compartment for over three hours. Would he still be himself, the boy I knew and loved? Or would he become a stranger? Perhaps he'd seem like all the other boys lumped together, ordinary and unknown.

When they finally came out, however, my son seemed so happy that I reproached myself for not having had the treatment done sooner.

"How are you, Nyong?" I asked, anxious to see the results of the PA.

"Fine, Mother," he answered firmly. "I've never felt better in my life."

"Why, he is better, isn't he?" I said, tears coming to my eyes. "And he's stopped stuttering."

The doctor set down his portable equipment. "Yes, I was sure it was merely a temporary condition brought about by psychological suppression."

"Suppression?" said my husband.

The doctor appeared embarrassed. "Did I say suppression? I meant depression."

It was a surprise and a great relief to me that Nyong really did seem happy. At the same time, he seemed not to have lost his own personality, judging from the way his eyes blinked out a rhythm of thoughts. Why, it was almost as if there'd been no PA at all.

"Are you ready to return to the Academy, son?" asked Phegmor.

Nyong cast a quick glance toward the doctor and then turned back to my husband. "Oh, yes. I want to make a record that will please you and Mr. Andiers."

"That's right," said Phegmor, obviously satisfied with the results of the PA. "And you'll try to improve the speed of your Computscript, won't you?"

Nyong squinched his eyes. "I'll become a whiz at it, Father."

"A whiz," said Phegmor approvingly. "That's the kind of cooperative attitude I like to hear. Just like your sister."

No, I reflected. Not like Adanza. He didn't appear to have changed that much.

"I think you'll find," said the doctor, "that Nyong will be most cooperative from now on." He went on to explain that, as a follow-up to the PA, it would be necessary for him to treat Nyong regularly at his office.

Nyong smiled the shy smile I had come to love. The prospect of continuing to see Doctor Markois seemed to please him.

Picking up his medical case, the doctor said cheerfully, as he patted Nyong on the shoulder, "Perhaps before you have a Technician blot out Nyong's mural, it might be well to photograph it—for the medical record, of course."

"Oh, no," I said, laughing. "You might try to sell it to that friend of yours on the other planet!"

As I watched the doctor leave, I decided that it was probably true he was one of the best medical men in the city. But how carelessly he dressed. And you would think that he'd keep himself cleaner, for I noticed colored stains on the fingers of his left hand.

Carol Farley:

The DILOPs Are Coming

IT SEEMS SO QUIET OUT THERE NOW," Nillet Gwarn said. She shifted her position on the swim blanket and stared out at the man-made island rising from the waves of Lake Michigan. "I guess I can't get used to the silence. When I was growing up, the roar of the machines was part of my life here."

Lazily, Larrick turned to look at her. He had sand in his hair, she noticed, for he'd been sunning with half of his long, thin body stretched beyond the edge of the blanket. "You must be thinking of the heavy equipment—it made enough noise to wake up my relatives on the moon. But we finished with the big machinery ages ago."

"Ages!" Nillet shook her head. "You sound like you're ancient! You're not *that* much older than I am."

"I've been working here on the project since you were a little girl." Yawning, Larrick sat up. He winked at her. "I have a few years on you, Child."

Nillet glared at him. Did he still really consider her a child? Being with him was the first joy she'd felt since she'd come home from school. She frowned at the thought that he might have asked her to share an afternoon with him simply because she was his supervisor's daughter. "I'm ready to start college," she reminded him.

"Still," he said, in a teasing voice. "You're not an *official* adult."

Nillet stiffened. "I told you I don't want to talk about that any more! I'm sorry I even mentioned that I haven't had my first educing yet. Don't worry—I'll be a full adult soon." She heard how tight her own voice sounded, and she felt ashamed of her obvious bitterness. She tried to shrug her shoulders carelessly. "At least I will as soon as my parents get around to taking me to the city."

After a long pause, Larrick cleared his throat. "I'm sorry I teased you about that first educing. I can see how much it means to you. Guess I'd forgotten how anxious I was to make my own PC program for the first time."

"I've been home for more than four days now. I've had my permit for nearly a week, but my parents still haven't mentioned a trip to the Educing Center."

"Maybe they're like me. Maybe they've just forgotten how it feels to have that school psychologist's permit without having a chance to use it." Larrick smiled and shook his head. "My own parents were that way, all right. I remember how my father . . ."

Larrick's words faded as Nillet felt a heaviness spring up inside her chest. The talk about first educings reminded her of her disappointment in her homecoming, and now her thoughts were blotting everything else from her mind. All those plans she had made in school—all those dreams—none of them were turning out the way she had imagined. She had expected that her parents would be as pleased as she was that her basic schooling was finished—she had thought that they would match her eagerness for her first educing, for only then would she be considered an official adult. But they hardly seemed to notice that she was home, they hardly seemed to care.

And none of her ideas for her future were any good now, either. She had expected to spend her summer on the preserved beaches of Lake Michigan while work on the island continued. But the project was being completed well ahead of schedule and all the plans were changing. Already many of the workers had left, and Nillet felt that her childhood home was being deserted. No longer were famous engineers and architects working together. Most of them were gone now, scattered to new projects, to new planets. Only her parents and a few other constructionists still remained; but they, too, would soon be leaving.

Nothing will ever be exactly the way it used to be, Nillet thought. Not for me, not for my parents, maybe not for anyone on Earth. She looked at the lake, and in her mind, she was sure that even it was stirring with new movements. The DILOPs are coming, the waves seemed to say. The DILOPs are coming, are coming, are coming.

"Hey, are you listening?" Larrick leaned closer.

"Oh, Larrick!" Nervously Nillet brushed sand from a corner of the blanket. "I guess I was daydreaming."

"You've done a lot of that these past few days."

"How would you know?"

"I've watched you here on the beach."

"I'm surprised you noticed me."

"Sure I noticed! Who wouldn't? You're not the same little girl who went off to school three years ago, you know."

Nillet felt her face flush. She had been so thirsty for attention that Larrick's words were like water in a desert. But before she could enjoy any pleasure, other thoughts drowned all her good feelings. "I wonder whether my parents have noticed," she said, and her throat felt so tight she knew that her voice changed.

But Larrick hadn't heard. She saw him reach for a handful of sand and stare at the yellow grains as they fell between his fingers. "You must be proud of them, Nillet. They've worked on DILOP almost from the beginning."

Frowning, Nillet turned her face away. Larrick was right—she ought to feel pride in the things her parents were accomplishing, and usually she did. But right now she felt only resentment. She'd come home from school for the first time in three years, but it seemed that they were hardly even aware of her arrival.

"I can remember when you didn't say DILOP for

the project or DILOPs for our alien guests," she said, urging the conversation back to Larrick. "I remember when you used the whole official title: the Delegation of Interplanetary Liaison Officers Program."

"I guess I did. It was all so new then, and I wanted to do everything exactly right. I must have been pretty formal. It's just that when I first reported to your parents, I was scared out of my wits. I was just a scared, skinny, shaky engineer."

"So what's changed?" Nillet asked, laughing and looking at him.

"Both of us." Larrick turned, and Nillet knew instantly that he was no longer seeing her as a small girl. Her laughter died as his brown eyes stared into hers. The sound of the waves faded, the swimmers were silenced, the sea gulls were quiet. For a moment the two of them seemed to share a special place of their own. Then everything slowly came back into focus again. Quickly turning away, Nillet pointed at the island.

"Is it beautiful out there?"

"Yes." Larrick's voice sounded strange, but he turned to follow her gaze toward the lake. Tree silhouettes stretched high above the horizon, and the rays of the sun made the water surrounding the island sparkle and glow, as though the waves were alive. There seemed to be perfect mingling of colors—green, yellow, white, all outlined against the blue of the sky.

"It has to be beautiful," Larrick said. "Earth wants its Reception Center for space visitors to be as good as we can make it."

Nillet saw his face radiate the same pride that her

parents had when they talked about the island. "We kept hearing last minute details at school," she said. "It sounded as though every area on Earth was involved."

"Everyone wanted to donate something," Larrick told her. He stood, and Nillet knew that his enthusiasm for his work had already blotted out the awkwardness of the silent moment they had shared. "People wanted to get their contributions here before the DILOPs started coming."

"And they're coming soon," Nillet said, rising beside him. "Sooner than anyone imagined when all of this was started."

Frowning, Larrick looked down at her. "Don't you want them to come?"

"Of course I do! This will give us a real chance for trade and study!" Nillet was startled at the volume of her own words. "Of course I want them to come to Earth," she said, lowering her voice. "Do you think I'm as narrow-minded as all those bigots who claim that only Earthlings should be allowed on this planet?"

"I never thought you were like that, Nillet. Never. It's just that you sounded funny when you said that—"

"Because the DILOPSs are coming sooner than we first thought, I have to change a lot of my plans, Larrick. I thought I'd be able to have more schooling or get my first job here on Earth."

"Well, can't you?"

"Well, yes, of course I can. But it won't be the way I'd always imagined. My family is going to Titan. I've been trying to decide whether I should go with them. My parents have a new job there."

"I didn't know that!" Larrick's thin shoulders sagged. "Most of the constructionists have signed up for new jobs here on Earth. I thought all of us had."

"Mom and Dad only decided this week. I guess that's why I'm so mixed-up right now. So many things are happening so fast that I—"

"Larrick! Are you ready?" Someone was shouting from the top of the hill, where three figures were waving.

"That's Bradlin and the others," Larrick said, touching Nillet's arm. "Listen—can I see you here tomorrow? I guess I have to report in now."

"Maybe." Nillet looked at Larrick's friends. They didn't seem much older than she was herself, yet their futures were firmly settled. She felt a flash of envy because her own—

"I'll see you here, then," Larrick said, moving away. "Unless your parents take you to the city for your first educing."

"They won't," Nillet called, but he was running through the sand, and she knew he hadn't heard her.

But then, who did hear her when she talked about her educing? Larrick laughed about it, and her parents ignored it. Sighing, Nillet lay down and settled herself on her swim blanket.

The heat of the sun on her back felt good. The beach, at least, seemed to welcome her in the ways she had imagined. There was still the same hazy mixture of senses that she knew from her early years: the warmth of the sun, the shrieks of the sea gulls and swimmers, the aroma of sun lube and snack foam, and the slight taste of sand and fish in the air. Why can't

The DILOPs Are Coming : 47

everything be the way I dreamed it would be, Nillet thought. Why do the DILOPs have to start coming so soon?

Fiercely, she shook her head, as though this movement could shake away her thoughts. Her long hair fell across her warm face. She pushed it back, and put her forehead against her arm. With her face buried against the blanket, she would not see the island far out in the water. Maybe in that position she could concentrate on something else. Or perhaps she could recapture the past, she could sink again into a lethargic trance like those of long ago, when the beach and the lake had worked together to make her unaware of everything except the sensuous consciousness of the moment.

"Hey Nillet! Watch out!"

She looked up just in time to duck a purple ovid. It bounced once, then rolled to a stop.

"Did it hit you?" her brother shouted, chasing after it.

Angrily she bolted upright. "See what you've done? You've kicked sand in my hair! Can't you watch what you're doing, Neylor?"

He had skidded to a stop directly beside her. "Sorry, Nillet." Slowly he back away from her. "I didn't mean to hit you."

"Well, try to be more careful." She leaned forward to brush away the sand. "Why don't you go play somewhere else? You don't have to play around me every day. I know Larrick wondered why you stuck so close to us all afternoon."

Neylor's round face dropped. "I thought you'd do something with me. Last summer when you couldn't be home, I used to think that this summer we'd have lots of fun together. Like we did when I was little."

"Last summer nobody knew that this summer would be so short. I'm busy now."

"You're not either. You're just lying there."

"I'm *thinking*."

"Oh." Neylor kicked at the sand, careful that none of it scattered near her blanket. As he stared at the ground, Nillet marveled at the length of his long, dark eyelashes. He had always been a beautiful child, a placid and undemanding baby. Although he was hardly the same chubby brother she remembered from the past, he obviously thought of her as the same loving sister. Even days after her homecoming, he still looked at her with the same mixture of joy and awe. Today, though, he seemed more solemn, more serious.

Nillet felt a sudden stab at the realization that she had hurt him. She was ignoring him almost in the same way that her parents . . . Impulsively, she leaned forward. "Want to sit here with me for a while?"

"Sure! Sure I do, Nillet." Eagerly Neylor sat down on a corner of the swim blanket. "I won't shade you."

"Aha!" Nillet laughed so loudly that she startled a sea gull. As she watched it fly away, she felt mild surprise herself. How long had it been since she had laughed so freely? Her worries about her first educing —her concerns about her future—her unhappiness with her parents—these were bonds that had held laughter and joy tight inside her. "I guess you have pretty clear memories of me all right," she said. "I remember telling you not to shade me lots of times when I was out here sunning."

Smiling, Neylor traced a circle in the sand. "I have lots of good memories about you. I remember everything."

"Oh, I doubt that," Nillet told him. "Your memory can't be that good. But you watch Mom and Dad's PC programs all the time. Maybe you get feelings and memories of me from them."

"Oh no, I don't. Mom and Dad educe programs on their perceptions of places for me. Or space machines or Earth's products. Or they buy some expert's eductions. There's no feelings about you in stuff like that."

Nillet looked out at the water. "I guess you're right. You couldn't get many memories of me from the PC." She narrowed her eyes, and she felt her throat tighten as she continued. "Besides, maybe Mom and Dad don't have many strong feelings about me any more, anyway. They hardly even know I'm home. They're too busy thinking about the DILOPs."

"That's crazy!" Neylor leaned closer, spilling sand on the blanket as he moved. "What's the matter with you, Nillet? We were so glad that you were coming home! But now that you're here, it isn't any good. You hardly say anything to anybody, and when you do talk, you sound mad. Mom and Dad have lots of feelings for you!"

"They sure don't show them."

"How can they? You act like you don't even care about us. You won't even go out to the island when they go to work. Children are allowed out there now— most of the things are safe enough for everybody to see."

Nillet clenched her fists. "Why should I go out there

as a *child*? I have my permit now—I could be a full adult if Mom and Dad would go with me for my first educing."

"Well, what's the difference? What's the difference if you go out there as a child or as an adult? You see almost the very same thing. It's still the same island."

"But it's the *idea* of the thing! Can't you see that, Neylor?" Then, as her brother's face grew more puzzled, Nillet slumped. "You can't understand what I'm talking about, can you?"

Frowning, the boy shook his head.

"Maybe it's because you're not old enough yet. Once you get to be my age, and all the basic schooling is done, you want to have the card that states you're an official adult entitled to all adult privileges. And the only way you can get it is to take your school permit to an Educing Center and make a PC program. Then, after the psychologists view your education, you're told to come back another day, or you get a card stating that you're a full adult."

Neylor leaned closer. "Are you worried that you won't get it the first time? Is that why you've been acting so funny?"

Nillet whirled around to stare at him. "Sure I'll get it! Why shouldn't I? I'm not a child any more—I'm mature enough to face my own perceptions. And I want to share them, too. Isn't that what educing is all about? We want to understand ourselves and others better."

She looked back at the blanket. "Besides, I haven't been acting 'funny.' I'm disappointed, that's all. Mom and Dad know that a parent or a teacher has to be at the first educing, and yet neither one of them has even mentioned a trip to the city. I'm sorry now that I didn't do mine at school with a teacher."

Neylor caught his breath. "But we always talked about you coming home for that! So we could go to the city as a family and make it a special day for you!"

"That's what I thought too. But now I see that nobody really cares about me at all."

Neylor forced his face closer, and his puzzlement had turned to anger. "Sure we care! But other things are happening too, and you don't seem to care about what's happening to *us*. The only thing you talk about is yourself! Does the whole world have to stop just because you're home now? You know what, Nillet? You're no fun any more. Those feelings I said I had about you—the good feelings—well, they're all from before you went away to school!" He whirled around, his feet throwing out sand. As he ran off down the beach, he shouted back over his shoulder, "Now I don't even like you! You're conceited and stupid!"

Staring after him, Nillet felt hot and miserable. Her brother's words vibrated around and around in her mind. Was she really as bad as he seemed to think? Slowly she lay down flat again and buried her face in the darkness formed by her arms. It felt good to hide her face in the shadows, and the wet odor of the sand smelled fine. She closed her eyes and breathed deeply, determined to forget the things he had said. But a familiar heaviness was beginning to churn around inside her stomach again. At the end of school, when she had first noticed it, she had thought it would disappear once she was back at home, secure with her family. But it hadn't. Being with her family hadn't made her feel any better at all.

Family—as the word passed through her mind, a picture flashed there too, a picture of the way she used to think of them. There was her mother, slim and serious, interested in and worried about her daughter's welfare. And there was her father, shorter, heavier, flushed with the laughter that always seemed to surround him. Her early memories were all like that— filled with contentment, laughter, and security. She had never doubted her parents' love and concern and her own ability to plan for her future.

But now everyone seemed different. She felt different herself. She didn't feel confidence any more in anyone or anything. She was sure that no one had ever been as confused and worried as she was. Angrily she dug her toes deeper into the sand. Growing up wasn't as grand as she had once imagined it would be.

"Oh, Nillie—doesn't that sun feel good?"

Only her mother still used that silly nickname. Quickly Nillet looked up, but the glare of the sun blinded her for a moment. When her vision cleared, she saw her mother's slender figure stretching out on a swim blanket beside her. Instantly she was conscious of her own awkwardness, her own graceless body. Her mother was perfect—perfect in every way. Her mother had always been perfect.

"I sent Neylor to help your dad with dinner," she said. "I thought we needed some time alone together." She hesitated a second, but when Nillet remained silent, she spoke again. "Don't you think we should talk, Nillie?"

Resentfully Nillet put her head back on her arms.

Her mother was always so sure of herself, so confident. She would never be able to understand the kind of thoughts Nillet had been having. Her mother was never afraid—had never been afraid. "Why should we talk? We've talked about lots of things since I've been home."

"But maybe not the right things. And not for long enough. It's my fault, I know. I've been so busy out on the island that I've hardly had time to think."

Nillet pressed her chin against her wrist. "I hadn't noticed that."

"Oh Nillie!" Her mother's laugh was so unexpected that for an instant Nillet felt her old joy at the happy sound. Then the strange ache flooded her again. "I didn't think I said anything funny."

"No, I suppose you didn't, Nillie. But you're so much like me that I had to laugh."

Nillet caught her breath. She thought of her mother's flawless complexion, her perfect figure, her obvious intelligence. "You think we're alike?"

"I mean that neither one of us is very good at hiding our feelings. Maybe because we both have them so completely." Her face grew more serious, as she added quietly, "That's why your first PC program might not be what you expect." She frowned at Nillet's sudden upright movement. "But you look so surprised! Didn't you think Dad and I had been talking about it?"

"You haven't said anything."

"But we thought you'd know we'd be making plans! We know how much the first educing means. And haven't we always said that we want your day to be special?"

"I just want it to *be*!" Nillet heard her voice quaver, and she frowned at her own weakness. Quickly she swallowed, forcing her tone to be firm again. "All my friends have probably educed by now. Most of them did it at school with teachers. But I wanted to wait to be here with you and Dad because I remembered all that talk about a 'special' day."

Her mother's dark eyes widened. "That wasn't just *talk*, Nillie. We still want it to be special. We want to go into the city as a family, visit the Educing Center, then have dinner out and come back here to have a few friends in. Some of the engineers are still here—they'd love to help us celebrate. I *know* Larrick would like to." She paused, obviously thinking of a new subject. "Did you have a good time with him today?"

"I thought we were talking about my first educing."

"We were. But I—"

"But now you can't be bothered. The DILOPs are coming, and that's all you care about."

"Nillie!"

"Then why haven't I had my first educing?" Even as she spoke the words, Nillet knew how childish they sounded, but still she had to blurt them out. She felt as though she could barely control her own thinking any more.

Her mother sat up straighter. "That's what I wanted to talk about, Nillie. I wanted some time with you alone before you did your first educing. I wanted to prepare you."

"Prepare me?" Nillet frowned. "Haven't I been prepared enough? That's part of our schooling, you know, Mother. I am mentally and legally capable of using an educing machine."

"Of course you are! I know that, but—"

"And my eductions should turn out fine. There's little danger that I may go blind or deaf," Nillet said in a singsong rhythm. "There's little danger of my eduction being one that might cause permanent aberrations. I—"

"Oh for goodness sakes, Nillet, I know the terminology! I've never worried about you in those areas."

"I will not attempt to educe my perceptions on God or Hate or Evil," Nillet continued. "I will limit my topic so that—"

"That's enough, Nillet."

Nillet stopped. She could feel the anger radiating from her mother. But her own anger was throbbing too.

Her mother took a deep breath. "I wasn't referring to any of those things, Nillet. I know you're perfectly capable. But I know how sensitive you are too, and that's what I want to talk to you about. Your eduction may not turn out the way you think it will."

Nillet shrugged. She wrapped her arms around her legs and looked out at the water. "I know that. Lots of beginners get blanks the first few times. I guess you don't want to keep making trips into the city with me. Is that it?"

"I wasn't talking about blank eductions either," her mother said. "We're alike in many ways, Nillet, so I know how you feel about things. I think both of us use our emotions more than our logic. In your educing, you may pick a topic that you think will turn out one way. But the PC picks up hidden perceptions as well as surface ones. I want you to be prepared to face the force of *all* of your feelings. I don't want you to be hurt."

"That's silly, Mother. How can our own perceptions hurt us? The psychologist who views my first coil won't give it to us if it could hurt me."

"I'm not talking about psychological damage, Nillie. I'm talking about something more subtle." Nillet saw her mother's face grow tight with some hidden memory. "Sometimes it can be horrifying to see and feel the strength of our true perceptions. Sometimes we fool ourselves into thinking we view certain topics in an acceptable manner, when really we perceive them in a very different way. I want to spare you the kind of hurt and shock I've had when I viewed some of my own eductions."

"I'd do just fine if I had the chance!" Nillet turned away. "Nothing is turning out right this summer. It isn't just my first educing. It's you and Daddy too—you're both all excited about going off to Titan. But what about me? What about my plans for college?"

"We can work that out, Nillie. There's plenty of time for making plans."

"But you haven't taken the time. I'm not that important to you any more, I guess."

Her mother drew back. "Can you possibly think such a thing?"

"You've hardly talked to me."

"Because we thought you needed time alone. We've both been busy on DILOP, of course, but you came first. You and Neylor always come first, Nillie. We thought you wanted time alone, though, so you could work out some plans in your own mind before we discussed them all together."

"I doubt it!" Nillet tossed her head. "I'll tell you what I think—I think you're so wrapped up in the coming of the DILOPs that you just don't want to be bothered with me."

As her mother's arm reached out, Nillet jerked back. "I don't want to talk any more, Mother. Talking doesn't do any good."

Mrs. Gwarn reached for her sun lube. "Well, then, we'll talk another time," she said. Her voice was crisp and emotionless. "I'll see you at dinner, Nillet. Maybe by then you'll be ready to listen to reason."

As she watched her mother walk away, Nillet wanted to call out, even run after her, the way she had done when she was a child. The figure moving into the distance looked so dejected and forlorn—it lacked the straight, purposeful carriage that her mother usually had. She glanced at her own long legs. For years she had believed that strength and wisdom came with size, but now she, herself, was taller and straighter than her mother. This realization had pleased her at first, but now it almost frightened her. She didn't feel any stronger, any wiser or less dependent. She wasn't a child any more by any means. But she didn't feel like an adult, either. It was awful trembling on the edge between two worlds like this. Awful . . . awful . . . awful.

The beach was empty now. Even the sea gulls had disappeared, and the sun was sinking behind the distant treetops on the island. Squinting her eyes, Nillet studied their silhouette. The trees were from all over the world, her father had explained. Stratifications of temperature kept each area of vegetation at its own native level. Nillet felt a quick yearning to forget her pride and rush out to view the wonders and the marvels of the island as a child, if necessary. Then stubbornly she stifled the impulse. Sighing, she settled herself on her blanket and closed her eyes. Soon the sound of the waves erased her thoughts of the present, for they were stirring with the familiar sounds of the past.

"Did I wake you?"

Nillet opened her eyes. It was nearly dark, and she was still lying on the beach. She saw her father bending over her. He was smiling in that lopsided way he had, and he was carrying a small basket.

"I called, but I wasn't sure you heard me," he said, pulling out a corner of her swim blanket. "You've been here a long time, Nillet. Larrick reported for work hours ago. Aren't you tired of the beach?"

Nillet rubbed her eyes. The nap had been good, she decided. She felt rested and almost happy. Somehow the bitterness she felt against her parents did not so completely include her father. "I couldn't ever be tired of being here, Daddy. Could you?"

"No. No, I guess not. I think I was born with sand in my teeth."

The joke was so much like all the childhood jokes he had shared with her that Nillet laughed with her old freedom. "Oh, Daddy! You didn't have teeth when you were born!" Hungrily, she leaned forward. "What smells so good?"

"Okay, so I didn't have sand in my teeth when I was born. But you'll have it in yours now, if you're not careful. I brought your dinner down here for you."

Nillet stiffened. "Where's Mother?"

"Oh, she and Neylor ate awhile ago." His silently arranged the utensils for her, moving his large hands in a surprisingly graceful way. "Your mother isn't feeling very well."

"Oh." Slowly Nillet reached for the food, but it suddenly seemed dull and unappetizing. "Guess I'm not as hungry as I first thought. I must have eaten too much snack foam today."

"That's not good for you." Her father settled himself with his knees drawn up, the way Nillet herself always sat. He took a deep breath and stared out at the darkening water. "It's hard for parents when their children reach your age, Nillet. For so many years they've said, 'this is good for you—that's not good for you,' and usually they're right, because the choices for children aren't very great. But suddenly the child is almost grown, and then the choices aren't nearly so easy. Sometimes parents can only guess what is good or bad, and sometimes they might be wrong."

"Mom talked to you about what happened," Nillet said.

Her father nodded. His face looked so dejected that she felt quick guilt.

Awkwardly she swallowed. The food tasted dry and stale. "I'm sorry if I hurt her."

"I'm sorry if we've hurt you too, Nillet." He made a movement towards her, then dropped his hand and looked out at the lake again. "Your coming home from school at the same time that we finished here has made it difficult for all of us, I guess. We thought you'd be all excited about the island—about the DILOPs coming—and you thought we'd be all excited about getting your plans in order."

Silently Nillet put the food back into its container. Her father's face was almost hidden in the shadows now, for the sky was growing darker. Already a few stars were visible in the blackness. "I *am* excited about the DILOPs," she said slowly. "But when I think about myself, I . . ." She hesitated, wondering how to put her strange feelings into words without sounding childish or foolish or shallow. "It's just that I—"

"Maybe I already know," her father interrupted. "You feel mixed-up, scared, maybe. I think I understand, because, in some ways, your mother and I feel that same way about your first educing."

"What? Why would you be scared about a thing like that?"

"Oh, not scared, really. I guess I mean apprehensive. It's a feeling I know you can't understand yet, because you haven't been a parent. It's just that once they've educed, children become full adults. Educing is a symbol, of course, but we all know its true meaning. Your mother and I know that your first educing means the beginning of a new life for you—a time when you'll make all your own decisions. And now, because of our assignment to Titan, we may not even be on the same planet with you any more. You may decide to stay right here on Earth. I know a certain young engineer who hopes you decide just that way, in fact." He shook his head and sighed. "So many things coming at once have overwhelmed us, I guess."

He turned to look at her, and Nillet listened so intently that even the sound of the waves faded. "We've always thought of you as a child, a person we could protect, cherish, educate. Even when we visited you at school, we still thought of you as our responsibility. We *liked* thinking of you that way. But once you've had your first educing, our responsibility is officially over." He gestured at the stars, slowly becoming brighter in the sky. "It's hard for us. There's a universe out there for you, and we want you to have the confidence and knowledge to explore it—we tried our best to give you that confidence and knowledge, in fact. But still, now that the time is here for you to be the adult we tried to make you, why, we both feel loss as well as pride. We love you so much we hate to give you up, Nillet."

Nillet caught her breath. During her father's words, she'd been so astonished that she'd forgotten to breathe. Her parents still yearned to keep her a child because they loved her so much? The idea would never have occurred to her! They had always seemed so fulfilled, so complete in each other and in their work. It seemed impossible to think that her mother—

"And we hesitated for another reason too, Nillet," her father was saying. "Your mother tried to explain it to you today."

Nillet felt some of her sudden happiness evaporate. Her father's words had been only her father's thoughts —she was sure of it. Her mother was too independent, too confident, too self-sufficient to care about anyone as much as her father cared. Her mother was so perfect herself that she could never understand confusion in someone else.

"You don't have to say anything more, Daddy," she told him, rising. Her body felt stiff and cold. "I think I already know how Mother feels."

"Maybe you don't." Her father was standing now too. He reached for the basket. "Maybe I'll have to show you."

"Show me?"

"On the PC. Your mother educed a program on you when we went to the city on our last visit."

"On me!" Nillet tried to see her father's expression, but he was stooping for the swim blanket. "But hardly anyone educes a program on a *person*, Daddy. Those eductions are usually blank. Most of our perceptions about people cancel each other out. Our good feelings mingle with our bad feelings, and everything turns out silent and gray."

"The one your mother did on you isn't blank, Nillet. Far from it!" The darkness hid his face, but Nillet knew her father was smiling as he folded everything into his arms. "Would you like to see how your mother perceives you?"

The idea erupted in her mind like a kaleidoscope spinning colors. "Oh yes! I'd like that a lot!" She grabbed her father's arm. "Come on—I'll race you to the house!"

Sitting in the Perceive Booth brought back a flood of early memories for Nillet. Even while the machine remained silent, her mind revolved with pictures of her parents. She remembered the hundreds of times she had come to them with questions. "How are babies born? Why is that a great painting? What was it like when you were my age?" Together her mother and father would share their ideas, and when they went to the city, they would visit an Educing Center and make a PC program for her. Sometimes, when they felt the need, they simply bought an expert's eduction for her, and Nillet would be able to experience someone else's perceptions of the topic she wanted. The PC would give out the sight, the sound, the smell, and the feel of the subject as perceived by the person doing the educing.

Watching her father's intent expression as he sorted through the eduction coils made her remember how often he had struggled to make special programs for her on musical compositions. He would have that same look on his face when he would give her a coil containing his impressions of music. Since he was tone deaf, his eductions were unlike anything she could ever have imagined herself, and she and her mother had shared their secret amusement at his efforts when they viewed them in their Perceive Booth.

Her mother—Nillet recalled that her mother's eductions were always clearer, more precise than her father's. It was strange, too, for in everyday life, her father seemed to show the stronger perceptions. At least he seemed to show more emotion, and Nillet was certain that deep emotion somehow tied in when making a PC program. Even though her mother had never tried to educe emotion, her factual programs had a clarity that was unlike any others Nillet had viewed.

"Here it is." Her father stepped to the second chair.

"We hadn't planned to show this to you—your mother simply wanted to see for herself how her perceptions of you could be transformed into sensory feelings. We didn't plan to use it for education, or anything. But I think you may learn from it all right." Quickly he placed the eduction coil in the proper slot. "Ready?" When Nillet nodded, he turned off the light and started the machine.

Instantly the Booth was echoing with music—beautiful music that combined the sound of waves with the movement of flowers. It was like a springtime breeze flowing across a field of daffodils. It swelled with the force of a waterfall, then ebbed to the beat of a butterfly wing. The music flowed out from every direction, and it had such a surging of hope, of joy, of love, that Nillet felt she should rise from her chair. At the same moment a fragrance unlike anything she had ever experienced drifted through the air. It was the aroma of pine trees and early morning fog and grass cuttings in summer. It was confidence, and a promise of hope for the future. Scenes burst forth now too. The Booth walls vibrated with visions of wild animals running freely through huge forests, mountain peaks rising through the clouds, babies reaching up for planets in a starlit sky. And there was Nillet herself, flashing through the years, growing taller and stronger and always laughing, radiating intelligence and brightness and love.

There was warmth, closeness, comfort, a tangible cushion of protection, and Nillet's senses sang out in recognition of the beauty that surrounded her. She filled her lungs with the wonder of it all. Then, gradually, the sights, the fragrances, the sounds, the feel faded, and she and her father were alone in the silent Perceive Booth.

"Well?" he said, flicking on the lights again.

Nillet shook her head. "It was beautiful," she whispered. "Beautiful."

He nodded. "Your mother loves you very much. Everything you saw, heard, or felt in her perception of you belongs in some way to all the things she loves most in life. In her view, you're a combination of everything good that the world has to offer."

"But I never—"

"You've never heard her say such things? You probably never will. Your mother rarely *tells* how she feels. She expects that you know it." He laughed. "Right now, though, I think she'd like to strangle you, Nillet. You've made life difficult the last few days."

His face reflected so many emotions that Nillet laughed too. "I guess I have! But I sure feel better now. I never dreamed that I could inspire an eduction like that. I thought Mother was ashamed of me."

"Ashamed!"

"Well . . ." Nillet paused, trying to get her jumbled emotions into words. "She's always so sure of herself, and I've been so mixed-up lately. It started the last few weeks of school when I tried to figure out what I'd do if you did go to Titan. And I've been feeling more worried all the time. I thought Mom was disappointed in me because I'm so unsure of everything. I know *I'm* disappointed in me!"

"You're expecting too much of yourself, Nillet."

"Maybe—maybe that's my problem." Once again Nillet felt the overwhelming comfort and love she'd known in the Perceive Booth. Eagerly she leaned closer to her father. "Listen, Dad, I was being silly and stubborn about not going to the island. I'd like to go there tomorrow when you and Mom go to work. Neylor can show me the things he knows about. Do you think Mom is still awake, so we can talk to her about it?"

"I can guarantee you that she's still awake. Let's go see her now!"

Nillet could not recall a time when her mother looked more radiant, her father seemed more proud, or Neylor talked more rapidly. The three of them were trying to pull her in three different directions at once as they pointed out sights on the island late the next day. Neylor started dragging her closer to the beach.

"See this sand? Mom and Dad spent *months* deciding what sand to put here."

"Well, we had to," Mrs. Gwarn said. "Daddy and I had to check through samples from everywhere on Earth."

"And the grass had to be the right color too," Neylor added. "And the trees, and the birds, and the—"

"Everyone wanted to contribute something," Mr. Gwarn put in. "Don't forget—this island represents the whole world."

"I can see that," Nillet said. "I can see it all right, but I still can't believe it. You must have plants from every zone on Earth." As she turned towards an exotic flower, she felt the temperature stratification. "It's incredible! Everything's so—so—"

"So perfect?" suggested her mother. "I guess Earth is trying to be the perfect host." Her eyes sparkled, as she pointed to the west. "All the cabins are over there. Each one is completely outfitted for the individual needs of the delegates. They'll only have to wear Earth suits when they meet in common convention."

"And lots of them will quickly adapt to the island anyway," Mr. Gwarn said. He shook his head and stared at their surroundings as though he, too, were seeing everything for the first time. "It's still like a dream, the answer to a dream. Imagine it! Think what an opportunity this place gives for study and understanding. Aliens can see every portion of Earth represented here, and they'll view everything in comfort. The idea of it all still takes my breath away."

"The *work* took your breath away!" his wife said, laughing. She turned to her daughter. "Oh, Nillie, you'll never know how hard your father worked out here for this! You'll never know."

Nillet gazed around the island. Her father was right —the idea of it was breathtaking. Even though she'd been listening to plans about the project all her life, even though she'd watched from the shore all those years, she still, still could never have imagined a result like this. Every leaf on every tree, every petal on every bush, even the feathers on the birds flying among the branches seemed shiny and new. It seemed like a miracle. Nillet glanced at her parents, and she felt she understood their reasons for pride and joy. But their accomplishments suddenly made her feel even more doubtful about herself. What would her own future bring? Success seemed to spring from certainty and sureness—she wasn't sure of anything any more.

"Nillie—" Her mother stepped closer. "Dad and I

have been talking. We think we can leave here tomorrow for the day. Would you like to do your first educing tomorrow? We can get a few people to come for the evening. Since you didn't see Larrick today, you can invite him for tomorrow night."

As fast as they had formed, Nillet's doubts vanished. "Oh, I'd like that, Mother! I'd like—"

"Are you coming or not?" Neylor was shouting. "I said that I got more stuff down here to show you, Nillet. Children are allowed down here too!"

Laughing, Nillet turned to her parents, then she whirled around and started running down the hill. "I'm coming," she shouted. "But this will be the last day you'll be able to call me a child, Neylor Gwarn!"

At twilight, they paddled back to shore in the manner of the ancients. It seemed fitting to Nillet that the island, which had been prepared especially for the delegates of the universe, still made use of crafts invented thousands and thousands of years before by Earth's first citizens. She liked to imagine the ages of mankind like links on a chain—it was only by the support and efforts of one era that a new era could begin. She looked across at Neylor, lying at one end of the canoe, with his left hand dragging in the water. Her father, paddling, faced her mother at the far end of the craft. They were talking in soft, low tones.

She felt warm and secure in the closeness of her family now, and she wished the feeling would never change. But of course, it *would* change—it had to change. The DILOPs were coming and her parents were leaving, while she—she . . . Her mind grew vague;

The DILOPs Are Coming : **69**

doubts about her future drifted through her thoughts like fog rising over Lake Michigan, and everything seemed gray and uncertain again.

"We must look just like pictures in history books," Neylor said suddenly. He splashed a handful of water. "Did you ever study much about the ancients here, Nillie?"

"Sure. Sure, I did. I guess everybody goes through that stage, Neylor. I used to have Dad and Mom get all kinds of PC programs for me."

Neylor leaned forward, and his round face was beaming. "Mom said you'd be making your first educing tomorrow! See? I told you it would be soon. I was right, wasn't I. What'll you do it on?"

Nillet watched the ripples left behind as she skimmed her fingers over the surface of the water. Its coldness felt pleasant on her hand, for suddenly she felt warm. "I'm not sure yet."

"Not sure!" Neylor shook his head. "How come? I've been planning my first educing ever since I was a baby. I've already got my topic."

"Well, I've planned for mine too, Neylor. I mean, I've thought of lots of ideas. But I've changed my mind a lot too. So I decided to wait until the night before I go to the Educing Center. Then I'll get my topic clear in my mind. I want my eduction to turn out right the first time."

"Oh, mine will turn out all right the first time when I get old enough to try. I'll get my permanent card from the Educing Center without any worry at all."

Nillet smiled at his sureness. "You'd better get a good topic, then. Most of us have mixed perceptions about everything. If you just get a gray color and a monotone sound, you'll have to do it again on another day. And if you try a subject you *really* feel strongly about, the psychologists may decide it might be too damaging to your senses when you view it. Everybody knows about that man who went blind when he viewed his own perception of God before psychologists checked first eductions."

"Oh," Neylor told her quickly. "I'd never try a subject like *that*."

"But you have to get a subject you've thought enough about to activate the sensory probes."

"Oh, I have a good topic all right. It's something I know about and I like a lot. But nothing I have really strong emotions about."

"What's that?"

"Sea gulls."

"Sea gulls!"

"Sure. I've been watching them all my life, and I've learned all there is to know about them. I've heard them and touched them and seen them and even smelled them. So that ought to be good, right? I may have the longest PC program in history because I know so much about my topic."

"You want a long program—is that it?"

"Sure. Isn't that what you want?"

Nillet shook her head. "I want clearness, I guess. At school lots of the kids said that the eductions we had from the teachers were clearer than the ones their parents did, but I thought they weren't nearly as real as the ones Mom and Dad did for me. I want my first eduction to turn out like one of theirs."

"So what will you use for a topic, then?"

"I'll make up my mind tonight," Nillet told him. "I'll have it all clear in my thinking before morning." Lazily she let her hand dangle in the water again, but she no longer felt the coldness. Her mind was filled with ideas for her first educing.

Late that night, Nillet lay on her sleep blanket and stared up into the darkness. Since the night was clear, she had rolled back her sliding roof, and now she felt she was lying high amid the stars. They were shining so close and so bright that she imagined they existed solely for her awe and her wonder. At school some classmates had confessed that they felt insignificant when they contemplated the millions of stars in the universe. But it was always the opposite for Nillet. She felt powerful and grand when she stared up at their splendor. The thought of other beings on other worlds made her feel, somehow, more important herself. There were beings from other worlds on their way to Earth right now, she thought. Nillet searched the sky and tried to find their planets. Then she closed her eyes. She mustn't let her mind settle on thoughts of the DILOPs, she decided. Her first educing would be in the morning—she had to find a topic where her perceptions were realistic, and clear and simple.

Smiling in the darkness, she recalled Neylor and his sea gulls. She, too, had wanted to do her first educing on a living creature at one time. Cats had been her first choice. But that subject was replaced by ancient tombs, and that became a sonnet. The topic ideas changed as Nillet grew older, and now, at the very moment she needed a firm decision, her mind was still wavering.

Did she dare do her first educing on a person? No— there was too much conflict involved there, and the facts were too few. She marveled over her mother's eduction on her. It took strong perception in order to turn emotion into tangible waves the way she had done. She wished that she had asked Larrick what topic he'd used for his first PC program. For a few moments, she let her mind linger on the memory of the time she'd spent with him. But soon she forced her thoughts back to her first educing. She recalled the subjects her schoolmates had used, then she discarded them one by one.

When it was almost dawn, Nillet reached her final decision. She chose the most sensible topic she could imagine: sand. It was boring too, she supposed—or at least it might be to someone else. But she was sure she could do a first educing that would meet any psychologist's standards. The eduction would be clear and concise, without any hidden emotions that might cause damage during a viewing. Most of her life she had enjoyed the sand on the beaches of Lake Michigan. She had studied it, played on it, felt it, and even tasted it. She knew exactly how she would feed the force of her perceptions into the sensory probes. Relaxed and happy, at last she fell asleep.

Her mother was nervous. Nillet had been aware of it on their way to the city, but now she felt her apprehension all the more keenly. It seemed strange, for Nillet was more eager than nervous herself now. Recalling her mother's eduction gave her security and certainty.

Happily she looked around as they walked down the long halls of the Educing Center. It was exactly the same as the pictures she had seen. People hurried back and forth to Educing Booths, and they looked busy and purposeful. Nillet straightened her shoulders, hoping she looked that way too.

Her mother gestured to the right. "This will take us to the Booths for the first educing," she said. She was talking faster than she usually talked, and Nillet saw that her face was flushed. "Don't be afraid now, Nillie. It's just the opposite of what you've done all your life. Instead of opening your mind to another's perceptions, you simply beam out your own. Remember, though, the probes pick up the topic your brain is *most* concerned with when the machines are activated, so you may not educe what you think you're going to. It gets easier all the time, but sometimes this first time—"

"Goodness, Mother!" Nillet shook her head. "I've never heard you chatter so! I know how the PC works. Don't you think I've studied it completely?"

"Oh, I know you have, Nillie." Laughing, her mother slowed her steps. "I'm being silly, I guess. It's just that I keep worrying that I should have talked to you more. Maybe we should have had Daddy come with us too. We could have left Neylor with friends here in the city, since children can't be in the Center."

"No, I only wanted you."

Nillet saw her mother smile in quick pleasure. Then her smooth forehead creased again. "But don't be disappointed if you don't get any reaction at all, Nillie.

That happens at lots of first educings. It takes strong perceptions, conscious or hidden, to make the mechanism function. Some people never get anything but blank PC programs on certain topics." She stopped and reached for Nillet's arm.

"Listen," she said seriously. "I want you to know—this isn't likely—but if the psychologists feel they can't give you the final permit for some reason, Nillie, it really isn't the end of the world. I don't want you to think that—"

"Oh, I'll be all right," Nillet told her. Then she had to smile at herself, because she realized how much she sounded like her brother. "I mean that I have a good subject, Mother."

As they turned another corner, they saw the corridor reserved for people educing for the first time. Young men and women with parents or teachers were mingling with white-coated technicians in front of the Booths. Nillet caught her breath in excitement. At last she would actually sit in a real Educing Booth—not the mock ones they used for practice at school, but an actual Educing Booth with sensory probes aimed directly at her! It seemed only then that she knew the real significance of the day. She rubbed her damp palms against her clothes, and she felt a heaviness loom up inside her chest.

She was sorry the preliminaries went so quickly. As soon as the proper permit was shown and the papers were signed, Nillet was guided to an empty Educing Booth.

A tall technician gestured her mother to a chair and beckoned Nillet inside the Booth. "You know how to operate the probes?"

"I've used practice controls lots of times."

"You wouldn't be here if you hadn't," he told her, smiling now. "The question is just a formality. Go ahead—sit down. Your mother and I will wait in the corridor. When you feel ready, activate the controls. I'll get your eduction coil and present it to the psychologist. You ought to have your final permit within an hour."

Nillet felt doubt grow heavier and stronger.

"Some people don't get them, though."

The technician laughed. "You young people listen to too many horror stories. I've never seen the psychologists completely refuse a permit. I've had a few youngsters repeat a first educing. But no one I've worked with has ever been completely refused." He ducked his head to go out the Booth door. "You'll do fine."

Nillet took several deep breaths as the door closed behind him. She'd been preparing for this moment for years, it seemed, yet now she felt rushed and hurried. She took the blank eduction coil from the desk in front of her and placed it in the proper slot. Then she stared at the four blank walls. Huge machines were concealed behind each one, she knew, programmed to record all her perceptions faster than her mind itself could thoroughly comprehend them. The single lever in front of her would instantly start them all.

She knew she would have to get her subject carefully set in her mind before she activated the machines. It would take only an instant for the probes to record all her perceptions, but it might take many minutes for her to narrow her thinking down to the one topic she had chosen. She would have to concentrate on her impressions of sand by bringing forth her conscious memories.

Closing her eyes, she visually recalled the beauty of the long, yellow, sandy beaches lining the preserved shores of Lake Michigan. Gradually she thought of how the sand felt when she walked on it—she remembered the heat of it in the bright afternoon sun and the coolness of it in the dark of the evening. There was a sound to it, too, a squeaky protest when it was warm, a squishing hush when it was cool. She thought of the smell of it when it was wet, the look of it glittering in the sunlight, the touch of it when the wind blew it slowly along the beach.

Soon all other thoughts had faded from her mind, and her consciousness was focused only on sand. Slowly she reached for the lever to activate the probes, but in the final split second before the mechanism vibrated, she lost control. Her final mental image of the beach had revealed the island in the distance, and her foremost thought as the machines flashed on was of the DILOPs.

"Finished?" Smiling, her mother rose from her chair. The technician stepped into the Booth.

Nillet nodded. "I'm not sure how it will turn out, though." Her stomach was churning. "I'm afraid I lost my topic at the last second."

"I'll take the coil downstairs for review," the technician said. "Wait here, please."

Nillet sank into a chair. She saw that her mother's

smile had faded. "Well, lots of young people get a blank the first time, Nillet. We can come back another day. Don't look so worried about it."

"I'm not worried about having a blank. I think I was concentrating on the DILOPs when I activated the probes."

Now her mother's smile was radiant again. She gestured at the technician hurrying away. "Oh, but that will mean a good eduction, Nillie! You just saw the island yesterday—you perceived with all your senses. You *know* that only good things can come from the program, so you're bound to have educed a worthy coil. You'll have emotions about your subject, of course, but they will be *good* emotions."

Still talking, she sat down in the second chair. "You're lucky, Nillet. I mean, even if you lost your topic, you thought of something good at the last instant. Some youngsters come up with a terrible thought at the end of their concentration, and their eductions are so horrifying that they can't be permitted to view them." She chattered on and on, but Nillet barely heard her.

It seemed to Nillet that hours and hours passed before the technician returned. "I have your eduction for you to take home," he said, smiling. "And here's your final permit."

"See?" Mrs. Gwarn said. "I told you it would be fine."

Nillet's hand was shaking when she reached for her permit. "They said you really picked an emotional subject, though," the technician told her.

"She picked a subject she's very proud of," Nillet

heard her mother say.

The man raised his eyebrows. "I should tell you, Mrs. Gwarn, that viewing this eduction may not be very pleasant. The psychologists only refuse to grant first coils that may be harmful to the viewer. But even though the senses will not be warped by this viewing, they *may* be disturbed."

"Oh, I know that," Mrs. Gwarn said happily. "Viewing emotional subjects can be difficult. But Nillet has asked me to view her first eduction with her. That's why we make PC programs, isn't it? So we can share our true perceptions and understand each other better? My daughter and I have similar feelings about everything. I'll understand her eduction."

"I wonder." The technician glanced at Nillet again; then he shrugged. "Congratulations," he said. "I expect you'll be visiting this Educing Center often now."

"Maybe," Mrs. Gwarn called, as they began walking away. "We have a lot of discussing to do about this girl's future, though." Then she laughed. "I mean, *woman's* future!"

They hurried from the Educing Center, and Nillet marveled at how excited her mother was. Her efficient, crisp manner was gone, and now she seemed to be the happy, eager woman Nillet remembered from her childhood. "I hope this eduction isn't going to disappoint you, Mother," she told her.

"Disappoint me? I couldn't be disappointed! I can hardly wait to see your perceptions of the DILOPs. Come on—let's hurry and get your father and Neylor so we can have that celebration dinner. We'll have time to view your eduction before any guests arrive

The DILOPs Are Coming : 79

too. Isn't this great, Nillie? Don't you feel fine about it all now?"

"I guess so," Nillet answered. Some of her mother's enthusiasm was spilling on to her, yet she still felt an unexplained sense of failure. She kept remembering the puzzled expression on the technician's face. Her honest perception of the DILOPs must not be as grand as her mother expected. Nervously she waved at her father and her brother. She felt eager to see this first eduction, and yet—and yet, she felt a terrible sense of dread about it too.

Hours later, Nillet and her mother were sitting in their home Perceive Booth. "Your father can get the last minute things finished now," Mrs. Gwarn said. Her face was flushed as she put Nillet's education coil into the slot. "I'm so glad that I can view a PC program of yours, Nillie. Of course I've always felt that I understood you—but eductions make understandings grow even more. This is going to be fun!"

Nillet shifted uncomfortably. "But you don't even know what it'll be like."

"Yes, I do. Don't we think alike? I guess we both could be called idealistic dreamers. We see good in things that look all bad to everyone else. Oh, Nillie— I'm glad you educed your perception of the DILOPs, even though you did do it by accident. We both know how important this project is for Earth."

The memory of the technician's face flooded Nillet's thoughts. "But Mother—maybe—"

"Shhh—it's starting!"

Instantly the Booth was plunged into blackness. Nillet heard her own heart begin to beat faster, for it wasn't the comforting blackness of night—it was a deep, clammy darkness that had an ominous, tangible, feeling of pain. A loud roaring noise came rumbling from its center and suddenly great glashes of color flashed like piercing swords across the air. There were slices of purple, brown, blood red-orange jumbles. The roaring became a screaming, shrieking cry that pounded and raced amid the colors. There were horrendous crashes, clanking, crushing, reaching out with dissonant screeches. And permeating the deepest darkness was a pungent odor, a billowing that reeked of sulfur, and it filled the room with overpowering pollution. Then everything faded and the Booth was normal again.

"Oh!" Nillet's head was pounding with the shock of her own perception, and her throat was tight with suffocation. "It was awful!" she cried, "awful!" She looked across at the other chair, and when she saw her mother's face, she staggered to her feet. "I'm sorry, Mother. I'm sorry!"

Now her mother was leaning over her. "Sit down, Nillet. You're nearly fainting, child. It *was* disturbing. I know your senses must be going wild. Take long deep breaths. Close your eyes."

"But don't you see what I've done?" Nillet cried. "I thought about the DILOPs and look how I viewed them! Look how I saw the project in my honest perception! It means all the world to you and Dad— maybe to everyone on Earth. Yet I've been thinking only of me. Now I see myself for what I really am— selfish and worthless. That's what I've suspected about myself for weeks. I'll never do anything worthwhile. Can't you see that now? I'm so wrapped up in myself and my own stupid problems that I can't even appreciate something as grand as the DILOPs. I'm as narrow-minded as those people who don't want them coming to Earth. It's no good, Mother, no good. I'm never going to be a worthwhile adult. Never—never—never—"

"Oh, Nillie—please, please." Nillet felt her mother stroking her hair. "You're not any of those things, child. Not any of those things. You're not selfish or stupid, and you *are* a worthwhile adult. Growing up is hard, though. I'd nearly forgotten how confused I was myself, when I was your age. And you have so much to think about now too. You have good feelings about the DILOPs, I know you do. But because they're coming so much sooner than we first thought, you have to change so many plans. You have—"

Her words abruptly stopped. She stared at Nillet. "But that's it!" she said. "That's the reason!"

Nillet blinked. "What? What's the reason?"

"It's the *changes*, Nillet! You're afraid of the changes the DILOPs are causing for you. That's what caused your eduction to turn out this way. It's not that you dislike any part of the project—it's just that you know, deep inside, that nothing will ever be the same for you personally, and your fears about the future have altered your perceptions of the present."

"I don't think so, Mother." Nillet shook her head. She felt hollow, empty. "I don't think fear could make that much difference."

"But it can! I know it can!" Mrs. Gwarn was silent

for a long moment, as though debating with herself in her own thoughts. Then she straightened. "I know fear of change can temporarily alter every perception. I'll prove it to you." She rose and stepped to the cabinet of eduction coils.

Curiosity replaced some of Nillet's misery. "I've never looked through that drawer," she said. She frowned as she saw her mother pull an eduction coil from a far corner. "That looks ancient!"

"Oh, it's not as old as that! But it's old by your standards, I guess. I made it before you were born." She paused. "Like you today, I was surprised back then when I saw my own perceptions."

Nillet felt instant hope that her mother's eduction had proved to be as disturbing as her own. And then she felt immediate shame for having had such a thought. It was a foolish idea anyway—no one as confident and mature as her mother could have ever educed anything as confusing as she had.

Mrs. Gwarn looked at the coil. "This is a strange eduction, Nillet. I can hardly bear to think of it, let alone view it again."

In the sudden silence, Nillet sensed her mother's hesitancy. "Maybe you shouldn't show it."

"Oh yes—yes, I want you to see it, Nillet. It won't be bad for you. Not as bad as viewing your own was, anyway. It's always harder to face our own perceptions. And I'll stay here with you. I have a good reason." Quickly she placed the coil in the eduction slot.

As Nillet settled back in her chair, the Booth darkened. A gray cloud swirled in, a thick, heavy mist that mushroomed into nebulous whirling. It hung in the air like an opaque fungus, then parts of it separated into long, boney tips pointing to directions that simply faded into empty dampness. And in the dankness and the slimy pall, a long, horrifying moan rang out, hovering in the murky gloom. The moan became louder as the grayness undulated in ever-widening circles, and a moldy odor drifted out from the oozing mass. It was a musty smell, tinged with decay and corruption, and it turned into the sharp stench of fear. The moan became more hollow, more filled with despair, and it vibrated with tones of anguish, lost faith, and unfulfilled quests. Nillet was seized with overpowering sadness, helplessness.

And then the lights flashed back on, and she saw her mother sitting rigid and motionless, her blank face glistening with perspiration. Quickly she rose and stepped to her chair. "Mother! Are you all right?"

Mrs. Gwarn shook her head, and Nillet saw the color gradually come back to her face. "It's just so shocking, Nillet. I can't believe it really was that bad. I'd forgotten how awful it really was!"

Nillet sighed. "Well, I think mine was worse. But maybe it's only because I didn't even know I had those awful perceptions. That's the part that hurts me about my own eduction—I wonder what kind of shallow, stupid person I must be. Because the topic that came to my mind isn't bad at all—only my perceptions of it are. But yours wasn't like that. You must have lost control of your topic at the last instant, and something frightening flashed into your mind."

Her mother looked completely normal again. She leaned forward with her old confidence. "But they were only your *temporary* perceptions, Nillet. That's the point I'm trying to prove to you. Your fear of change clouded your other thoughts about the DILOPs just the way my fear of change clouded the topic in my first educing. For I had a good topic too. And I *didn't* lose control. That eduction came from the very topic that I chose."

"But what was it, Mother? What was your topic?"

"The same one you viewed in here the day before yesterday."

Nillet scowled. "Oh, I don't think so, Mother. The only eduction I've seen since I've been home is the one you did on me."

"Yes."

"You mean this eduction is on me too?" When Nillet saw her mother nod, she caught her breath. "But that can't be! You couldn't have ever had perceptions like that about me!"

"I'm afraid I did, Nillie. Of course it wasn't really you quite yet. I was pregnant, you see, and I wanted to have a record of all the happiness and excitement I felt."

"But it can't be—it just can't be. I mean, I—"

"You wonder how I could have ever perceived an unborn child that way? Believe me, Nillet, I wondered about that myself, when I saw that horrible program. I was sick. I wondered, like you, what kind of shallow, foolish person I could be." She moved closer. "I thought I was thoroughly delighted about having a baby. Your father and I had been married for years, and we both were eager to start a family."

Shaking her head, she leaned back in her chair.

"We discussed it a lot, and gradually I realized what had happened. You see, having a baby meant great adjustments for me—it does for every woman. My subconscious mind was completely aware of the mixed emotions I had, even though I consciously refused to admit them. No human can accept drastic change without some anxiety. And this anxiety shows up in our perceptions on the machine. My apprehension about a future baby was similar to your worry about the DILOPs and your personal future. We had similar results because we're very much alike, I guess."

"And look at your perception of me now!" Nillet cried. Then she felt herself flush. "I guess that sounded kind of vain," she mumbled.

"It sounded just fine to me," her mother said, rising and smiling. "And I'll wager that your eductions on the DILOPs will be just fine someday too."

"Maybe," Nillet said, standing now. A strong, new confidence was surging through her body. She looked at her mother and saw—for the first time—a being much like herself. She, too, had been consumed with doubts about her own capabilities at one time, her own fears of the future. An idea flashed across Nillet's mind, and it etched itself on her brain: all thinking creatures must suffer doubts and fears about change— it must be the price of awareness. "The DILOPs must be worried too," she blurted.

"Of course!" Nillet saw her mother's eyes light up. "And those people you called narrow-minded—the ones who are concerned about the DILOPs coming— they're simply reacting to their fears too. But these fears won't last, Nillie. It's the thinking process that gives us our lasting perceptions, our permanent view of reality."

"And I'm thinking I have a great future ahead!" Nillet said, hurrying to open the Booth door. "Come on—let's go see if the guests are here yet. I've got to tell Larrick he can't call me *child* any more!" Laughing, she turned to take her mother's arm. "Haven't you heard? This is a special day for me!"

Shirley Rousseau Murphy:

The Mooncup

KEB LAY ON HIS BACK IN THE TALL grass listening to the harsh calls of a flock of skeeba birds; their cries dropped down from the cliff above him. He was in the Cut. The bare sand cliffs rose sheer and tall and ten times his height on either side of him. Beside him the river that had carved out the Cut ran like a silver snake, making its way to the sea across the wide, wet delta. He stretched out his hand and trailed it in the cool, fast water. The wind across his face was damp and tasted pleasantly of salt; the grass blew down against his cheek; the wind above on the desert tableland would be dry and harsh.

Only here in the Cut did Keb feel really alive; only here was he able to free himself from the worries at home, and from his stepfather—though even here, not entirely. The restlessness gripped and troubled him so he thought he could never be free of it. He watched the wind hustle a lone zantha tree and sweep the heavy tall grass, tearing at the seeds so they scattered across the delta. Two waterbirds dipped and guzzled in a shallow, and he could hear a thrush call from somewhere back inland where the Cut was tamer, and farmed; the rich silt land of the Cut was the only source of food for the sparse Karrach nation, for miner and slave alike; nothing would grow above on the high desert.

Here at the end of the river, the farms could not be seen; the little huts and crudely plowed fields were left behind, and Keb was surrounded by a vast stretch of wild green—weedy, tumultuous, and satisfying. Here the river separated into seven fingers that thrust between the cliffs to grasp the open surf, the marsh dark green with sodden growth. Keb tried to imagine for the hundredth time how the land would look from the sky, the way the gods would see it as they soared and banked effortlessly on the winds above Ere; Keb had never seen them, but he knew how they must look, light as birds, their wings catching the sunlight.

From the sky one would see Karra and Moramia as a pale, flat expanse of sand bordered on the one side by mountains of the unknown lands, bordered on the other by the Rim. The Rim, the abrupt edge of the high desert shelf, dropped sharply to the more civilized countries of Ere. From the sky one would see the drop like a scar across Ere; and one would see the high desert scarred in the center, slashed through by the Cut carved deep by the river, like a knife wound filled with green. The pale dry desert slashed with the green cut, then stopping abruptly at the Rim; and below, all the lands green and lush.

But strife-driven, too, just now, the civilized countries of Ere. For it was a time of war in the countries below the Rim, a time of blood and killing and of people fleeing their homes to go begging in strange towns like thirsting birds in a drought. It was the fifth such time of war since the beginning of Ereian history. And the men who weathered it and profited from it were the grandsons and the great-great-grandsons of the men who had weathered and profited through all the wars of Ere.

Always it was the Kubalese who attacked the weakest nations, killing and plundering. A few of those who escaped fled east, to Carriol, for protection; but most were driven in the opposite direction, to the desert shelf. And if they climbed to the high desert, they ended too often as slaves in Karra. Trussed and bound together like animals, they were driven to work in the bowels of the earth, mining silver and gold. Many who were sold thus were Cherban, for the nations that flanked Kubal were heavy populated with men of Cherban blood.

Keb's mother was the granddaughter of a Cherban warrior taken in battle and sold to a Karrach miner for gold. Keb's father was a Karrach, gentler than most, who took her from slavery for love of her and made her free; so Keb was half red-headed Cherban and half the dark Karrach that showed in his eyes, black as night under his red thatch. His father had died when he was four, and his mother had married a Karrach slavemaster, Sherrick, a taciturn man. She had little choice: a woman freed from slavery by marriage was still of lower class and had no way to make a living and feed a child save by her charms. Josiam was a beauty then, before the illness wasted her, made her pale and weak.

Keb didn't know what had changed Sherrick in late years from a tolerable stepfather to the beast he had become. Perhaps it was the loss of comeliness and vigor in his wife that goaded him, as if he had been deceived in the bargain of marriage. These last years he had driven Keb mercilessly in the mines— and in something worse. Keb could have gone away, he was old enough to be called a man, for the young grew up early in Karra; but he could not leave his mother to the Karrach's mercy. Too often had Sherrick threatened harm to her if Keb did not use his gift of seeing to spy for him.

The Cherban were known for their seeing: the ability to look into the mind of another. The Gift of Ynell, it was called, and Keb had inherited that strain in the blood, though his mother had none of the talent. On much of Ere the penalty for such gift was death, for it was said to be against the gods. But the men of Karra cared little for the gods and their ways; and seeing, when it was used to steal, was too valuable to taint with foolish covenants. Keb was adept enough at seeing to seek out the best mines of their neighbors and direct his stepfather to the rich veins; and he was skilled enough, when the Kubalese massacres began, to spot wealth among the refugees who fled into Karra with jewels sewn into their clothing and braided in their hair to pay for freedom.

He hated it, hated the killing that ensued, for Sherrick's raiders gave no quarter to the pitiful bands that fled before the Kubalese hoards up the clifflike Rim. The Rim stopped the Kubalese raiding tribes; they would not climb into the desert lands. Those they pursued did, and many died there; the strong, unwounded were captured, tied on a trot-line like a string of ponies, and driven over the parched desert to the mines; the rest were left to struggle on to Moramia if they could, or to die, and it mattered not to the Karrach raiders whether they died from their wounds or from thirst. Keb hated his Karrach stepfather, and he hated himself for the spying he did. But when he tried to refuse, the old man beat him; he took it soundlessly so his mother would not know, for she would have killed herself to free him had she known the depths to which he had been driven.

Only here in the Cut could he be free, could he imagine himself as any better than the real slaves of Karra. Here he could dream of the low countries and of other ways of living; here he could dream of Carriol on the far eastern coast of Ere, Carriol, fabled for its freedom. No man was slave in Carriol; and her rulers had shown long ago that theirs was a fierce response to attack. Carriol would remain free. Here in the Cut Keb could dream of such freedom, and he could dream of the old ruined cities; he could imagine the winged gods, half man, half horse, moving as lightly among those ancient towers as the stilta birds moved on the breezes around his mother's cactus tree.

Keb was not like his stepfather and the men of Karra, for he did not believe that the gods were myth. He dreamed of them and watched the cloud-driven winds for them, and he thought that the great volcanic fires that had once covered Ere had in some way truly been called forth by the gods, as most of Ere believed. Only in Karra did men say that the great flames that had risen into the sky were naught but the bellies of the mountains burning—surely they were mountains burning, but what *made* them? Keb dreamed as the other men of Karra did not.

He lay in the shelter of the grass, slept, and woke ravenous to finish off the dried rabbit and seed bread he had carried with him. Alone he was, always alone—though he felt more alone with his stepfather than here on the delta, for the loneliness in the Cut was a satisfying one.

He turned to stare into the depths of the river and could see the clouds reflected and colors like sapphire and amethyst where dead grass had fallen and washed deep against the rocks; when a dark shape moved there, he thought it a fish and held still. But it passed across the rocks, a shadow with no source. It was no fish; it was a shape reflected from the clouds, was utterly unfamiliar. He rose and stood staring upward, expecting to see the gods, their wings outspread, yet knowing in his inner being that this was no god.

A strange shape he could not understand was there in the clouds. Where had it come from? Only a moment before he had been staring at the sky. There were cloud banks where it might have hidden; he saw it catch the light of the sun in an orange flash, then begin to move downward toward the dunes that lay on the table land high above him. The sky began to brighten as if the light of the sun had increased, though that was impossible. The light flared up, and he stood perplexed and excited as the brightness blazed around the object and slashed across the sea too fast for any natural thing, turning the dunes white.

The thing within the light was like a star but bigger, growing quickly. The light shone into the Cut and touched him; he stood transfixed with it. The silver-white object poised in its own radiance over the desert that lay atop the cliff: light so bright he could hardly look, light that was all around him, and in its vortex the silver *something* glowed and whirled so that his breath caught hot in his chest. This was not a god, this was a thing of metal as smooth and polished as a silver ingot from the smelter. And yet it came from the sky. The feel of wonder that it gave Keb swept him in a shudder of passion as he stood in the delta staring upward.

Slowly it drifted down, so slowly. Even before it came to rest above the cliff, he had begun to climb, heedless of danger, and when he reached the dunes at the top, the silver thing towered above him upon the sand: a silver shaft resting in its own light.

When at last its glow faded, the metal within seemed more solid: as sharp-cut as a diamond he had seen once worn by a king of Moramia. He was not a lad to be easily frightened, dark mines and Sherrick's killing had seen to that; but this silver thing made a fear in him and a yearning terror of eagerness that he could not unravel. He stood staring, then hunched down into a sandy womb between two dunes to watch it. Something more was going to happen: there were feelings coming from the object, muddled feelings, human feelings. Amazed, he tried to finger them out gently with his quiet-sense.

But nothing was clear. Was the emotion he sensed eagerness, or fright? He could not make it out. When at last the silver side of the creature began to move, it was a movement of light rather than form, as if his eyes had blurred. He realized he had been holding his breath, and let it out slowly; an oblong space yawned in the burnished side, and green light glowed from within: light that shimmered, and he could see the outline of something intricate with nobs and protrusions like jewelry.

Then a figure stood in the green glow, and he crouched lower between the dunes.

It was a woman stepped out. She was clothed in something very thin so he could see a great lot of her, and she was young, perhaps no older than he; she was smooth and finely groomed, so beautiful he forgot to try to sort out the clear emotion that was a part of her, the terrible, engulfing sadness that came from her.

Her hair was as pale as the silk of the painon trees that grew in the civilized lands, and her movements, as she stepped out of the green light onto the sand, were lithe and graceful. She seemed surprised at the feel of the sand under her bare feet and knelt to take a handful and examine it, then let it run through her fingers slowly, with obvious delight. She was golden all over, as if her skin held the last light of the setting sun. The aura of sadness that clung to her was strongly overridden, now, by her growing excitement as she studied the vista of dunes and sea; oblivious to all else she was in her intense embrace of this land, as if she had searched for such almost in desperation.

Keb slipped farther back into the shadow of the dunes and sent his mind out more probingly, seeking to know her, to learn who she was, to touch her memory and her knowledge of herself: and the vision that engulfed him almost made him reel. The mind-pictures came sharp, the sensations of her journey still flaming bright in her consciousness: he was in space, not the sky, but a deeper space than he had known to think of, and below him Ere lay like a spinning green ball jeweled with the blue of the sea—not just the eleven countries fading into the unknown lands, but more of Ere than any man imagined. He could see the silver wash of desert that must be Karra, where he stood. Then suddenly the spinning world was engulfed by cloud, and only the wonder of it remained; then the dunes and sea rose swift in blinding light as the ship landed.

Only the gods could see Ere from the sky thus, could move above the earth thus, though he had dreamed of seeing it so. Could this girl be of the gods, then? Were there god-women of mortal shape?

As he watched her, trying to sense something of what she was, he felt again the sadness he could neither plumb nor understand, a great wave of it, and of bitterness, though her wonder at this new place overlaid it. He felt her absorption as she walked to the edge of the cut to examine the delta where it met the sea below her, knew her rapt pleasure at the seven fingers of river, at the raucous cries of a rising flock of skeeba birds. She stood for a long time thus, drinking in the wind as if she were possessed of something wonderful, of life itself suddenly; he could not quite touch or understand the meaning she gave to what she saw and felt.

Then with a surge of eagerness, she began to run down the sloping narrow path Keb had worn into the side of the cliff. He rose and followed her, going past the silver ship with a shiver of curiosity, then stood looking down as she ran along the delta like a wild thing suddenly unleashed, toward the surf. He watched her strip off her thin garment and dive into the water, heedless of what might lie in wait. He felt a surge of fear for her, yet he knew the sea creatures were harmless enough, and the sea god, SkokeDirgOg, was truly only a myth and not like the gods of the sky. Though it was only the dark stories of SkokeDirgOg that seemed to stir belief in his stepfather, as if the great flying gods of light he could disbelieve, but the dark one, being closer to his own nature, was more real to him.

Keb wanted to go nearer, but, undecided and uncertain of himself, he stayed where he was, watching her as she swam and dove then floated face down on the surface. He caught the sense of the underwater beauty, then her thoughts were obscured. Once he turned to look at the tall silver creature: a sudden desire to examine it tore him in fierce competition with his pleasure at watching the girl, but he stood still, touching now and then her delight as she played like a fish in the sea.

When she came out of the water at last and climbed the Cut, he had gone back, but his footprints were there in the sand. Hidden in the dunes, he felt a heat of apprehension as she came to the sand and stared in puzzlement at his path.

She followed the prints with her eyes, never moving. Then she knelt to examine one print closely, and stood at last to place her own bare foot over it. She was smiling, and, though he could not comprehend why she would think it, the humor of her thought burst in his mind like a bright bubble: she was pleased there were the same number of toes!

She began to follow his footprints toward the dunes where he was hidden. Did her mind touch his? He held his breath. He must be imagining it—her pale gold beauty had befuddled him. She walked slowly and quietly, with her face down a little, and her hands loose at her sides. Why wasn't she afraid?

Often on the desert he had stood so, loose, hands at his sides, looking at the ground before him as if he did not know of the frightened band hidden beyond; stood and felt out their deepest secrets and hiding places among the pack animals and the pitiful bundles; stood spying silently, then told his stepfather where lay the riches Sherrick lusted after. He had seen the jewels ripped away from the refugees and felt their terror and the desperation of those captured for slaves; he had watched Sherrick kill those who resisted, then sweep away at last with his saddlebags laden with diamonds and topaz and emeralds, and the captives led like thirsty dogs across the desert lands.

She raised her eyes. They were blue and they looked into his, and she was not afraid, or even surprised. His blood pounded with the look of her. Blue as otter-herb flowers, her eyes, gazing into his as if she had known him always. And he knew she saw the killing he had been thinking of, and that she felt his shame. Bright and clear her look, but the shock and sadness with which she greeted his thoughts were as if she greeted a wounded brother.

When Pama entered orbit after the terror and discomfort of passage through hyperspace, she had pressed herself against the glass of the sight-port with a hungry longing for the greenness of this tiny globe that hung before her, a longing for the wash of blue sea and the richness of heavy air. Her hand on the ship's controls was comforting; this ship had housed and warmed her, had restored its own strength and so hers, too, at the very breasts of the worlds that she had touched, built its fuels in the warm rays of those worlds' great suns. But still it was only a ship, and she longed for the solidness of rock and earth, for greenness, and for the water of rivers and seas; none of the worlds she had found yet had been meant for humans. Then at last she had awakened to see this planet in her sight-port, a sphere bedecked with the blue jewels of lake and sea, and she had thought of music; in her head great chords of Loomiusian symphony had burst forth. This world was beautiful. She let the ship down into the swirling atmosphere with wonder.

She wished she had the power to slip into a stream in time, so that she might see the planet as it had been when it formed, molten and whirling; she wished she could have watched its cooling, and the slow rise of its continents and of its life; could have given herself this spectacle as a fitting introduction—

In spite of her joy she was so tired, so desolate and lost; in spite of her eagerness, her mind was like something limp and her body weak from the confined traveling, and from the unhappiness before. When finally she set the scout ship down on the deserted coast, she stepped out onto the pale sand, so like the skirting sands of Loomiu's moons, felt the wind and the healing sun with a great pleasure, and stood for a long moment simply *being*. She was on a solid planet at last, standing on a solid depth of sand and rock, feeling this world's very breathing and aliveness as if the earth itself spoke to her.

At last she roused herself, walked over and stood looking down at the green, lush growth that surrounded the seven fingers of river, and she felt soothed; this was a human's world, there could be no doubt of it: she could feel the size and rightness and that infinite sense of something that made her know there were men here.

And the sea—she could smell the salt, she had not seen a sea like this since her babyhood on Treavorreau; her body longed for the cold freedom of it after the confines of the ship. She ran down the cliff to the water, stripped off her garment, and plunged in—delicious and salt it was, buoying and cold—she swam and dove and then floating face down she felt the presence of another. She started, afraid, but then she relaxed as the sense of him came clear: a young man, she could feel his eyes and mind on her as clearly as if she had faced him; he had been there all the time! And she not knowing, so enraptured was she with this world. A creature like herself, who watched her innocently—from the cliff, yes. A terrible thrill shook her, engulfed her so she thought she would cry out. A long time in space without another human, a long time without her own kind . . . Though most of those she had left were cruel enough, cruel as stone.

This human would not contrive to use her as her own kind had done, she felt the privacy of his mind as if he did not want to be touched, did not want to be too close to men. And yet she felt, too, the wonder of his mind, a sense of something *other*, something he searched for with longing—a sense of gods, she thought, a sense of something flying, and a sense of her mixed with it because she came from the sky. She smiled and came ashore, and when she had climbed and found the footprint, her joy was whole and eager. A footprint like her own. But she followed his track with head bent, for he was as uncertain as she.

Her parents had left Treavorreau when she was small, and gone—to serve the State, of course—to the outpost of Loomiu. Ships were slower then, and the journey had been a long tedious void in her life; she had boarded that ship as little more than a baby, and left it a young girl pushing adolescence. She could remember little else of her childhood so vividly as that time of confinement, of controlled air and controlled places and controlled sights, as if all the world outside the ship were one with the fairy tales they read to her: make-believe. She had come out of the airlock onto Loomiu terrified of the openness that swam before her, like a caged animal set free. But soon enough she had quickened to Loomiu's beauty, to the meadows that surrounded their spaceport home—her father was a ship's engineer. She had stood at the window longing to run free, aching for a liberty she had never known, a liberty that now beckoned. And then she had discovered that it was not only shipboard life that was confining: sparsely populated as Loomiu was, the edicts of Treavorreau were observed. It was considered suspect for a child to play alone without a group, to go alone into the untamed places—considered aberrant. Children's lives were planned for them, there were long hours of lessons and longer hours of youth work and meetings and games—almost, she thought, as if a child left to its own devices was a threat to the State. Her teachers and leaders considered the wild areas of Loomiu useful only as laboratory assignments, as organized walks so dull they destroyed all sense of exploration, walks kept close to the plastic safety of the science compound. Her parents did not help, they were submissive to the will of Treavorreau. She was organized and herded and molded, though the mold did not take very well.

And the children—if there were any who shared her longings, they were clever indeed at deceiving; they seemed only staid and serious; children like their elders, obedient and grim. They made her feel more out of place and lonely than ever; there was no one she could speak with about the things that mattered, even had she dared try.

Though meadows were inaccessible in the daytime, at night there was no one about. The few guards spent their time walking to and fro in front of laboratories and confinement houses; dull beyond description, their nights, for there was seldom need for their services. So at night she crept through her window and into the fields and wandered for long hours under the moon-washed skies of Loomiu.

In those long hours she learned to love the freedom of solitude, away from her fellow creatures, away from prying State officials. And she learned to hate, too— to hate the regimentation, to hate the thoroughness with which Treavorreau ruled its subjects. Very early her life work had been chosen for her; not because of talent, but because the need for medical assistants was fast increasing as Treavorreau explored and settled new worlds. Her studies had been channeled in that one direction at the cost of the classes she loved. No more history or music; these would not be needed. Who had the right to say what you needed in your life!

It was on Loomiu that her thought-probing skills began to show themselves. Perhaps it was her age, for the talent often appeared first in adolescence. Or perhaps it was her turbulent state of mind, her very rebellion that made her more receptive. But whatever the cause, it happened, and she could not undo it.

The first time had been when the Master Engineer came to supper. She had seen in his mind his intention of promoting her father to a higher rank, and she had blurted it out, "You'll be wearing a blue uniform, Father, I can see you by the hangar all fine and shining—"

They had all stared at her, then her mother had hustled her off to her sleeping chamber with such frantic haste that Pama had been frightened of her for the first time in her life. After that, whenever *the power* came on her—they called it *the power*, they said it was a special privilege but it terrified them all the same—whenever *the power* came on her, her parents became distant and cold. Admiring, yes. But so cold. Soon she learned to hide her talent, for she needed her parents' warmth; she learned to keep her visions to herself, not easy for a child as exuberant as she had once been.

They never let her forget that because of *the power* she would go back to Treavorreau, to join the Council, when she reached her first adult birthday; and adult birthdays came far too early. Her parents already looked on her—since they had learned of *the power*— as adult in many ways; and they tried to shield their own thoughts from her as if they feared her, tried to shield their minds in a crude, inept way that hurt her terribly. Though perhaps she couldn't blame them: all Council members were feared. Council members came to Loomiu periodically to examine, telepathically, teachers and leaders and workers, to see that all was in order. They would return those who were suspect to Treavorreau. The rigid hierarchy of the State made a fear in Pama that she could not cope with, that left her feeling trapped and desperate.

By the time the fateful birthday drew near, she had

become a secretive, quiet girl, the joy stilted, her visions private and painful. *Must* she go to serve the Council? Her father said it was the law. Why must the Council know, then? Why must her parents tell them? It seemed to Pama that the good in the civilization she knew, the arts and the music that were so beautiful, were far overshadowed by the rigidity of the tenets under which people were made to live. *"Why must I?"* she had demanded of her father in a painful rage.

"Because it is the law," her father said again. "You can't hide from the Council." It was plain that he thought the Council Seers could detect Pama's talent from as far away as Treavorreau; she did not believe that, but she could not convince him. And he was right that *the power* she possessed might have been sensed during any one of several visits Council members had made to Loomiu, touched just as surely as she in turn had felt the icy quality of those she had tried so hard to shield against. Had that shielding been as useless as a child's toy sword would be against sophisticated weapons?

There was no need for the Council to notify a young person who had *the power*, he was simply taken on his majority day. Did the State know about her? Others with *the power* made it known at once, or so she had heard. Made it known and were proud of it as the State expected. One who hid such a talent from the State would be executed as a traitor. No talent, no skill could be used except as the State directed; no personal choice was allowed. In her desperation, Pama could only repeat to herself that she was not one of them, not in spirit; that she could not go to the Council. She had seized her only chance to escape twelve days before her birthday. That night her father had worked late on a two-man scout ship for the space botonists, and when he finished the last of his work and left the ship, she climbed aboard, locked the entrance behind her, and sent the ship at once into space like a Mooran bird-steed leaping toward the sky, tense and eager. She had watched the spaceport dwindling beneath her, then at last she had watched the planet of Loomiu disappear, feeling a terror of loneliness, and feeling, too, her father's incredulous fury as he watched the ship vanish and realized how she had learned to fly it: from his own mind, from bringing his meals and staying around the hangars and tie-ups while he worked. She had not asked questions, but had simply followed his thoughts as he sorted out the jumbled electrical systems and made the repairs that would allow starting, throttling, transference and structuring of fuel. She had learned it all silently, and now she felt a deep, aching sweep of righteousness toward her father: despite his adamancy, she had escaped the life the State had so doggedly intended for her. But she felt a terrible sadness, too, that this must be so.

One thing she had taken with her that was frivolous, that she did not need to sustain herself: the mooncup. For now she would not receive it at her majority in one of the few rituals her people had kept alive; now the cup would not be ceremonially passed from her father's outstretched hands to hers, his eldest child—his only child—to be carried forth into another generation as, in the dim past, their simpler ancestors had

carried the symbolic light of the moons to commence
a new life. The Council called it barbaric, but it was
a beautiful custom, and the cup was delicate and
lovely; she had taken it without her parents knowing,
to begin a life her parents had never dreamed for her.

She looked up and faced the boy where he stood in
in the shadow between the dunes.

His hair was as red as the safflow flowers of Loomiu,
and his eyes were like coals, so black they shone. He
was staring at her as if he could read her thoughts,
and certainly when she thought deliberately that he
was a handsome young man, his face flushed pink and
he looked away with embarrassment.

She grinned, her blue eyes lighting, and she said
her name, then waited. "Pama. I am Pama." And her
pulse quickened as she felt his mind read the sense of
her language. Both were reaching out, and their minds
touched in a way that shocked and excited her, the
reality of such a contact making her tremble.

"Keb. My name is Keb. Are you a god, then?"

"Not a god!" She couldn't help but laugh, embarrassed at such an idea, her thoughts filling with delight
at the ease with which their minds met. "I am
from . . ." She paused, and showed him the space beyond Ere's sky, showed him her long travel confined
in the ship. He grew white with seeing it, with feeling
what she had felt: the uncertainty at some of the controls, the sense of being trapped in space with no way
to break free save through death or the finding of
another livable world. She gave him her thrill at seeing this green world, and he knew again her wonder

at the sand, at the sea. The languages flowed between them, their minds learning as they spoke, touching the loneliness each had felt at being so without another like himself. The surprise and recognition of such like longing, such like bitterness, made them suddenly shy. Never had either been so exposed, so without defense. He touched her weakness and her strength and recognized them as similar to his own.

He took her hand at last and led her down the Cut, and made a fire for her. They gathered scropples in the shallows of the river and laid them in mud and coals to bake; he made a meal for her of roasted scropples and lily roots and honeypods from the branches of the lone zantha tree that stood in the Cut. They sat before the fire gazing at each other intently as each laid the color and fabric of his life before the other to explore.

He showed her the hot dry sands of Karra, waterless and cruel; the barren black holes down into the mines; the feel of weight over his head as he descended; the utter darkness as if his eyes could not remember what light was; the backbreaking work as he chopped with the metal claw, fearful always of collapsing timbers and caving walls; the pain of the beatings when something went wrong; the face of his stepfather as dark and cruel as the Cadaver eagles of her own world; the refugee caravans and the blood. How strange that he was not ashamed to speak so of his private fears and hates—and of his private dreams. He felt her frustrations as clearly as if they were his own: the inner torment she had known on Loomiu; her unease when she had touched the disturbing thoughts of others, thoughts grown twisted and awry in stifled minds. He felt her anger that such could happen, and her sense of hopelessness for the worlds of Treavorreau, her impotent fury with a tyranny she was powerless to change; he knew her hate as if it were his own. Nothing was held back: it was as if they had known each other always. And nothing was said with shame.

She went up once to her ship, and brought back the mooncup; she knelt and filled it with river water that became as light-filled as the cup itself. She gave him its name, and indeed it was like the moons in its opalescent luster. Cut from a gem called tyrion it was, a pearly jewel sliced by some impossible ray of light that Keb could only try to understand. And the paper thin slices, like iridescent butterfly wings, were laid round and overlapped and joined with gold to make the shape of an opening flower, as delicate, as brilliant as a breath of light. She handed it to him, and he held it in his palm fearing he would crush it; then carefully he drank from it.

"And you've never seen more of Ere," she said at last, "you've never gone down below the Rim into the green lands. But you can see them in your mind as if you've been there," she whispered, studying him.

"I see those lands in the minds of the refugees— before they're killed," he said slowly, "and in the minds of the slaves, their longing is sharp for the lands below the Rim. And my mother was the grandchild of a Cherban warrior; he kept the stories alive to tell her, and her to me. It is not such a primitive land as this, not all of Ere. Nor such a cruel one. Beyond the raided countries, and the raider Kubal, lies Carriol. And in

Carriol—lucky the hunted who can cut back through the Kubalese lines into Carriol. In Carriol men are free, and they trust each other; there men are slave to no man. Carriol is the only country of Ere the Kubalese will not attack—though they shun our high, cruel desert. The caravans of Carriol go out to trade made up of the finest horses and the ablest warriors. No Kubalese would be fool enough to challenge Carriolinian soldiers, they are too skilled and too finely armed. They ride over all of Ere in peace. And their tradesmen carry silks and linen and fine weavings, and even ride up the Rim to trade, though the Kubalese will not. I have never seen them, but I know they bargain for gold with our miners unharmed, and in spite of their strength, it is said they never steal or cheat us. It is like a city of light, Carriol. The sacred city still stands on the shores of Carriol in ruins, and the gods are said to come to it still.

"But the rest of Ere—there are cities where men are free, but they are small and vulnerable to the Kubalese. And in Karra . . ." He paused, and a sense of the narrow, dry lives of Karra lay in the air between them. He seldom spoke so much, and a surge of self-consciousness touched him; but his need to show her all of Ere was stronger, his need to put the sense of Ere's history into words as lucid and clear as her own; for though their thoughts touched, the contact was not constant; and in their minds they found that words were sometimes easier to call up than complete pictures, that words were essential when ideas were expressed. Pama saw his world, as she saw her own, as a thing evolving; she thought of man as a creature evolving, though slowly. The idea was new to Keb.

She had thought at first his people might be akin to her own, so far had the Treavorreau races traveled into space; but now she was sure they were not. This was an indigenous race: the very things he showed her of Ere's religion, of Ere's history, told her that Keb's people had evolved on this one world. Its autonomy and simplicity made her envious in spite of Kubal's aggression, in spite of much that was primitive. This was a civilization's childhood, its formative time, and she was warmed by the sense of wholeness, of completeness, that its very isolation gave her. "And you would not go to Carriol?" she said at last. "Yes— I see—if your mother could travel that far."

Keb watched her. The firelight caught her face and rounded the shadows of her cheeks so her beauty was earthier. "A trip like that," he said slowly, "I've thought of it often enough. But it's too long and hard for an invalid, it would be many days' ride before we were safe. She could not manage it even if I could steal Sherrick's mounts unseen."

"Are there no other mounts to be had?"

"No miner, no friend of Sherrick, would sell me so much as a lame pony, had I the gold. And the refugees come on their own feet, sore and blistered."

He told her of the gods then, and he thought she could see them as he did in the gallery of her mind, winged, shifting images lifting on the winds above Ere. She said they were like the mythical beings of a world she had heard of, but she did not scoff at him or call his gods mythical.

In the back of his mind he could feel the black unease that was Sherrick searching for him; darkness had come and he knew he should be leaving, but he could not leave her. He sat wondering at her, at her courage, for he could not fathom how she had come alone so resolutely and not crumpled under fear. The very idea of worlds beyond, of a space infinite, dizzied him— worlds spinning incredible distances above Ere, below Ere, in a space where there was no up nor down, no east or west and no hand to reach out to. He took her hand suddenly and looked so long at her that her face began to redden; and yet he was only thinking what any normal man would think and feel. . . .

When at last he left her, it was very dark, indeed, and Ere's two moons rode pale as silken scythes in the sky. She put into his hand the mooncup from which they had drunk, light as gossamer and seeming to give off its own radiance. His eyes questioned hers, but she bid him take it. He held it gently, and they climbed to where her ship waited like a dark animal caught at one point with silver—and he kissed her lightly and wonderingly once, planning how soon he could return.

The desert was cooler at night, but still the air pressed heavy after the breezes of the Cut. Keb held the mooncup out before him so it caught the moonlight with a slash of rainbow color; and not even the thought of Sherrick's fury at his late return was as painful as his progress away from Pama. In his mind the soothing quiet of the delta was heightened and given new dimension by her presence there, life itself given new dimension; and the ugliness and flatness he had known before Pama seemed, by contrast, as parched as the sand over which he trod.

Bleached featureless in the moonlight, the desert had its own cruel beauty, colored the pale stain of saffron. The sand huts, strung out now and then along the shallow creases where neighborhood mines went down to honeycomb the earth beneath the very bedrooms and scullers—the huts were little more, themselves, than heaps of desert sand. Sand, water, and ogre-bone—the strange, pale dust from the edge of the unknown lands—was combined into a thick mixture and shaped over bent boughs and thatch to make the low, domed huts and pony stables: hardened sand that would keep out the sun and the night-bats, and an occasional few droplets of rain that would have been welcome enough to come in.

Keb thought how Pama had awakened once in the open spaces of Loomiu at night and found a rare, dark shadow slipping through the sparse growth close to her: a Loomiusian scammon, a creature resembling the Ereian fox. It had been a rare sight; she had sat staring after it silent with wonder, willing it to come closer. But it had only paused and looked, then slipped into the night; a nearly extinct little animal. He felt Pama's memory, her wonder, within him as if it were his own. How could he and Pama be so close, two who had once been separated by a distance impossible to comprehend? If Keb had ever dreamed of knowing another like himself, it had been only a dream. The other Children of Ynell had seemed very remote from him, the idea of knowing another so closely quite beyond the hard reality of life. Now as he crossed the moonlit desert he felt her thoughts touch him, comforting and yet exciting beyond anything he had known. And when he neared his hut he paused, concentrating all his efforts to give her a picture of the moon-washed dome and the emptiness of the pale, stretching desert all around it. The hut was dark at the entrance, the curving top bright with moonlight. He felt Pama's pleasure, then felt her sudden concern: he had sensed Sherrick there and so had she. Sherrick hidden in the shadows of the door.

Keb went forward, his contact with Pama quite gone. He held his anger tight, fingering Sherrick's fury where the old man waited for him. What right had Sherrick to stand bidding him back, to watch and begrudge his every movement! And yet Keb knew Sherrick had the right because he had been strong enough to take it, because Keb himself had not resisted.

But there was something else, something beyond the feel of Sherrick's fury, something—Keb thought fleetingly that his senses were heightened tonight, were made the sharper for what he had experienced—something there beyond Sherrick in the night . . .

And then he knew. Above Sherrick's temper he could feel the fear and confusion of the refugees, far away but painful for all the distance. They were struggling up the Rim. Harsh as a wound he could feel their exhaustion as they climbed; he poised to listen with his mind, and he could feel the straining of their bodies where their packs pulled at their raw shoulders, he could feel their desperation for they had been traveling hard, Kubalese soldiers close on their heels. Hungry they were, and sore fearful for what they carried hidden among the packs and in their clothing—fire-pearls! Keb started. This was a rich band indeed, carrying fire-pearls more valuable than gold.

To all the bands that climbed the Cut, their secreted riches were a passport to freedom and a new life. Driven from their home countries, they knew if they could slip through Karra and into Moramia, they could buy safety and land to start anew; the Moramian herders were of gentler nature than the miners of Karra, and the Moramian high desert was fruitful, with grass to pasture on. Keb shuddered and tried to put the vision of this band from him, tried to pretend he had seen nothing. He felt sick and trembling.

Before this night, he would have told Sherrick, lest Sherrick's own raiders spy out the band or hear that it went through, and Keb's silence bring him a beating and threats. But now he could not do so. Before this night, his life had been like the desert, mined under with black holes—flat, parched, riddled with emptiness. There had been no more to it than that, he thought. Now because of Pama his life was another thing, now Keb's inner world was the shape of Pama's smile and of the curving winds of space. Now he had looked at infinity and knew there were other lives and other ways of living, ways he had never dreamed— and that there was another like himself, whose mind reflected his thoughts. He had looked at Pama and now gentleness was a dimension for Keb, love was a dimension, where before these things had been only isolated feelings. Right was a dimension, right, and hatred of that which oppressed. He looked up at the dark door of the hut and knew he could not spy for Sherrick.

He started to go in, ignoring Sherrick, but Sherrick reached out from the shadow and gripped his arm; the ring on his hairy hand glinted in the moonlight; he stood staring down at Keb with fury. Black framed, tall and smelling of sweat and mine dirt and drink.

"Where have you been this night! I gave you no leave to come crawling back with the night half gone when there's work to be done, boy!"

Sherrick knew about the refugees, then. "I—I was swimming in the sea, then I fell asleep," Keb said, palming the mooncup in the shadows. "I dreamed of SkokeDirgOg," he lied. "I thought SkokeDirgOg rose up out of the sea and came here to kill us—"

The man's eyes flashed with a quick fear that he put down at once. He shoved Keb toward the dark doorway, spinning him around so Keb, in raising his hand to catch himself, let the cup flash bright in the moonlight.

Sherrick froze. He grabbed Keb's arm again, bent his fingers back, and took the cup from him. It lay in the Karrach's swarthy hand, the mooncup, so frail, transparent and shimmering. "What's this?" Sherrick hissed covetously, staring; then fear grew large in the Karrach's eyes. He watched the glinting colors and seemed to shake himself. "Where did you get such as this! Diamond!" He said with wonder, "It's made of diamond, boy! *Where?*"

"Not diamond," Keb said with disgust. "I found it in the sea." He lied sullenly, wanting to snatch it away, but afraid they would break it in a struggle.

Sherrick's fury leaped and his hulking form seemed to swell and pulse. "Insolent!" He roared, "Insolent

slavy child! If you were there in the sea ..." He
pointed, his hand quivering slightly, "There was a light
there over the sea." He stared at the mooncup. "A
light in the sky that shone like this, a light ..." He
drew his hand back as if to strike. "What was that
light, slavy boy? Where did you get this?"

"I'm not a slavy boy, my mother is free," Keb said
evenly. Then, "I saw no light. How could there be a
light in the sky, except the moons! What, a light from
the *gods*?" He snorted.

Sherrick's voice shook as if he was losing control,
and Keb could feel a spinning terror from him that
centered around the light. A fear of something in the
sky. A dread of the gods! Keb watched him with interest: so Sherrick believed in the gods enough to fear
them! The man's confusion and temper were like a
wildfire in him, he began to curl his fingers slowly as
if he would smash the cup; Keb stiffened.

"Tell me where you got this," Sherrick growled, and
then, as if he could accept no other answer, "Have you
been poaching refugees, boy?"

Keb looked at him and laughed. "What refugees
would make a light!" he said derisively. "I found it in
the sea."

The Karrach's face went black with fury, he raised
his fist and his ring flashed as he knocked Keb against
the door jamb. He lifted the mooncup, his expression
terrible, and hurled it so hard against the entry stone
that it smashed with a small explosion; the shards
glanced away and lay gleaming on the stone. Keb
stood staring, too shocked to speak or move.

Pama. It had been Pama's. The one thing she had

kept from her world that had meaning for her. Why had he taken it, brought it here to be smashed?

"If I find you got it from refugees," Sherrick said in a terrible voice, "if I find that, son of a slavy, you will die for it. Understand you? Now go in, she's worse," he finished shortly, speaking of Keb's mother.

The shattering of the cup had shattered something in Keb, as if Pama's very soul had been wounded by Sherrick's action: her trust in giving him the cup had been shattered. He stepped through the dark doorway hearing Sherrick's cold words echo: *Now go in, she's worse.* He could feel Sherrick's disgust for his mother's weak condition. Keb scowled. How could he ever have thought the lust Sherrick felt for Josiam was love? His tenderness for Pama helped him see truly for the first time the real quality of Sherrick's emotions—it was as if Pama had pulled aside a curtain obscuring his vision; he knew an aching sadness for his mother.

He went slowly toward the back of the house, and as he did, he felt again the pain of the refugees pushing into his own pain, heard again their torment; the shattering of the cup seemed to have focused their agony into him more strongly, as if, if he should reach out, all the unhappiness of the universe would thrust into his head. The pain of his mother was with him often, but only as the dim swirling of unrelated senses and memories her constant suffering created in her mind. The plight of the refugees was the sharper for being sporadic; and it was twofold: now he felt the fear and impotent fury that hunted men feel; later, after Sherrick attacked, he would know the horror of death and enslavement.

The Mooncup : 121

Sherrick's men were preparing even now, Keb knew. A small band they were, half a dozen, but cruel when armed and mounted. Could Sherrick force him to tell of the fire-pearls? The hiding places the refugees had invented were diverse, and if they were attacked helter-skelter, the treasures would be swallowed, buried, thrown down over the Rim while Sherrick's men searched and were forced in the end to go scampering and scrabbling in the dirt. It was a matter of pride for Sherrick, a matter of manhood, to be able to herd the refugees together and pick and choose among them the very ones, the only ones, who concealed treasure, pick them and have them strip and slit open boots to dump jewels out of the lining, unbraid jewels from the women's hair, take them from places more secret still. Sherrick's men would gloat at his skill, no more wise than the refugees as to where his real source of knowledge lay.

If Keb did not tell where the treasure was hidden, he knew well enough that Sherrick would order the whole band killed before he would let any refugees see his men scramble like jackels among the sand and rags for their take. Sherrick was as unreasoning in his pride as he was cruel in his treatment of Josiam.

It did not help to know that Sherrick might have killed more refugees without Keb's spying, would not have left the small and old and infirm to take their chances on the desert. To have been a part of the raid, no matter what the circumstances, sickened Keb.

He ducked his head and entered the sculler, then ducked again as he entered his mother's room.

The candle was lit and Josiam seemed to be dozing

under the thin, worn cover. Keb stood looking down at her. Her red hair—mark of a Cherban—seemed to fade a little more every time he saw her.

She gave a little sigh, then opened her eyes and lay watching him. There were dark shadows across her cheeks, and he knew she had been coughing; the salve crock was open by her bed. He felt a pang of guilt for having been away when she needed him, for having been touching another life, touching joy. He knelt by the bed and put his hand on her arm. He knew if she looked at him reproachfully he would break, would want to turn on her. Her weakness and pain made him seethe with a fury of helplessness and indignation that was almost unbearable.

The door-hide had been pulled back to let in the cool air, and he could see out into her little sand garden that lay cupped between two domes of the hut; white as a lizard's breast it was in the moonlight, and the lone chivvy cactus made grotesque lace in the center. In the daytime his mother spent long hours watching the tiny stilta birds and oteros that came to the cactus for insects and for water. The stilta birds, from the unknown lands, were her special joy. He wished—he wished the birds could heal her as he could not. As nothing could.

"He's in a temper," she breathed, her voice no more than a whisper. Her skin seemed transparent, more so in the candlelight perhaps, and her eyes were huge. He could see her bones pressing like ivory. She looked up at him with concern. "He doesn't know I heard, but the scouts told him there was fighting again in Cloffi and there would be refugees. What does it mean? Why did he tell them to find you, Keb?"

Her rare lucidity stirred him terribly; he stared down at her, appalled that she had heard. "He—nothing. I don't know, some errand he wants, he said I was to come to him in the stable," he said stupidly.

She shook her head, not believing him; but she asked nothing more, and soon she seemed to fall into the more confused state that was natural to her illness.

He stayed as long as she expected him to, his face stone-innocent, and to still the further questions that might occur to her, he sang a Carriol ballad softly; when she released him at last by falling into a light sleep, he backed out the door silently. What had she understood from the words she overheard? Her pain-dazed mind was hard to follow, and seemed to confuse his own seeing sense so he could never read her thoughts clearly.

He stood in the sculler, his back to the light of her room, thinking. No matter what his mother thought, and no matter what vow he had made within himself to Pama, he knew he must go with Sherrick. Not to go would mean more deaths among the refugees, might mean his mother's death, or at best Sherrick's increased unkindness to her; and yet to assist Sherrick in his venture revolted Keb even more this night. To betray the commitment he now felt to Pama shamed him as nothing else could have. If I were clever enough, he thought, I would stop him somehow; I would find a way. Torn with revulsion, he half turned, looked back over his shoulder at the candlelit room where his mother slept, then went out. At the entry he paused to scoop up the butterfly-wing shards of the broken mooncup that lay scattered across the stone. He tied them in a bit of linen from the cupboard, and dropped the whole deep in his tunic pocket. And he felt Pama reach out and touch his shame—at the broken cup, at the broken promise—felt her tenderness, felt as close to her as when he had kissed her; he closed his mind abruptly and turned away in his thoughts.

He went out to the stable, to Sherrick.

The raiders were already mounting. Sherrick turned and gave Keb a look as black as the shadows under the horses' bellies and shoved his pony at him; a poor ragged beast used in the day for dragging the mines and not capable of much more than a tired amble through the night; not a mount of fire like the band of six rode, great plunging horses bred from the Kubalese stock that had once come stolen into Karra. Keb climbed astride and followed the others obediently into the night.

It was a long ride to the Rim, and they had to cross the Cut, of course, fording the river between two farms; there were no farm huts to be seen from the ford, but Keb could smell mawzee grain in the field on his right and could hear a horse whinny far off. The splash of the river, as they crossed, made Keb want to slide off his pony and slip away through the waters like a fish, silent in the darkness, out of Sherrick's grasp. The moons began to set, and in the formless night ahead, Keb knew that the refugees had at last topped the Rim where their Kubalese pursuers dared not come and had settled down in a makeshift camp for the night. He could almost taste the dried mountain-meat they chewed on, could sense the babies crying. He could feel their terrible fear at being in Karra. Why did they come here? Why didn't they stand somewhere in Cloffi or Aybil and fight? Keb did not know. Nor did the refugees, he thought, except that here the Kubalese would not venture. Their desperation was so bitter in him that tears of rebellion at the unfairness of life—and of men—escaped his clenched lids. He could gladly kill Sherrick and his men if he were armed—if I were man enough, he thought furiously. Keb carried no sword, nor did Sherrick allow him to lay hands on one. I could have stolen one, Keb thought, gritting his teeth. Now it was too late.

When they neared the refugees at last, Keb knew that most of the tired band slept, and that the few guards stood nearly asleep, too. They were camped among a series of low ridges that ran like a rippling skin to the Rim. Keb could sense, he could feel—he pulled up his tired pony and sat staring into the night, amazed: there were others there in the night besides the refugees! Then he kicked the animal to go on, so as not to draw suspicion. There were other men at the Rim! Kubalese soldiers mounted and alert, climbing silently, tracking this poor band. Kubalese soldiers coming into Karra! The glitter of fire-pearls burned hot indeed in their lusting minds to make them climb the Rim.

Keb's hands shook with excitement, with the eagerness that was leaping in him.

The moons had sunk; it was so dark that Sherrick's band showed around him only as lumps of black in the night. Keb felt Sherrick close to him, and heard mumbled words; but Sherrick had learned to be still, to let Keb feel out in his own way, uninterrupted, and now the Karrach only muttered with suppressed impatience and moved away, his horse mouthing the bit softly. Keb sat silent for a long moment, then he wound his reins around the pommel and slipped silently off the pony, who had begun to crop futilely at the sand for fodder. He slipped behind the animal, using it for cover, then out into the humping desert; there would be only minutes until he was missed.

Crouching low, he moved along a ridge as if he were one with it, then ran silently across empty space the long distance into the refugee camp. Too soon, Keb knew, Sherrick would turn in the saddle to hear his directions. He was glad he had always delayed the mind scanning so Sherrick thought it took a long time, and had taken longer still at the telling, hesitating, uncertain, when in reality his mind saw it all as clear as the ears of his pony in front of him.

He could sense a sentry ahead as he stepped between sleeping people too exhausted to awaken. Keb slipped up quietly, clapped his hand over the man's mouth, and drew him down to where he could whisper to him.

And soon enough it was done; the refugee camp roused in a silence born of terror, the people moving off across the dark sand of the desert without pack or blanket or shelter, the babies' mouths muffled and the women silent, their fear washing over Keb.

When they had fled, he made his way to where the pony still nuzzled at the sand, moving about restlessly,

The Mooncup : 127

and mounted him and drew closer to where Sherrick was fuming with impatience; the night was still as death. "I can't seem to—it's all confused," Keb whispered. "I think they—I think there's precious little, but I can't . . ." He stumbled and stalled with it until at last, as welcome as water to a thirsting man, came the first shout and the slash of a sword against metal as the Kubalese warriors, remounting their horses after climbing the Rim, found the refugee camp. Cries of bloodlust rang out, then cries of chagrin as they found themselves battling empty blankets and packs, and Sherrick's raiders who, surprised into wild, lunging fighting, cried out more in confusion than in lust. Keb slipped away, his pony tense and skittish, and rounded the battle to join the refugees.

He led the pitiful little band toward a place of low sand hills that ran along the edge of the Cut and up into Moramia. He could hear the babies' irritable grunts behind muffling hands, could feel the exhaustion and desperation of those who followed him so silently. They were cold, he could feel the chills as if they were his own, and they were desperate at having lost their blankets and food and meagre possessions, though the fire-pearls were safe in their clothing. They seemed almost too discouraged to care that they were still alive. He guided them away from the mine neighborhoods, and kept them clear of the Cut itself, going slowly, resting more often than he would have liked. Fear marched with him, and the raging of the battle stayed in his head, the cries of the dying seething in his mind, as if the battle followed him and exploded all around him as he made his slow way across the desert.

Then, at last, as dawn began to come, the ragged band crossed over into Moramia and safety, and Keb turned back, exhausted. The incongruous idea that he should have tried to save Sherrick haunted him. Yet what could he have done? See the refugees die in Sherrick's stead? The sense of guilt was terrible; no matter how he reasoned with himself, mindless dark emotions continued to battle within him, exhausting him: guilt that was not logical, guilt that he had led Sherrick to his death, guilt that confused him even though his strongest desire had been to get the refugees away before Sherrick should come after them.

And the pain of loneliness that gripped him, too, during that dark forced march across Karra was terrible: his mind was in such turmoil he could not reach out to Pama, and the breaking of the mooncup seemed to Keb to have broken the contact between them so that perhaps he could never touch her mind again.

Pama had followed Keb in her mind after he set out from the ship, had followed him home with her thoughts as lightly as a moth in summer, so that she saw the moon-white desert over which he moved and sensed Sherrick there in the shadows of the door, felt Keb's fear of Sherrick; knew Keb's resolution to defy Sherrick, born of what he felt for her.

She saw the cup smashed on the stone and felt Keb's pain and saw his little mother pale in the bed. And she saw Keb mount and ride away toward slaughter he was powerless to stop.

She had sat on the edge of the cliff, looking down over the sea, and had felt the lift of Keb's mind when he sensed the Kubalese soldiers climbing the Rim.

The moons had sunk and the night was dark, and Pama knew what he planned to do: she knew he hoped Sherrick would die.

She rose and went to the ship and drew on a cloak, took a few oddments from the vaults, and set out.

In the blackness the sand felt as if it would give way to nothing under her feet and let her fall. Keb's rising pulse at the fighting, she felt only sporadically; for a few moments she could not touch him, then would come the cries of battle reflected from his mind and the surge of death and killing—then all would be silent again and she could not make him come to her. She was losing him, his preoccupation was too great, the strain of his effort too great to allow anything left for her. Then in the silences, she began to sense the muddled thoughts of the frail woman who slept lightly on her couch, began to touch her dream of small, bright birds. She could feel the woman's fear and the knowledge she had put back, tumbled among the confusion of her pain: Keb's mother knew, in the dark parts of her mind that she would not willfully touch, that Sherrick laid evil upon Keb, knew that Sherrick had a hold over Keb that she could not understand, nor yet bear to puzzle out.

As Pama neared the hut, she stopped and let all her senses reach out to Keb over Josiam's rattling mind. But she could not touch him, she did not know what was happening to him, she had lost him utterly. Fear swept her. Nothing came, nothing, the night was emptiness.

She went into the hut at last, taking hold of her emotions, went directly back through the sculler to

Keb's mother's bedroom. She woke the woman with the light pressure of her hand against her shoulder, and smiled down at the tired, dazed eyes. "I have come for you," she said. "To help Keb, you must come with me. Do you think you are able?"

The woman's hair was a pale version of Keb's, and her eyes were dark and large in her thin face. "I am Josiam," she whispered with the simplicity of a child as she gazed up at Pama. "What is happening to him? Is it Sherrick, then? Where will you take me?"

"If Sherrick dies this night, there will be no need to take you," Pama said without explanation, wondering at her own curtness and feeling a terrible need to be alone, to try to sort out her feelings and Keb's loss of contact. She looked down at Josiam, and took the woman's hand. "If Sherrick comes back, then—then we had best be away when he returns," she said softly.

She helped Josiam to rise; the woman seemed to trust Pama, though the sense of her thoughts was fogged and unclear. "You are a beautiful girl," she whispered hesitantly. "Will Keb come?"

"Yes." Pama helped her to dress, to draw on boots and a cloak, not daring to think that Keb might not come. She half supported, half carried Josiam out through the sculler and through the main room, then out past the door shadows into the night. There were no ponies in the stable, she could feel the emptiness of it, and they began to walk slowly across the shifting sand.

"When he comes..." Josiam began, "when Keb comes back for me..." Then she turned to stare blindly at Pama in the darkness. "He *will* come?" It was as if she were drugged and only very late in making sense of anything. "When will he come? Where is Keb? He's not hurt?"

"Keb is fine," Pama said softly. "He will find us, he will come to us . . ." She did not want to say the truth, not here in the night so far from anything that could give peace. What would this woman do if she knew the grisly work that Keb had been made part of? If Josiam had a right to know, then it was Keb who must tell her—if Keb came back.

Josiam's frantic, pain-fogged mind filled Pama's own with changing images and smoky uncertainties that would not let Pama focus her own thoughts or reach out to Keb with strength; and when she did reach, there was nothing; her frustration made her tense and upset so her power was diminished further, and this in turn frightened her. She tried to think of Keb as if he were close to her, to make a warm depth of thought he could touch; she thought of what it was between them, how strange was their meeting. Never in her life had there been another with whom she had spoken in this way—she could not lose him now, she thought with panic.

On Loomiu she would not have dared reach out to another as she had to Keb. Perhaps there was no other with *the power* on Loomiu, save the Council members who came, evoking in her the terrible fear of discovery. She thought their minds must turn in on themselves like convoluted seashells, heedless of human feeling. They must see others' lives only as one-dimensional pictures cast upon a screen, with no understanding; for if they truly understood and cared, the worlds of

Treavorreau would not be as they were. A Council that judged precisely by rote the punishments, the executions—she shuddered.

Keb was not like the Seers of Treavorreau. His very pain, when the cup was smashed—she thought no Seer would feel thus. And his shame at breaking his own vow had racked him utterly. Had she come all across space at some silent beckoning, some drawing of an invisible cord that existed between herself and Keb? He must come back to her. She sought for him in panic, but there was nothing in the night, no sense of him. And then a feeling of blackness and confusion swept faintly through her; was it Keb? Her spirits lifted in spite of the blackness: he was there, somewhere in the night.

Josiam was growing weaker and leaning more heavily against Pama; their progress, slow and difficult, seemed almost to cease; the sand was full of stones and ridges to trip them, and Josiam's breathing had become harsh and fast. As they paused to rest, Pama felt out again and again toward Keb, but the sensations she received were formless and swirling, then were lost utterly in the thrusts of emotion from Josiam's pain-clouded mind.

When Josiam stumbled and could go no farther, Pama knelt beside her in the blackness. Vast and empty the night, so empty she thought she could feel the planet spinning under her; she and Josiam were in space here just as much as if they had cast themselves off in the ship, two creatures clinging to a small globe that spun in blackness and infinity; she made herself dizzy with the thought; she sat silent, half-fearful, listening to Josiam's breathing ease and slow at last; she felt the woman's mind calm and grow clearer. Keb will come, she thought to herself. But she could not reach him—she could not reach him at all.

The night spun out and died, and the sun came; it was nearly noon before Keb returned to the scene of battle, to stand sickened, staring at the death that spilled across the desert sand. His pony was so spent it hardly shied at the smell of blood, and at the two crippled horses that hobbled away, one falling in a heap over a dead Kubalese warrior. The broken bodies of Kubalese and Karrach alike were flung across packs and cookpots and soiled blankets; those who had escaped death must have fled long ago.

He found a small shovel in a pack that was half-wedged beneath a slaughtered horse, and began to bury the dead. It was all he could do to drag the bodies out of the rubble, exhausted as he was. The sand was soft enough to dig, but it kept sliding back into the holes; and the sickness he felt at the mutilated bodies made him retch.

It had been a slow, nerve-straining march to Moramia, and a slow journey back, leading the pony most of the way, and Keb's mind confused with the dark thought that haunted him that he should have saved Sherrick. The desert heat had sapped the last of his strength, his mouth was dry as the sand, and his waterskin hung empty from the saddle.

When he had buried five bodies, pausing twice to be sure those he knelt over were truly dead, he came into the bloody, debris-strewn battle area for the sixth, sickening at the sight of a slashed-open horse, and saw that the body he stood over was Sherrick. But Sherrick stared up at him, his eyes smoldering with hate.

He lay beside a child's blood-caked doll, and his arm was twisted in an unnatural way, with a sliver of bone sticking out. There was a long gash down his side that laid the flesh open and was bleeding badly. And Sherrick's stare held a fury that made Keb go cold. "You—" Sherrick croaked hoarsely, "you knew." The seething of his hate made Keb want to back away from him, though the man could not get up, mortal wounded he was. Keb stood for a long moment staring down at him. Sherrick tried to speak again, but his words were little more than a crude rasping, though the hate in him was plain.

At last Keb brought the pony and stood over Sherrick, then lifted him up. The man pulled a little to help himself, and the pony staggered with the weight. Finally Sherrick slumped in the saddle, limp and unwieldy. The bandage Keb had wrapped him with was already oozing blood. "You will promise," Keb said, afraid Sherrick might really live, against all odds, "you will promise not to harm my mother, nor to touch her. Not ever."

The Karrach said nothing.

"You will promise, or I will drag you off this horse and leave you to the carrion hawks," Keb threatened.

Sherrick nodded slowly, hardly a motion, hating him, and muttered something Keb could not make out. Keb took the pony's rein and started slowly across the desert under the afternoon sun, toward the Cut. Sherrick swayed in the saddle like a sack of meal, held himself upright with a will few men possessed, Keb thought. The Cut would be the worst test, down that steep bank for a quarter of a mile. But at the Cut there would be water, and food bartered from a farmer, perhaps.

The sun was a great ball of searing flame in the white sky. Keb's body was sore and parched, the exhaustion gripping him like a weight; beside him the pony was nearly as bad, his head swinging low to the ground and his feet unable to place themselves solidly on the sand, as if his legs were almost out of control. Keb's desire to lean on the pony was so strong that when the tired animal plunged against him, Keb laid his weight into the pony's shoulder; they struggled together across the desert, animal and man, Sherrick lurching and leaning above them like some malevolent wraith of death.

By the time they sighted the Cut, the sun had sunk to a bloody smear of red behind the western mountains. As they started down, Keb had to call forth the last of his strength to keep the dying Sherrick upright in the saddle on the steep grade as the pony slipped and struggled.

When they reached the blessed green valley, with its cool, fragrant breath drifting up to them, the sky was darkening fast, and Ere's two moons were risen like silver blades, curved and sharp, in the east; Keb helped Sherrick down, to lie beneath a tree, and filled the waterskin for him. Keb and the pony drank, the pony sucking up great mouthfuls then turning at last to graze frantically along the river bank. The long field of mawzee, south of the fording place, smelled like fresh baked bread, making saliva rise in Keb's mouth. To the north was a tall stand of miner's barley, and some zantha trees. Keb knew that a farmplace lay beyond that.

The Karrach was bleeding badly, his skin clammy and his eyes dull with pain. He clutched at his side helplessly, and Keb pressed the edges of the wound and tightened the bandage, but he knew nothing else to do. He turned from Sherrick at last and gazed down along the Cut toward the sea. His exhaustion was great, the spinning in his head like the buzzing of Doonas bees, and he had never been so hungering for sleep.

As he stood staring blindly northward, he heard the shrill cry of a peonskill cock. Then it seemed to him that he saw Pama standing beside her ship. How bright the ship, almost pulsing; though the vision was fogged and unclear. Then superimposed across it, almost a part of it, a second image appeared, sending a dizziness through him; he saw his mother sleeping between the dunes. But that was impossible. He had never seen a false vision, his mind had never betrayed him before. The images misted and converged further, then both faded, were gone.

He wanted Pama, but he could not seem to collect his mind enough even to reach out to her. He drew the shards of the broken mooncup from his tunic and stood looking down at them, then turned to stare again at Sherrick. Shaken, he bent uselessly over the dying man. At last he lay down nearby, caring not that he might wake beside a corpse, too tired to think of it.

He closed his eyes, and the aching of his body spread around him as if it flowed into the very earth itself, in a delicious sensation of rest. Spinning, dropping, he let a swirling blackness engulf him, let sleep engulf him.

Josiam slept in a nitch between the dunes, covered with a filmy sheet; she had drunk the medicine Pama offered and was comforted. Pama watched over her, her thoughts spinning; the discipline of her mind seemed to have ebbed; she was utterly shaken, uncertain. She could not reach Keb, could not sense what was happening to him. She was afraid as she had never been; alone on a strange world, utterly alone. How could she ever have thought to bring herself this far? Could she not have coped, somehow, on Treavorreau? Couldn't she have tried? Fear gripped her: fear, and confusion.

If she had not met Keb, she might have remained stoic, decisive; she might be making her way now into gentler lands than Karra. But she had met him; her emotions had tumbled her; now she needed him. Now she felt she was not *able*, not *whole*, without Keb. Alone, with a sick woman—with Keb's mother—in a hostile desert country. Someone I must care for, she thought, glancing at Josiam's frail, sleeping form. Perhaps she could make Josiam well; the illness, though not understood on Ere, was like a common one of Treavorreau, might respond to Treavorreau's medicines. They were remedies that worked on all of Treavorreau's planets, on people of different worlds. Would they not work on Josiam? The medicines could be left with her . . .

Josiam had not seen the ship. What would she think? Pama had kept her among the dunes; the ship stood just beyond where she slept. She might never need to see it. Pama sighed. She was terrified for Keb. Had she really touched his mind after the fighting began? Or had it been another's dark, confused thoughts reaching out blindly? There were others with *the power* on Ere, perhaps among the refugees. But such a one would have known the Karrach band was waiting, would have seen—she did not know, her mind seemed muffled, everything unclear, her very skill damped and unsure.

The Gift of Ynell, Keb called the seeing. Such ability was said, on Ere, to be against the gods. Keb scoffed at that: he felt it was one with the gods. But he felt the gods were *beings*, living creatures, on a higher plane somehow. He did not see them as spirits, but as a mortal part of this world, rare and wonderful. He had a yearning for them, a burning curiosity that lifted her, too, in its intensity. If Keb believed they were real, perhaps there were such on Ere, dwelling upon the winds. Beings who shared *the power*, as Keb believed they did; beings who were, themselves, a part of something larger. Was there some greater force that encompassed all sentient creatures? She was not taught so on Loomiu. But her people had believed it once. Was there, through all the vast depths of space, a force that linked all life? A force of which her skill, Keb's skill, were a part?

She settled deeper against the dune, watching Josiam idly. On Loomiu *the power* had been used for evil just as it was in Karra. Used to control men, to destroy their freedom. But not all the nations of Ere were so corrupt. In Carriol, Keb said, the Children of Ynell were free; they were not used, their own wills ruled their lives.

The power could be turned to evil, but perhaps it was not meant to produce evil—if there was meaning in life. Meaning. She had not known how she had longed for such a thing, until now. Perhaps the power was meant for the opposite of evil; maybe those who possessed it were intended to bring good from it. The idea gripped her, excited her.

Her head swam with questions. She could not bear to be quiet in her mind, for she feared what she might then know within herself: that Keb was dead. He could not be dead.

If she had not left Loomiu, could she have helped the Treavorreau worlds, turned the tide of repression? Could she do so now if she returned? Go undiscovered among the Council, influence the Council? Hide her true feelings and subtly make its seers begin to abhor the ugly power they wielded? But that was madness. What made her think she was stronger and more skilled than they, who ruled all the worlds of Treavorreau with their minds?

Were there others who would help? Others like herself, who cared, somewhere in the State's environs?

She cared now, where she had not before, where before she had wanted only to escape the subjugation. If she went back—she glanced at the ship, silvered and waiting, and she was more confused and shaken still.

She bowed her head on her knees. Keb is dead, she thought bleakly. He would come to me in his thoughts; even if he found he didn't care for me, he would tell me that he lives.

If Keb was dead, she was truly alone, more alone than she had ever been in her life. For now she knew what it was not to be alone. And if he had forsaken her, she was more alone, was desolate. *If I went back*, she thought, and then, *I could not. I could not do it alone.*

One person against a tyranny colder and more efficient than the killer-limpets of Killeamme. One person against worlds ruled by the unfeeling machine called the Council: a machine that could quench her parents' lives if she returned. The theft of the ship and her escape, those crimes could mean death for all three of them.

And yet if Treavorreau were ever to change, there must be a beginning, people must be made to care. Children must be allowed to grow up caring and not be suppressed into joyless robots.

But for one alone to battle such a thing before the tide was ready to turn, could be suicide, a death with nothing accomplished. Shaken, she sat staring, her hands clenched tight. Not knowing what to do. I love him, she thought suddenly. And he is dead. Or he does not love me in return, will not answer my thoughts. If he is dead, what is left for me then? Nothing. But my own people, my own kind. Oh, Keb, I cannot bear it if you are dead, to be without you.

This planet, his planet, what will happen to it in the time that will come after my life is over?

The Mooncup : 141

Ere is like Treavorreau was in centuries past. One planet with small countries, none of them as powerful as the octopus Treavorreau has become. With small separate countries, could a despot be overcome before he could grow into something too big to challenge? If they aren't stopped, will the Kubalese rule, or the Kubalese and the Karrach as one, brought together by their lust for cruelty? Will the Children of Ynell be used as our seers are? Or could they guide Ere in another direction?

She felt the spinning planet beneath her, clutched her arms around herself, and, defeated suddenly, desolate, she put her head on her knees and thought that she was truly alone in the universe.

Keb woke to hear groaning, was confused, did not know where he was. The moons lay low on the horizon like slanted eyes watching him. He turned on his side and saw Sherrick, a dark shape.

The Karrach was drawn with pain; Keb tried to quench the bleeding with his hand, pressing, but it was like trying to stop the river. He thought it impossible the man had lived so long; but he did live, and his expression, tense with suffering, still showed hatred for Keb; Sherrick would damn him if he could. Keb wanted to leave him there, yet he could not. Then as he knelt, staring into the Karrach's face, the man's expression changed abruptly, looked suddenly amazed, shocked. Fear came into his face. He tried to sit up, pulled himself up with an inhuman effort until he leaned against the tree, the blood from his wound spurting. He was staring over Keb's shoulder, and his face was lighted from some source behind Keb, as if the moons had brightened suddenly. Keb turned to look.

The sky was lighting; brightness blazed in the night and slashed into the Cut so the pony shrieked and reared, wheeled off; light slashed across Keb and turned the cliffs white. Keb's breath stopped in his chest.

The object within the light rose, blazing, washed in its own radiance; he saw it lift quickly, growing smaller until at last it disappeared.

He turned away and tried to block the sight from his mind by staring down at Sherrick. The Karrach's black eyes were wide. "The gods—" he said, rasping, so low Keb could hardly hear, "the gods bring fire from the mountain." He gazed hard at Keb, and remained staring, unmoving as stone.

Only at long last did Keb realize Sherrick was dead. He touched the Karrach, and the man slumped forward until his face lay against the grass.

Keb buried him where he lay, thinking it irony that Sherrick, who had scoffed at the gods, had died believing in them because he was deceived in what he saw. And irony, too, that Sherrick the hard, the cruel, should lie now in this gentle place. Well, Keb could not lift him, a dead weight. And to drag him home behind the pony would be not only impossible, but an indignity. Sherrick, dead, seemed to deserve more than Sherrick alive had deserved.

Only after the Karrach was buried did Keb give himself to the blazing light that still filled his mind, and to the meaning of it—to the receding ship and to grief. He did not reach out to Pama: she was gone. Why try to touch her mind there in space? What good would it do? He knelt on the grass, twisted with grief, and his eyes, under clenched fists, saw Pama's face— Pama—the pain of her leaving shook and battered him. When he imagined he felt her thoughts, he knew it could not be true, and anger surged over him.

Why had she left him? Fury gripped him at his own treacherous mind that could see her now, but had not been able to reach her when it mattered; and fury at Pama, who had not had faith enough that he would return to her.

He stayed so for many hours, beneath the tree where he had buried Sherrick, thinking sometimes that Pama reached out, then pushing the delusion aside. He heard farmers in the distance calling to their animals in the night, as if some creature had strayed, and once he thought he heard Pama's voice so clearly that he stared with hope into the darkness around him; then he clenched his mind and body tighter, to shut everything out.

Had Pama seen that he wanted Sherrick dead and learned to hate him for that? Had her beginning love for him, if ever her feeling had been love, been quenched? He heard the pony grazing near him and felt the animal's warm breath; he turned away, as if the pony would bring him back to a life he did not want any longer. When again he imagined he felt Pama's thoughts reaching out to him, when he thought he heard her voice, he wished he had died instead of Sherrick.

And guilt wrenched him, too, that his thoughts were

all for Pama when his mother lay alone—how could he have imagined that his mother had been with Pama? What groundless hope had made such a thought?

He saw them again in an aberration so real his stomach warped in pain with it, saw his mother walking beside Pama. He imagined that somehow Pama had healed her; he turned from the vision and bent his face into his hands, sick with the strength of his delusion.

When he looked up, he still thought Pama and Josiam walked hand in hand through the mawzee field with the moonlight on them; he thought Josiam was stronger, he could see it in her walk, he could sense from Pama's mind the ways of healing with which she had treated Josiam. He stood up and stared at the two figures coming toward him: they were not imagined, they were *there*. Pama was supporting Josiam. The ship had gone empty, sent away: he could feel the rhythm of it through Pama's mind as it spun in an endless path around Ere.

And then Pama's joy touched him, her wild, terrible joy that he lived. Joy that he wanted her—how could she have doubted? Yet *he* had doubted, too.

They came together and held each other, and it was all right. The world was all right—worlds could have been born and died, the distance they had been from each other; but now it was all right.

He took the linen wrapping from his tunic and held it a moment, then opened it. The shards of the broken mooncup gleamed in the light of Ere's moons—something of her life that had been shattered, something she cared deeply about.

"It will mend," she said quietly. "It will mend with gold, each piece set into gold from the mines of Karra. So it will be of two worlds. And we will go to Carriol, will we, Keb? Where we need not fear. Where we can make a life of—of meaning, perhaps. For us, for all the Children of Ynell."

"We will go to Carriol, to the city of the gods."

They helped Josiam astride the pony and began to make their way south, along the river. They would come out by the seven fingers and go along the coast into Zandour, Keb thought, then Aybil and Farr, along all the coastal countries traveling by night; then into Carriol, where the sun could light their way.

Rick Roberson:

The Astoria Incident

NO FIELDS CHOPPED OUT OF THE forest," came the voice from behind him, "no gaping pits to dig out ore, no sprawling city on the river. Nothing but endless wilderness and the freshest air we've breathed for months." There was a contented sigh as Yulette finished, "It's beautiful."

Captain John Walker wordlessly adjusted his binoculars and continued to scan the treeline of the sluggish river before him. Its full length lay in his view, from the spectacular waterfall on the north mountain ridge to the point where it flowed out of sight into the mists of the opposite horizon. Thousands of square kilometers of green forests bordered the river's banks on both sides, stretching unbroken to the wooded hills that formed a valley with the river at its center. Walker and his crew had landed on the highest of these hills, and their vantage point was excellent. Nothing could have been missed; he lowered the binoculars and closed his eyes to think.

What now? They weren't due on Earth for another three weeks; their assignment to map a dozen newly discovered worlds had gone unusually well, and they were ahead of schedule. Lingering on this long-abandoned planet was thus a possibility—but there was no reason to do so now that both colonizing sites had been checked and no sign of its lost expeditions had been found. The only logical thing to do was dock with their orbiting ship *Wildfire* and continue on the return trip. And yet, while he was anxious to get the data in *Wildfire's* computers back to Earth Central, Walker could not help but think of his tiny bachelor apartment, and of the lonely days he would spend there waiting impatiently for another space survey assignment. . . .

"Is something the matter?" Yulette asked, a trace of worry in her voice.

Walker opened his eyes with a start. "No," he answered, a bit hastily. "I was just . . . considering."

"You should try to relax while we're here, John." She looked at him for a moment and turned her gaze back to the valley. "After all, we seldom get such a golden opportunity. This planet is so much like Lacaille IV—"

"Well, it's not," said Walker firmly. "Something here

caused the *Astoria* and *Saratoga* to vanish without a trace; that's a jinx your home world never had."

The *Astoria* had been the second starship in a row to disappear on this planet; the first had been the *Saratoga*. Since both had been designed to land and unload cargo and colonists, the possible search area for clues as to what had happened was millions of square kilometers of the surface and not just the few standard-type orbits that all starships used. But Earth Central, the organization in charge of the space colonization program, had deemed the effort of a full-scale search too low priority, in view of the countless other worlds where failure was less likely, to launch such a search. That decision had stood for twenty years, and Walker had questioned its wisdom ever since he'd first heard of it back in his Academy training days.

This unforeseen chance to solve the mystery of the two missing starships had come when the *Wildfire* had run low on water during the return trip to Earth. As a liquid, water was used as a cooling fluid; broken down, it provided needed oxygen to breathe and hydrogen to fuel their fusion reactor. His decision to stop on this particular planet for water would raise a few eyebrows but cause no criticism back at Earth Central, and justified this welcome side expedition to an otherwise off-limits planet.

It was too bad, reflected Walker sadly as they loaded their scattered equipment into the lander, that no clues had been found. They had stopped without incident to fill the lander's water tanks at the ocean beach where the lost *Saratoga* colonists were to have landed; from there it had been a routine flight to the hills of the *Astoria* site. Since these double-check trips to the landing areas had been fruitless, and *Wildfire*'s orbital survey was almost complete, there would be nothing further to do on the surface unless Beck and von Nimen had found something in their trek to the river. The two men had not called on their communicators to report anything unusual, so Walker was not surprised to see them emerge empty-handed from the edge of the woods a few minutes later. The fatigued look on their faces told him all he needed to know about their unsuccessful forage.

"The river samples check out as normal," Beck panted out when he reached the lander. The climb up the hill had been a steep one, and the engineer gratefully accepted the canteen Yulette offered him. Taking a long sip, he continued, "We didn't see anything out of the ordinary; this is a textbook pastoral planet as far as I can tell."

Von Nimen downed several noisy gulps from the canteen and turned to Walker. "So where do we go now, John? Back to the *Saratoga* site?"

Walker paused at the scientist's question, remembering the vast expanse of sandy beach to the south where they had initially landed. By now the sea surf had washed away even their footprints—the first the beach had ever known, he was somehow sure. The lonely image faded from his mind. "There was nothing by the sea," Walker said flatly, speaking to all his group. "We'll go back to the *Wildfire* and break orbit. We've done what we could; it's time to go." They nodded solemnly in acceptance and Walker led the slow procession up the steps of the squat lander.

Beck, the last one in, busied himself with the hatch; Yulette and von Nimen moved to the control console and deftly began preparing the spaceship for flight. Walker surveyed the proceedings approvingly and turned to his own station at the communications board. Somewhere overhead their mother ship *Wildfire* orbited; he pressed the button to signal it.

At first there were only faint pops of static; then suddenly the hum of a carrier wave came from the speakers, and the amplified voice of Janet O'Neil, *Wildfire* biologist and medical officer, filled the crowded interior of the landing craft. "*Wildfire* here. We were just about to call you, John. On our last orbit we scanned a nuclear crater that is on the same entry path the *Astoria* would have taken to reach the landing site where you are now. It's only about two hundred kilometers from your present location."

"You're sure it's nuclear?" queried Beck.

"No doubt of it, Steve," O'Neil answered the engineer. "The only question Mark has is whether or not it's radioactive. Our orbit is too high for us to tell."

"Well, we're going to find out," Walker said grimly. "Does Mark have the coordinates plotted yet?"

The voice of Mark Sutton, navigator and final member of *Wildfire*'s crew, replaced O'Neil's. "I'm here, John. Bear 72.9 degrees west for 192 kilometers. You can't miss it."

That was for sure, Walker vowed. He would scour the entire planet to find that crater if he had to; it should have been found twenty years ago. Signing off on the radio, Walker settled down into the pilot's seat and throttled the flight engines to life. Within seconds the lander was heading west at full speed towards the remains of the *Astoria*.

Yulette could feel the aura of excitement around Walker as he piloted the ship, and she was worried by the intensity of his emotion. It was not the restrained enthusiasm he usually displayed; it was more like a desperate attempt to escape the dull routine that had dominated their lives these past few months in space. Yulette was willing to accept that routine for the rewards it brought: the satisfaction of knowing that mankind was advancing through her efforts to explore. She wondered if Walker still felt the same way. He had once, not so long ago; but on the past survey trip he had seemed increasingly disenchanted.

She wanted to help; Walker was a dear friend as well as a starship captain who commanded her loyalty There seemed to be nothing, however, that she could do. Even understanding Walker's unhappiness was difficult for Yulette. She was satisfied with her life, though he was apparently becoming disillusioned with his. Lacaille IV probably had something to do with that, she reflected; the research-oriented colony in which she had been reared, and still called home, was not shackled by the superficial limitations that Earth put on its other colonies. When she returned to Lacaille IV, she would be free to do what work she wished using the data she had gathered on this mission, with all of the help she could use from her friends and colleagues there. Since her home was not controlled by the rigid authority of Earth Central, she could only begin to comprehend the bureaucracy that Walker knew all too well from his life on Earth.

Yulette roused from her reverie and stared out the window at the passing terrain below. Walker was flying high, and from this altitude the trees looked like thick moss covering the ground. As they flew on, the woods slowly began to thin; tiny blotches of open clearings showed through the forest. Before she could examine them more closely, Walker nudged her shoulder and pointed wordlessly ahead.

They passed over the edge of the forest and into a vast expanse of golden prairie. Broken in places by tiny knolls topped with scrubby, twisted pines, the area was astonishingly flat after the gentle curves of the forest. Swirls of motion flowed as the wind blew stalks of grass about. The sun was not far off the horizon, casting long shadows from the low bushes that dotted the land. As Beck and von Nimen crowded the window from behind to catch a glimpse, Yulette had a sudden desire to just watch the sunset.

Yet she could see that the beauty was not unmarred. To the right, at the limits of her visibility, lay a single dark scar. Walker nudged the controls and the ship turned towards it. As the minutes ticked away, little progress was seemingly made towards the ugly blotch; then Yulette made the mental shift in perspective, and the grim truth was suddenly evident to her.

The crater was huge, a gaping wound in the soil fully a kilometer across. Reaching the edge was taking so long because it was still kilometers away. Yulette could see upon drawing closer that the walls of the crater were jet black and seemed smooth, almost glassy. The grass and shrubs around the rim were very sparse;

probably, she thought, they had been destroyed by the heat of the blast and were only now growing back.

"There is no residual radiation," said von Nimen, looking up from his instruments. "I'd say it's a clean fusion crater."

Walker nodded. "We're going down."

They landed at the point along the rim closest to the distant forest. Von Nimen and Beck went off together in search of plant and soil samples that might yield clues to what had happened, leaving Walker and Yulette to record the scene with the video camera. Walker was switching from a wide angle to a zoom lens when he said disgustedly, "Earth Central could have found this crater years ago. But no—it was too busy dreaming up bogeymen because of the *Saratoga* disappearance to consider the possibility that the *Astoria* might simply have blown up." Turning on the videorecorder once more, he finished scornfully, "I suppose they will be sorrier to hear about the planet they've wasted for so long than about the people who were killed in the blast."

Yulette considered his remarks sadly and began walking the hundred meters to the rim. Without a word she sat down, dangling her feet over the edge and into the yawning bowl. The far wall of the abyss was hidden in featureless shadow; the part that was visible in the sunlight sparkled with flashes of orange and red. Walker came from behind and settled down beside her. "What's wrong?" he asked.

"You can't blame Earth Central," Yulette said quietly. "They sent search probes—"

"*Unmanned* probes, and only *two* of them. Two for

this whole planet!" exploded Walker. "What kind of a search is that? Admit it, Yulette; they were too busy with the colonies that succeeded to worry about the ones that failed."

"There was more to it than that. Earth Central was afraid of the unknown, and anything that can cause the disappearance of two colonizing starships like the *Saratoga* and *Astoria* is certainly an unknown to be feared."

"Exploring the unknown is what *Wildfire* and the other survey ships should be for," Walker argued. "Instead, all we're supposed to do is go out and find planets for Earth to colonize. Never mind about finding something new; just find someplace for the masses of Earth to settle. That's all Central cares about." He picked up a stone and threw it angrily down the slope of the crater. "The dozen planets we've surveyed on this mission will be overrun by colonists in the next ten years. After Earth builds the cities and imposes the export quotas on those planets, they won't be new worlds—only mockeries of old ones. That's what always happens."

"Not on Lacaille IV," said Yulette calmly.

Walker grinned sheepishly. "Your colony is one of the few I would consider living in," he admitted. "But I'm not a scientist; I'm an adventurer. There aren't any settlements for my breed, unfortunately." Yulette could think of no reply, and an uneasy silence settled.

Beck found them watching the sunset when he returned to the lander a half hour later. "John," he called out, walking towards where they sat, "we need to take some samples from within the crater. One from the bottom and at least two from the wall."

"Hm?" said Walker. He turned his attention away from the spectacle before him and concentrated on Beck. "It's too dark to start rappelling down to the bottom, and I don't want to take the lander down there. We'll just have to wait until morning."

"We're going to spend the night here?"

Walker paused, then nodded. "I think it's safe enough. We'll stay in the lander and somebody will be on watch at all times."

Darkness fell swiftly once the sun had set, for though the planet had two small moonlets, neither would rise for several hours. Von Nimen got the first watch upon drawing straws; next came Yulette, then Walker and Beck. O'Neil and Sutton were contacted in *Wildfire* and told of the decision to stay for the night. After a brief dinner of concentrated foodstuffs, the surface team bedded down.

Sleep did not come easily for Yulette; she knew that spending the night here was an unorthodox decision for Walker to have made, and wondered what his real reason for staying could be. To brood over the crater, perhaps? That seemed unlike Walker, but she had to admit he had not been his normal self ever since they had found this crater. She considered the matter without reaching any conclusion for over an hour before a dreamless slumber overtook her.

Walker awakened fully alert at von Nimen's touch. "What is it, Fritz?"

"There are people outside the lander."

He was out of his bunk and at the control panel in

fifteen seconds. "Where?"

The scientist pointed wordlessly to one of the TV monitors. One of the moonlets had cleared the forest, casting a dim glow upon the area—enough for the image intensifiers in the TV cameras to work with. Walker could see the men as if they were in broad daylight. There were half a dozen of them, using the bushes for cover as they worked their way towards the lander. At a distance of fifty meters they stopped; standing erect, their shoulders and heads showed above the shrubs as they watched the lander from the illusory security of darkness. Walker noticed one man pointing at the lander, shaking his head and talking excitedly to the figure beside him, who listened quietly.

He needed to act before they did, Walker realized. "Fritz, call *Wildfire* and tell them what's happening." Beck and Yulette had entered the flight deck by this time, and he turned to them. "Steve, prepare to get us airborne. If they bolt and run, I want to be able to follow them to their base. Yulette, on my word, hit them with the searchlight." He picked up a microphone and waited until his crew was ready. "Now."

The beam lanced out from the landing craft and onto the intruders. Walker hit a switch on the front board, and his voice boomed out into the night. "THIS IS CAPTAIN JOHN WALKER, COMMANDING THE SURVEY STARSHIP WILDFIRE. STATE YOUR IDENTITY AND PURPOSE, PLEASE." He turned on the outside parabolic mike and waited.

The men did not flee. Their arms up to protect their eyes, one spoke out in faint but intelligible words: "Turn off your light. We aren't goin' to hurt you."

The Astoria Incident : 159

"Survivors," whispered Beck.

Yulette turned to Walker. "How did you know?"

"It was only a guess," he replied. "Any survivors would have heard our lander and hiked out to meet us."

Beck removed his hands from the flight controls and relaxed. "Well, let's not just sit here. I'll open the hatch."

Von Nimen stayed inside, relaying the proceedings to the two still aboard *Wildfire,* as the other three went down and took a stance at the foot of the lander. The group of survivors shuffled forward to meet them.

Walker did not know what he had expected, but certainly not this. There was no happy laughter from the approaching men, or even smiles. They came grimly, silently, and stood before the *Wildfire* people as if sizing them up. He became aware of a sharp, sour odor; suddenly he realized that it was the smell of human sweat. There were large, wet stains under the armpits of the shirts the men wore—probably from their exertion in reaching the crater. In the subdued light bathing the lander, Walker could see more clearly the rough and baggy clothing the group wore. Made of some native fiber, it stood out in stark contrast to the trim uniforms the surface team had on. All in all, the band was very unkempt.

"I am Walker," he said. "Are you from the *Astoria?*"

The tallest of the men cleared his throat and spat upon the ground. "Yes." He looked around at his companions for a moment and continued hesitantly, "I'm Bill Johnson."

"Glad to meet you, Bill," said Walker. He extended his hand.

Not one of the men moved.

"This is my engineer, Steve Beck," Walker continued smoothly, though unsure as to what was going on. "And Yulette, one of my scientists."

"Yulette who?" someone in the back snickered.

"I have no other name," she stated simply. "I am from the colony of Lacaille IV."

There was a moment of silence as the men absorbed this; then Johnson said, "Well, this is Tom Harris, Phil. . . ." Walker didn't hear the rest of the introductions; he recognized Harris as the man on the screen who had been waving his hand at the lander. Now Harris was standing beside Johnson, and the look he gave Walker was one that brimmed with contempt. Wondering what could cause such instant dislike, Walker decided that Harris was one he should keep an eye on.

"And that one pawing around on your spaceship is my son, Zeke," Johnson was saying. "Get over here, boy."

Zeke looked up from where he had been examining the outer hull of the lander. He was a tow-haired boy who looked to be about fifteen years of age with eyes that gleamed excitedly. "Aw, Pa, I'm not hurtin' anything." He reached out to touch the white surface once more. "It sure is smooth metal."

"I said get over here," came the command again. His head lowered, Zeke took three steps and rejoined his father's group.

"Are there any more of you?" Beck asked. "I mean, other survivors?"

"There's a hundred or so in our village about three

hours from here," said Johnson, "and several times that on the farms."

"So many? What happened to the *Astoria*?"

"Mr. Beck, that's a long story." Harris was speaking, a thin trace of sarcasm in his reedy voice. "We're tired. I suppose you'll be wanting to see our town tomorrow, and that will be a long walk back. The questions will wait."

"There's no need to walk," began Walker. "We can fly all of you back in our landing craft—"

"No," Johnson interrupted firmly. "The spaceship stays here."

Taken aback, Walker could only agree.

Pointing to a large knoll half a kilometer away, Johnson said, "Me and my men will set up camp over there. We'll head back at dawn." And with that, the group began to move away.

"Mr. Johnson," Walker called, and when the man had turned, he added softly, "Good night."

There was a barely perceptible nod of Johnson's head; then the men picked up stuffed camp bags they had dumped in the bushes and walked off to their knoll.

"Well, one thing's clear," Walker said when they were out of earshot. "Tomorrow is going to be a long day. The watch is still in effect; it's your turn, Yulette. Let's get some rest."

Walker controlled his rising anger with effort as he mounted the lander's steps. He remembered Yulette's defense of Earth Central earlier in the afternoon and winced. Hundreds of colonists, Johnson had said. That meant not only that many had waited twenty years in vain for Earth to rescue them, but that to their children, Earth was only a fairy tale. If this was the kind of progress Earch Central was responsible for, Walker thought bitterly, he wanted no part of it.

At dawn the surface team downed a quick breakfast and trudged over the rocky ground to the knoll. Walker introduced von Nimen, who had been in the lander the night before, and without further ado the group started off for the distant line of trees.

It wasn't long until Beck raised the question that was on everyone's mind. "Well, Mr. Johnson, last night you were going to tell us about the *Astoria*—"

Johnson sighed. "There really isn't that much to tell, Mr. Beck. We had some problems with our fusion reactor on the trip from Earth; I don't know what it was, I'm only a farmer, but they told us it wasn't serious.

"The trouble really started when we tried to land. Comin' down through the air, here, some shield or other overloaded and burned out. Well, Captain Scott —that was our captain's name, Scott—he got on the intercom and told us not to worry, that we didn't have enough power to reach our landing site by the falls but that we could land short of it all right. Pretty soon we did land—an awful bumpy landing, it was.

"Not long after that they opened the hatches and told us to assemble outside. We'd been cooped up in that ship a long time; it was good to get some fresh air. But then Captain Scott came out and told us that he was going to hold a conference with his crew and do some work on the engines so we could get to where we were supposed to be. He said a walk would feel good after being cramped for so long, so why didn't we take a walk over to a creek they'd spotted by the woods? It was cool and the air smelled just fine; the idea sat good on everybody. So we all took off—it was like a Sunday picnic.

"We were about halfway to this creek when I looked around and saw them unloading the cargo holds. I turned to Tom," Johnson slapped Harris on the shoulder and continued with his tale, "and I said, 'Tom, there's something wrong. They're unloading the seed and the cows.' We ran ahead to tell the other men; we thought maybe one of them would know what was going on.

"All of a sudden there was this big flash of white light, just like the sun. Me and Tom, we covered our eyes, and then this big thunderclap just knocked us right over. When we got up, there wasn't anything there but a big black hole.

"Well, the *Astoria* was gone; Captain Scott and the crew were gone; the cows and chickens they'd unloaded were burned along with most of the seed. They hadn't even gotten around to unloading the machines and the shelters—only a few hand tools. We were all alone.

"It was a race with winter after that. We hiked up the creek into the woods, built log houses, hunted and smoked meat, planted what little seed we had."

"That must have been rough," commented von Nimen.

Johnson looked at him like he was a crazy man. "Rough? Yes, it was rough, Mr. von Nimen. Have you ever tried to plow with a wooden plow pulled by human beings? It's not as easy as pushing a button. No, sir."

"But we made it." Johnson's voice, haunted and drawn before, took on a note of pride. "We didn't lose a single person that winter—in fact, gained quite a few babies. Went on to make log cabins and farms for all the families. We did all right."

"What did you name the planet, Mr. Johnson?" Walker asked quietly.

Johnson laughed. "The planet? Shoot, we never did get around to naming it, I guess. I'm mayor of Astoria —that's the name of our town."

"How about you, Captain Walker?" Harris interrupted. "When did you spot our cornfields?"

"Cornfields?" replied Walker, surprised. "We haven't noticed any cornfields. My two crew members still in orbit spotted the crater when we had to make an unscheduled stop on this planet to take on water."

"Hmm." Harris sneered, glaring at Johnson for some reason that Walker could not discern. "If you didn't see our cornfields from the air, then you didn't know where to find us, did you? Well, you must have your two people come down and see us. They could probably use the vacation."

"I'll take it under consideration, Mr. Harris."

Overcoming his uncertainty, the boy, Zeke spoke up. "Are you really all the way from Earth?"

Von Nimen reached forward and ruffled the boy's hair playfully. "We sure are, buddy."

"What's it like on Earth?"

The boy's elders looked at each other uncomfortably

as they walked along; Yulette winked at von Nimen and said, "That's a pretty big question, Zeke. What would you like to know?"

Soon the two of them were deep in conversation. The men of Astoria, evidently curious but unwilling to admit it, listened attentively; Walker could not tell whether Zeke or his elders were more interested in the past twenty years of Earth's history.

Several hours later they reached the creek that Johnson had mentioned in his story. Walker and his crew unpacked their hiking rations, but Johnson intervened with his rough frontier hospitality. "Put that stuff away," he said, handing them long strips of jerky. "As long as you're our guests, we're going to feed you."

The jerky was as tough as it was dry; the *Wildfire* crew could barely swallow it. By unspoken agreement, however, they did not refuse the food. Yulette began repacking the field rations kit, but not before Zeke spied the bright yellow of a squeeze tube. "What's that?" he asked.

"Peaches," she replied, examining the tube. She saw the blank look on the boy's face and realized he had no idea what she was talking about. "Here. Put this straw in your mouth—like this—and squeeze here gently."

The youngster's face lit up in pleased surprise. "Hey, this is good!"

Yulette smiled. "You'll find lots of good things you never knew about when Earth brings your group fresh supplies and new people."

Walker noticed that Harris and Johnson traded worried glances at these words. Before he could probe the mystery further, however, Johnson had started the group onward again. They followed the creek into the wooded wall of the forest, which sloped upward at a slight but detectable angle. Walker was unused to such stamina-draining marching after months in space; he was too breathless for conversation as he hiked up the shaded trail.

The path through the woods grew gradually steeper as it followed the stream upward. In several places boulders had dammed up the creek, forming shallow pools where fish darted back and forth. Walker noted several crude baskets made of branches and vines in the water. At a welcomed rest stop, he mentioned this to Johnson.

"They're fish traps," he replied. "We can't eat just grain; we've got to have something that'll stick to our ribs. Those fish are pretty good. We've also caught and domesticated a type of wild bird—like a turkey, I guess—that we can get eggs and meat from. And we've tamed several unicorns that we caught as colts—they have one horn and look like horses, a little, so we call them unicorns. Of course, we've cut their horns off— too dangerous otherwise. We don't kill our tame unicorns; they're too useful as field animals, for pulling plows and wagons.

"You'll see all of this when we get to Astoria," promised Johnson. "Which we won't do unless we get started." With that, the leader got up and forged ahead once more.

It was high noon before the village of Astoria came into view. Nestled into the windbreak formed by banks rising on both sides, its packed dirt path led in a straight line between two rows of primitive shelters, each about forty meters long and made from felled trees chinked in mud. These were the original log houses Johnson had mentioned, Walker realized; but instead of protecting castaways from winter cold, most housed craft shops and lodgings for the people who ran them. He could see the glow of a blacksmith's fire from within one stall, hanging quilts in another.

His attention was drawn to a crowd at the other end of the village, a group of perhaps thirty people. Their attention was drawn to him, too, he realized suddenly. They began to stare and murmur uncomfortably as Walker and his crew came into their view, all except a few intent on some center spectacle. "Something's wrong," Johnson muttered and began to run forward. Walker, panting, followed close behind.

"What's happened?" the mayor cried, pushing his way into the center. Walker stopped at the fringe of the crowd, where he could see a figure lying painfully on the ground amid the circle of people.

"It's Will Abrams's boy," someone said, relieved to have the burden lifted from his shoulders and placed upon Johnson's. "A log rolled off the woodpile up at the new grain barn and broke his arm."

"His bone is sticking out, Bill, and he's been bleeding something fierce," came another voice. "We put a tourniquet on him. But we lost Harry Wilson like that four years ago, when all of that pus and infection set in."

Johnson nodded unhappily, and an uneasy silence settled. "Perhaps we can help," Walker said, feeling compelled to speak.

"This is John Walker and his group from Earth," said Johnson as they pressed through the crowd to its center. "There are two more of his people up there in orbit somewhere."

Walker watched the boy struggling to master his pain. "If you had to use a tourniquet, there's probably an artery torn," he declared. "He's got to have surgical treatment."

Johnson nodded and turned to the crowd. "All right, folks. We'll take care of this; go on back to work, please."

Four men gently carried the Abrams boy into one of the log buildings and eased him into a bunk. Walker knelt by the boy, not even taking time to notice his surroundings. "What's your name, son?"

"Barry," whispered the boy through gritted teeth.

"All right, Barry, we can fix your arm, but it's going to hurt for a while longer, till we get some pain-killers."

"Pain-killers?" he gasped. "You mean corn mash?"

Walker turned and looked at the Astorians behind him. "What's he talking about?"

"Whiskey," Johnson replied, entering the room with a large clay jug. "Here, Barry, take a swig of this."

Yulette reached out to stop him. "He's in bad enough shape now; he doesn't need that stuff."

"Yes, he does," argued Johnson. "Setting that bone of his is going to hurt."

"Not if I can help it," said Walker. "Put that jug away, Johnson. If you try to set his bone before his arteries are sewn up and he gets a blood transfusion, you'll kill him for sure. We'll wait for my medical officer to get here."

"Go ahead and give him the mash, Bill," said a graying woman from the corner.

Frustrated, Walker began, "Wait a minute. I want to see this boy's father—"

"My husband is dead," the woman said evenly, her gaze unflinching under Walker's stare, "and I will not have my boy suffer any more than he has to while we're waiting for your doctor, sir. Is that understood?"

With a curt nod Walker turned to unzip his shoulder pocket and withdraw his communicator. The tinny words "*Wildfire* here," were almost drowned out by the sound of Barry coughing as the whiskey went down his throat.

"Janet, I want you and Mark to come down here," said Walker. "We're in the survivors' village, and they have an injured man. Put the ship on automatic and bring a Unit III surgical kit. Set your lander down at a creek bed about ten kilometers northwest of the crater, then hike up the creek into the woods until you reach the village. Got that?"

More than an hour passed before the medical supplies reached Astoria. After repairing Barry's arm and inflating a plastic air cast about it, O'Neil injected sedatives and antibiotics into his body. "I got the tourniquet off before any tissue died," she reported to Walker when she had finished. "There is no chance of gangrene setting in."

"Thank God!" exclaimed Johnson. "All our medical supplies and personnel were destroyed with the *Astoria*; injuries are the one problem around here we can't deal with. We're sure grateful to you."

"We're just doing our job," Walker replied.

"Well, we'd better get on with ours," the mayor commented to the Astorians around him. "We've got to get that grain barn finished before the harvest ends, and we were shorthanded before Barry was injured. What's more, I suppose somebody will have to tend him; Edna certainly can't care for him all the time. She's got work of her own to do."

"We have time to assist your people," said Walker. "We're ahead of schedule."

"I can stay with Barry," said O'Neil. "I'm sure there are plenty of other things around here to keep me busy," she finished, glancing about the dirty cabin with her suspicious medical eye.

"And we can help with your barn," Beck added, with a motion to von Nimen and Sutton, who both nodded.

Harris started to say something unpleasant, to judge from his sneer, but Johnson interrupted him. "That would be mighty nice, Captain Walker." He turned to Harris. "Tom, take these men to Fred Tinsley. Tell him to set 'em to work and put them up tonight." The mayor extended his hand to the men from the *Wildfire*. "We sure do appreciate this."

Led by Harris, the workers left. Johnson continued in a light tone, "Well, Captain, I suppose that leaves you and Yulette to tour our humble village and make your reports. Let's get on with it." But the words did not quite ring true to Walker's ears; there was a tone of wistfulness, even sadness in them.

The two from *Wildfire* saw it all: the barns made from logs cut by hand, the primitive looms on which cloth was woven, the blacksmith shop where metal hand tools were made, the crops that were being harvested on homesteads carved laboriously out of the wilderness. Johnson showed them everything with pride in his voice and the mists of memories in his eyes. He always had a story to tell, whether he was showing off a storehouse of food sealed in clay jugs or the waterwheel grist mill on the creek where the Astorians ground their cornmeal. Yulette listened attentively to every word; but Walker noticed that the mayor spoke in past tense when he referred to the things he showed them. Evidently Johnson did not expect to use the cloth or mill or canned foods ever again. Which was understandable—Earth would ship in fresh equipment and men as soon as the existence of Astoria was known. Yet Johnson did not seem gladdened by that prospect.

It was night by the time their tour was over. The three walked down the deserted main street of Astoria in darkness, shadows of candlelight and echoes of laughter from the distant cabins the only indications of human presence. The gloomy village was almost like a ghost town; Yulette shivered, and not entirely from the cold. "Zeke will have some hot supper for us," Johnson commented abruptly. "He's become a pretty good cook lately."

"What about your wife?" Walker asked.

Johnson sighed, a faraway look in his dim eyes. "Sarah . . . she died five years after we got here. Fever."

"I'm very sorry—" Yulette started.

"No need to be. I've come to accept it." The man crossed the street and opened the door to one of the village houses. "Come on in."

The interior of Johnson's house was no different from that of the other cabins they had seen. The four bare walls were illuminated by the flickering flames of the fireplace where a pot of fragrant stew hung. A rugged wooden table was in the middle of the room, and two bunks lined the corner opposite the door. Zeke looked up at the sudden rush of cold air; he had four steaming bowls of broth on the table ready to eat.

"It was a hard life in the beginning, all right," Johnson said over a piece of cornbread minutes later. "Seems like we lost a lot of our best people back then, too. Things have gotten much better since those first years; we have a pretty comfortable life now. Every once in a while an accident will happen, though." The man put his hunk of cornbread down and waved at a mounted unicorn head above the mantle of the fireplace. "Take that monster up there, for instance. That thing gored old Will Abrams to death last year—the injured boy's father, that is. Almost got me, but I shot him with my crossbow."

Walker looked at the stuffed head with renewed interest. It projected from the wall in brash splendor, a noble specimen matted with soft, snow-white fur. The eyes had been sewn shut, but in all other respects the features suggested a subtle cross of a variety of Earth horses. Only in legend, however, had Earth horses had such a deadly, meter-long horn atop their crowns. Below the trophy was the equally deadly weapon that had brought it down: a hand-crafted crossbow with a beautifully finished stock and frighteningly powerful bow, another example of the ingenuity the Astorians had displayed.

The Astoria Incident : 173

"Your people have done well in the past twenty years," Walker commented. "Everything you've shown us today proves that."

"We were mighty proud of all we did," said Johnson. "We had to be, after giving the best years of our lives to it." His words took on a withdrawn tone. "I only hope the people they send from Earth will have the same pride."

Yulette noticed the catch in his voice. "You don't sound very hopeful."

"It . . . it will take some getting used to, you know." The man stood, his figure straight in the light of the fire. "Let's get some sleep. Zeke's brought in two mats for us to sleep on; you two can take the bunks."

By this time Walker knew better than to suggest an alternative more convenient to the man. "Thank you, Mr. Johnson."

Johnson doused the fire as the others bedded down, then stretched out on his mat. He yawned loudly and turned to face Walker, the reddish glow of the dying embers playing across his face. "Let me give you a word of advice, Captain Walker. If you want to understand why we lasted so long, don't look at our barns and cabins and fields. Look at the people who built them—they're the ones that did the surviving." With that, Johnson curled up into a ball and went to sleep.

Walker's corn shuck mattress rustled gently as he reached to scratch the itching it caused on his legs. Lying quietly once more, he could feel as well as hear the cold wind swish through cracks in the log wall on its way about this empty, lonely world. Total darkness fell as the last of the embers flickered out. Yet somewhere humans dared to challenge the chill blackness, and they challenged it by ignoring it. Walker could hear muffled singing and faint laughter as the Astorians gathered around one another's hearths, bringing a close to another day.

Walker awoke the next morning to the smell of fresh scrambled eggs, a mouth-watering aroma after months of freeze-dried meals aboard *Wildfire*. "Good morning," Johnson said quietly from the fireplace. "I was just about to wake you up so we could get off to an early start."

"What's happening today?" Walker asked, swinging quietly out of his bunk so as not to awaken Yulette.

"I'm going to go lend a hand with the grain barn," Johnson answered. Moving to the table, he continued, "It's a rush job, since our old barn burned down last week and the harvest has already started." He gave Walker an appraising glance. "The work is rough, and I wouldn't ask my men to do anything I wouldn't do, too."

Walker raised the mug of hot tea Zeke gave him halfway to his lips before Johnson's hidden meaning penetrated his sleepy mind. "Oh, I couldn't agree with you more, Mr. Johnson; I treat my people the same way." With a trace of bitterness he added, "I know how mad it makes me sometimes to be doing the dirty work for some desk-jockey back on Earth."

Johnson smiled and pushed a plateful of eggs to Walker. "I know just what you mean. Here, eat up."

"So many eggs?"

"You're hungry enough to eat all of them after that

hike yesterday," drawled Johnson. "We have plenty of food for everyone, Captain Walker; we have to work for it, yes, but that only makes us appreciate it more." Grinning, he added, "You'll see after you put in a good day's work on the grain barn."

After breakfast they started to the construction site to do just that, leaving Zeke to clean up their dishes. As the stream curved deeper into the forest, Walker could hear the slow but steady pounding of axes on wood; upon reaching the clearing where the barn was being built, he could see that von Nimen and Sutton were chopping away the branches of a downed tree. A small crowd of workers looked on in silence.

Walker moved to speak with Beck, whose haggard face and grimy, blistered hands added much to the quiet tale he told. Fred Tinsley, in charge of building the grain barn, had given Beck, von Nimen and Sutton the job of felling a tree to use in the wall of the structure. Sutton, with overconfidence born of inexperienced youth, had bragged that they could finish the job in half an hour; after a few swings of a ten kilogram ax, he'd made no more promises. The three *Wildfire* men stuck doggedly to their task long after their arm muscles screamed for rest, though, for they understood the unspoken rules. They were being tested, and knew that the Astorian workers would be the judge of success or failure with their sidelong appraisals of the strangers.

After four sweat-drenched hours, the tree had finally fallen at dusk. They were only now chopping away its protruding branches under the silent stares of the frontiersmen. Minutes later, Walker watched as the

Wildfire men sheared off the last limb—and were suddenly whisked away by the Astorians and thrown laughingly into the icy waters of the creek. They had passed the test and were part of the group.

Walker waded in to help his soaked men reach dry land, almost doubling over from laughter. As he extended his hand to them, though, Beck and Sutton exchanged a sly glance and tackled him mirthfully into the chill stream. Wiping away the wet hair plastered to his forehead and eyes, Walker turned to where the Astorians were roaring at his own unexpected baptism into frontier life. He splashed a mighty wave at Johnson, who retreated to the frame of the barn with a grin. The horseplay was finally broken up by Tinsley, whose proddings to return to work were finally heeded.

Things went better for them after that. Shingles for the roof had to be cut from the waiting logs; Walker and Johnson joined the work party to the lilting tunes of lively, bawdy songs that relieved the drudgery of the task. A contest was organized and to everyone's surprise, Sutton came in third after his companions had hollered themselves hoarse from giving encouragement. The Astorians were so impressed that they threw Sutton in the creek again before they stopped for lunch.

As morning slipped away into afternoon, Walker became increasingly involved in the mood of the men working around him. The solid feel of wood under his hands, the smell of fragrant rosins, the rhythmic pounding of axes in his ears: all combined to make the construction of the building an end in itself. The barn was more than a structure to be thrown together; it was the source of a pleasurable experience. The blood flowed vigorously in Walker's veins, a feeling of life he had known only during the high points of his career in space. It was, he reflected wryly, a satisfaction he could never obtain from the construction of an Earth Central standard-issue prefabricated shelter. By evening, Walker knew firsthand the pride that the Astorians shared, and his respect for them grew.

"What are we going to do tomorrow?" Beck asked Tinsley when they finally stopped working at sundown.

"See those logs over there? We'll use them to put up the walls come morning."

"Without nails?" said Beck, eyeing the huge hardwood timbers.

"Well, yes, since we don't have any—and we sure can't use wooden pegs on those logs," Tinsley replied with a touch of irritation.

He started to turn away, but Beck grasped his arm lightly. "Wait a minute. I'm an engineer, and I don't see how you can do this. You're talking about a wall ten, fifteen meters high—you can't just brace the corners of logs that heavy like you do on your cabins."

The Astorian looked at Beck in disgust and headed for the woodpile, picking up an ax as he went. He rolled two logs off the top of the stack and began chopping away at their corners. When the wood chips stopped flying, he motioned Beck in to see the result.

"Come here, Mr. Engineer," Tinsley said with unhidden sarcasm. "This notch is especially designed to hold up heavy walls. With it, we will put up four heavy walls tomorrow." He threw down his ax. "And we're going to do it with or without your help, whether or not you believe we can." Throwing up his arms in a gesture of hopelessness, the man stalked off to the waiting campfire, muttering, "We build barns for twenty years, and he tells me it can't be done. Next he'll knock down this barn and put up an aluminum igloo to store the grain in."

Walker followed him to the campfire where the other workmen were gathered for supper intending to deliver an apology—for what, he was not quite sure. But Tinsley was nowhere to be found. Mystified, Walker settled down and began to eat.

His thoughtful reverie was broken a few minutes later when the low murmurs of the others' conversations died away. Only Sutton's voice was left, suddenly loud in the quietness around the crackling fire. "And so there we were, no gravity, no power for the lights and only four hours of air. . . ."

The young man stopped short, confused at the sudden silence. "Another ship picked us up, though," he finished quickly and turned his attention to eating. The others stared at him for a time, then went back to their discussion of the weather, the current harvest, and other community affairs.

But Walker understood. The Astorians, it seemed, were happy with their own ways and did not want to be overridden by Earth authority or outdone by Earth affairs. And the two cultures, he reflected sadly, were on a collision course.

"I always like to come up here and watch the sunset," said Zeke.

Yulette could see why. Her legs ached from the hour

of uphill hiking behind them, but the view ahead was worth it. A rocky knob broke clear of the trees and jutted free into empty air. Zeke settled into a familiar, well-worn spot and leaned back; Yulette followed his example, and they hung suspended in space hundreds of meters above the forest that hid the foot of Zeke's cliff from sight. The lander O'Neil and Sutton had used was at the edge of the forest, looking like a miniature child's toy. Endless prairie extended beyond the boundary of the woods, a muted orange wasteland in the light of the waning sun. Far away was the dark splotch where the *Astoria* had met her doom; Yulette could see a tiny spot beside it, the other lander.

Shifting to find a smoother stretch of rock to lean against, Yulette concentrated on relaxing her knotted muscles. The heavy fatigue she felt surprised her. She and Zeke had spent the day helping a farm family gather corn from their fields—a job that had been harder than her first glance had led her to believe. The sun had been sweltering on her shoulders, and there had been no respite from the itching leaves or noonday heat. Blisters, many of them already broken, showed on her soft hands where she had carried basket after basket of ripe ears out of the patch.

It is such a waste, Yulette thought. They work so very hard here, and could be accomplishing so much more for their effort. Even the satisfaction they apparently derived from their work was unreasonable; their bountiful harvest would have been an equal accomplishment had it been gathered by machines. But the family she had helped hadn't seen it that way when Yulette had mentioned the new technology being used in the latest colonies—a topic that Zeke, too, was evidently thinking about.

"How many other colonies has Earth tried to set up?" he asked suddenly.

"Oh, I don't know," she said, relaxing. "Fifty or sixty, I guess."

"Most of them had ships that didn't blow up like ours did, right?" At her nod, the boy continued, "What are they like, Yulette?"

She closed her eyes, sunlight warm on her face. "Well, some of the older ones have upwards of a million people now. There are machines to do everything your people do by hand, letting the colonists work on other things—building cities, or building another starship to go and colonize the next planet out."

"Why would they do that?" the boy inquired. "What's wrong with the land they have?"

"Nothing is wrong with their land. They do it for the people on Earth that are crowded and want to move on to new worlds." She frowned thoughtfully. "Unfortunately, most of the colonies' cities end up just as crowded as those on Earth."

"Are all of the colonies crowded like that?" asked Zeke, a touch of awe in his words.

"No," Yulette told him. "The one I come from isn't."

"Where is that?"

"Lacaille IV," she said, smiling at the thought of her homeland. "Our planet doesn't have enough resources to support a colony of its own, much less start on another one. We produce knowledge instead—or specialize in training scientists to produce it. That is our contribution to Earth."

Zeke threw another stone over the cliff. "That doesn't sound like much of a contribution to me."

Yulette racked her mind for an example this boy would understand. How could she describe the sights in the universe she had been fortunate enough to see, wonders that had made her short life so meaningful? She finally had to settle on an analogy that left much unsaid. "You've seen a unicorn, Zeke, but have you ever seen a dragon? No? Well, I have, on a planet named Komodo. Don't you think I'm a better person for having seen that? Don't you think you'd be a better person if you saw it?"

"What's wrong with me the way I am now?"

Dumbfounded, Yulette stared at Zeke for a moment, then reached out to grasp his wrists in her hands. "You're *limited*," she replied insistently. "Zeke, you can't be your true self as long as you limit yourself to Astoria; you're meant to be more, and you can only know how much more by going to find out."

"What about the other colonies?" asked Zeke. "I'd be limited in most of them, too, wouldn't I?"

"Yes," she admitted reluctantly, "but that's not what I'm suggesting. The people of Earth are limited to the colonies, but they don't have to be. Neither do you, Zeke; you can go into space exploration for its own sake. In the future that will be commonplace, but it's a choice that is available now to those that want it. And I believe that's important, more important than colonization, even. Only by pushing back the limits of ability and knowledge can mankind find what it is truly meant to be."

He considered her words for a moment, then said

quietly, "I've always wondered what was out there among the stars—but Pa and the rest said that Earth and its colonies weren't worth seeing, and that everywhere else was just the same as here. The other kids believed them, but I've always thought there had to be something else." She saw the anticipation that gleamed in his eyes despite the growing shadows. "I wish . . . Yulette, do you think I'll ever get to see the things you have?"

"Yes," Yulette declared solemnly. "There are more marvels out there waiting for you than you could imagine in your most wonderful dreams."

"I'm glad," Zeke answered. "It gets awfully boring here in Astoria, with the same old routine day in and day out. Pa says it was different in the old days, when people were fighting to survive—but it's not like that now. I was wondering what I was going to do when I got older. I didn't want to be just a farmer; I always wanted to be something *more*." He glanced at Yulette. "Then you and your friends came along. I don't understand all of the things you say yet, but I can see you're more than just plain old farmers." Zeke pursed his lips to continue, then stopped.

"Go on, Zeke," Yulette urged.

"Yulette," he said reluctantly, "I want to be like you, and do the sort of work you do. Is that crazy?"

"No," she said gently. "You're young, and young people look for challenges. The challenge of space exploration is a far bigger one than any you have in Astoria."

Zeke considered her words with a silent nod, then rose to his feet. "Well, it sounds great, but right now

I've got to get back and cook supper or Pa will be madder than blazes. You coming?"

She regarded Zeke with a smile; his sudden switch from the profound to the practical amused her. "Oh, I think I'll stay up here a little longer—don't worry, I can find my way back." With a wink she finished, "I like to watch sunsets, too, but I don't get to see very many of them while I'm in space. I'd better enjoy this one while I can."

"Sure," he grinned. "See you."

When Zeke had left, Yulette turned her gaze skyward once more. The satisfaction she felt pleased her, for chances to help someone on a person-to-person basis in her travels were few and far between. They were worth waiting for, though; certainly this one was. She knew instinctively that Zeke had the qualities to become a space explorer if he wished, and she was prepared to help him in any way she could to see that he got that opportunity. Because of his limited background, he had no idea yet of the stakes involved; but that would come. That would come.

It was almost dark when she reached the trail that led back to Astoria. Walking in the dim light that filtered through the trees, Yulette suddenly stopped when she heard voices floating down the trail from around the bend ahead.

"You were right, Tom," someone said. "That engineer, Beck, came right out and said the barn wouldn't even stand. He thinks he's so smart, and he don't know *nothin'.*"

Yulette eased up to the curve in time to see Harris

nod solemnly in the gathering gloom. "I told Bill they might not know we were alive and that we shouldn't go out to that lander. But he didn't listen, and now we've got people like Beck in Astoria. They're all like him, too."

"That Sutton sure is," said another man, picking up a stick and flinging it into the surrounding brush. "A braggart for sure. Said he could down that tree in half an hour—ha!—and then tries to sell us on some story about how brave he was in some space mission of his."

A voice of protest came from the rear of the group. "Now wait a minute. Those men have really helped us the past two days. They're good workers, strong—"

"Yes, they're strong," Harris interrupted. "It's because they are strong that they are dangerous. Earth is so strong that their people will crush us when they get here."

There were disquieting mutters of agreement. "There's only one way out," insisted Harris, taking control of the group. "You heard what Walker said yesterday morning—that people were afraid to come here because they didn't know what happened to us. If *Wildfire* doesn't get back to Earth, they'll *still* be afraid to come."

"But we can't do anything about that spaceship," a man objected. "It's still up in the sky."

Harris smiled. "That's right. But the two landers aren't." There were scattered grins of understanding as he continued, "If we wreck their landers they're stranded with us for good. Word of our existence will never get back to Earth."

"Shoot, let's do it!" someone yelled. "I don't want

anybody coming in here and taking away my farm."

"Are we agreed, then? To destroy the landers, for the good of Astoria?" plugged Harris, and a cheer lifted from the men. "All right. Go get stone mallets and fresh torches, and let's get it over with tonight. We'll meet at midnight at the grist mill." With that, the men scattered in all directions into the forest on their way to fetch weapons. It was only by luck that they did not stumble on Yulette, hidden precariously in a clump of bushes she had picked in her effort to remain undiscovered.

Walker listened quietly to Yulette's story, glancing about at the muted faces of the other *Wildfire* crew members as she talked. They seemed surprised but not frightened, Walker noted approvingly; they were a good crew. He was depending on that fact for the decision he had already made.

At last Yulette finished, and everyone turned to Walker for his comment. "We've got to move the landers," he finally said, "to some place where they can't be found."

"*Move* them?" cried Yulette. "Why not go back into orbit and out of reach entirely?"

"No," Walker said flatly. "Not yet."

Yulette started to protest, but held her comments when she saw that the rest of the crew was ready to support his decision. Walker had the final say, but only very, very rarely would he override the majority wish of his crew; their divisions of rank were mere formalities, and they were all close friends. In this instance, however, the breakdown was clear: Yulette was a minority of one person, and she had no choice but to accept being overruled gracefully.

Walker knew that in principle Yulette was right, but he felt sure of what he was doing. After only two days of observation, he could see that in comparison to the colonies Earth Central had established, Astoria was not only vastly different—but in many ways better than average. He wanted to see more of what Johnson was willing to share so freely, and knew the others in his crew felt the same way. They would stay.

"All right," Walker continued, "Mark, you and Janet will pilot the lander you came down in; take Steve and Fritz to the one by the crater, then all of you move the landers north of here. Use your judgment and come back to Astoria when you've finished. Let's go."

The six of them started down the creek and reached the plains without incident. The second lander there was unharmed; soon the two flight crews were airborne, intent on their mission. Yulette and Walker stayed behind and watched as the craft moved out of sight quietly under low power, then settled down to wait.

They spoke little during their long vigil. "If Harris finds those landers," Yulette said quietly, "we'll be stranded here for the rest of our lives, and the Astorians will remain undiscovered. Are you willing to take that chance?"

"I already have," answered Walker, glancing up at the stars from which he would be banned if the landers were destroyed.

He was the first to hear faint voices as the men made their way down the creek; soon the flickering lights of the torches showed through the cover of the trees. He and Yulette shifted uncomfortably in the bushes and waited.

By the time the band reached the prairie both moons had risen high into the sky, shedding a soft glow over the level land. Harris emerged from the forest and scanned the area as the others gathered around him expectantly. The small man finished his survey and swore loudly. "I don't understand," he said, pointing to a smooth, empty stretch of ground. "The second lander—the one O'Neil and Sutton brought down—was right over there when I came down here this afternoon to check on it."

The group walked over slowly and stooped to see the dim imprints left in the soil from the lander's footpads. "Where is it now, Tom?" asked Tinsley.

Harris thought fast and replied, "They must have moved it to the crater, by the other one."

"That's a two hour hike," someone grumbled, shifting his stone mallet to his other shoulder.

"We were going to have to make it anyway to get to the other lander. Come on, let's get started."

"You can make the hike," Walker called out, "but you'll be wasting your time."

They whirled towards the sound in time to see two figures rise from the bushes. "Walker," Harris hissed.

Walker started forward slowly; Yulette followed only a step behind. "Hello, Harris."

The sound of air rushing from Harris' nostrils was the only sound to be heard. "What are you doing here?" he finally demanded.

"Oh, we were just moving our landers to a safe

place," Yulette said with undisguised contempt. "There's no telling what dangerous animals are out prowling around tonight."

"Don't try this again, Harris," warned Walker with blazing eyes. "Even if we don't get back to our ship, in six months our autopilot computer will return it to Earth anyway with the log tapes intact. You'll really be in trouble if a second survey ship finds you've destroyed our landers." He took Yulette's hand and led the way through the hostile group of men without waiting for a reply.

They had not quite reached the woods when they heard the sound of someone's voice echo to them, the cool night air causing his words to carry. "What are we going to do now, Tom?"

There was a pause, and they heard Harris' faint response. "I don't know—but I'll think of something."

Walker led the way back up the creek to Astoria, trying to relax his edgy nerves. The threat of the autopilot computer had been a bluff; while such things existed, outfitting the entire fleet with the devices had been deemed too expensive. Making such a ruse believable had been hard for Walker to do, but his anger had helped. Now if Harris found the hidden landers, he wouldn't dare wreck them—or so Walker hoped.

Ten minutes of hard walking in the cool night air soothed his tension. He became aware of Yulette behind him, and wondered why she asked no questions. He knew that she did not fully approve of his actions tonight; surely she had something to say! It was with a shock he realized that her silence was probing him more deeply than her words ever could.

The Astoria Incident : 189

Yulette realizes she can't sway me, thought Walker, so she's trying to make me doubt myself. Even as he recognized this, he knew the reason why her tactics would not work.

He had glimpsed a feeling of camaraderie in Astoria, an esprit-de-corps that he knew he must pursue wherever it led him. As an astronaut, Walker had made many new discoveries—not as many as he could have if Earth Central had given him free rein, of course, but enough to keep him from quitting altogether. The one thing he lacked was permanent friends to share these high points, the fruit of his work. Nobody on Earth cared about such, and unlike Yulette, he couldn't bear the restrained atmosphere of the various science institutes. In space there were transient friendships, but crews changed from mission to mission. Only in Astoria had Walker ever seen the free-wheeling, carefree but lasting sort of group unity that had always been missing from his life.

Despite his watchful eye, or perhaps because of it, Walker could see no indications of trouble from Harris in the days that followed. Tinsley made no mention of the night confrontation; Walker and the men in his crew helped with the grain barn without bringing up the subject themselves. Strangely enough, it was Johnson that felt responsibility for the occurrence.

"I don't really know what to say," he told Walker in the shade of the finished barn when everyone else had gone. "Tom is pretty radical sometimes, but he gets along with most everybody okay." Plucking a shoot of hay to chew on, he continued, "I'm glad you didn't just up and leave us."

"Well, we aren't planning on leaving at all . . . for a while, anyway," Walker said, snuggling into a bale of straw. "You've still got work for us, don't you?"

"Do I ever! Harvest is our busiest time of the year."

"Then we'll stay and help you. My crew can use the change of pace; we've been in space for a long time . . . too long, I sometimes feel," Walker finished, shaking his head.

"I think they're enjoying it here," Johnson observed hopefully.

"I think so, too," agreed Walker. "I know I am; helping on the barn, using my two hands, the friendliness you extend to strangers . . . very nice."

As they ambled along side by side on their way back to the village for lunch, Walker realized that he felt enthusiasm that had been lacking during his past few months in space. When Earth Central sent him to verify the reports of several other ships, as it had on this mission, it was hard for him to be enthusiastic; he would rather take his ship and prowl uncharted regions. Planets had advantages, though. *Wildfire* lacked the room for much exercise, for example, and on Earth his workouts were confined to the sterile confines of a gym. He wondered if. . . .

The race began with a tap on Johnson's shoulder, and ended with both men hugging the columns of his house to keep from collapsing from laughter as well as exhaustion. Johnson had won . . . but not by much. In a week, perhaps less, Walker would be ready for the rematch.

In the meantime, though, there were crops to harvest. It was almost impossible for a single family to gather a year's worth of food from their fields during the short span of ripeness; it was up to the neighbors to help, and the response of the Astorians was tremendous. In the spring neighboring farmers had agreed to stagger their seed planting so that now, in the fall, they could help each other bring in the crops. Walker admired the ingenuity of this arrangement, and the cooperation that made it work.

Cooperation made the harvest not only possible, but bearable. Work in the fields was a sweaty and toilsome job; winks of encouragement sometimes meant as much to Walker as a cool cup of water. He went to bed exhausted every night, but awoke in the morning refreshed and even eager to meet the family he was to help that day. The more he saw of the Astorians, the more he came to appreciate their easygoing ways, their earthy humor and contented lives.

The men of his crew took a similar view. Beck, von Nimen and Sutton, he noticed, joined zestfully in the elaborate folk ballads sung during the day—ballads less ribald, because of the women who worked in the fields, than those sung while the barn was being built. They were glad to help these people; the arm-wrestling contests, lazy evenings spent fishing, and all-too-frequent drinking sprees were a welcome vacation from their duties aboard *Wildfire*.

O'Neil took a more professional look at things. Walker dropped by her makeshift clinic one afternoon, and after she finished dressing a young girl's cut foot, she flopped into a nearby chair. "Whew! They've really kept me busy, John." A glimmer of happiness shone in her eye. "This is so much different from the colony hospital where I interned. There, the computer kept track of the patients; I just treated the symptoms. But here, I have time to get to know the people. It's really nice." She pointed out the door at the pigtailed girl who had just left. "Isn't she the cutest thing?"

Walker watched amusedly as the girl threw a handful of dirt on her playmate, a boy of the same age, and both scurried from sight. "She sure is."

O'Neil sighed. "You know, I'm going to be a bit unhappy when that computerized hospital gets here."

There was a pause, and then Walker heard himself say, "Me too, Janet."

He went back to the fields thinking about just what reopening this planet for colonization would mean for the Astorians. There was no way of escaping the fact that their way of life was doomed. In all probability Earth would place them on a collective farm, housing them in a prefabricated apartment unit; but even if by some bureaucratic miracle they were allowed to keep their primitive farms and cabins, they would be a laughingstock to the thousands of colonists who would overrun them. Walker knew that ridicule would destroy their proud lifestyle just as surely as would a bulldozer razing the village of Astoria.

After supper in Johnson's home that night, he still had not thought of a solution to the dilemma. Yulette, he knew, believed he could help the Astorians most by returning at once to Earth to send back aid, but as usual she did not raise the subject. She and Zeke, to whom she'd been devoting most of her free time, set up a checker board and were soon lost in thought over the square of wood. Johnson looked over the scene approvingly and cleared his throat. "You know, now

The Astoria Incident : 193

that the harvest is about finished, we have a little festival to get ready for—"

"The Harvest Festival," said Walker. "I've heard several people talking about it."

Johnson nodded. "In the past couple of years some of our younger ones have decided it's about time for them to get married." He paused and said, "Won't be too long till that one over there gets the same idea—"

"Aw, Pa—"

"Anyway, we always get 'em hitched at the Harvest Festival, and when we do, we want them to have someplace to go." Johnson took a sip of tea and continued, "That means a house-raising; four of them this year, in fact. We've got enough men lined up for three, but Strom Adler is still out in the cold." He looked at Walker. "You want to help, or finish up with the harvest? Your men want to work on the cabin, but it will work out either way."

Walker considered. "I think I'll stay in the fields, Bill," he said, trying to keep the emotion from his voice. He knew that he could not bear to work on a home that would be destroyed by Earth Central in a year's time. It would be bad enough, he thought, when they tore down the grain barn.

"Well, you're certainly doing a good job there," Johnson was saying. He gave Walker a meaningful look and ended, "We could sure use some more men like you, John."

Walker averted his gaze before his eyes betrayed him. "Thanks, Bill," he choked out.

There was an uncomfortable silence that Johnson broke by pushing the dishes aside to clear a spot on the table. Placing his elbow in the center and holding his hand into the air, he said, "Ready to take me on in a bout of arm wrestling?"

Forcing a smile, Walker replied, "Sure."

He unsnapped his shirt cuff and placed his elbow beside Johnson's; grasping the other's hand, he began to push with all his might. The two men locked stares, and as the taut strain built up in his arm, Walker suddenly realized that he had found the sense of belonging he had never before found on any world.

The struggle lasted for a very long time, swaying back and forth between the two men until one seized his temporary advantage and pressed on to victory. As the cheers from Yulette and Zeke died away, Walker's concentration drained from his mind and left an empty void. What difference does it make which one of us wins? he thought. Soon Johnson is going to lose his cherished way of life, and I'm going to lose a beckoning oasis in space where I can stop during my travels and rest. We're both going to lose in the end.

The harvest was over. The men who had cut the silage from the last cornfield scattered into the lazy afternoon heat, their tired chatter filling the still air. Walker went to the back porch of the adjacent cabin, got himself a cup of water, and went off to lean against one of the bundles of brown cornstalks. It had been a long day; closing his eyes, he dozed off for a nap.

The shadows were noticeably longer when he awoke, somewhat refreshed. He was just about to go around to the back of the cabin for more water when he heard

Harris's voice. "Bill, they're going to spill the beans when they get back to Earth. This place will be swarming with greenhorns, noise, schedules, all sorts of commotion." There was the swirl of the ladle in the water bucket, and then, "We won't be in charge any more. What are we going to do about it?"

"What are *we* going to do about it?" cried Johnson. "What do you mean, *we*? Did *we* try to wreck those landers? No, sir. *You* did, you and your buddies, and you failed. The only reason you've come whimpering to me is because you haven't got any more tricks left up your sleeve." There was a brief, contemptuous pause. "I believe you would even murder those people if you thought you could get away with it. You'd make it look like an accident, sure, but you can't stop that spaceship of theirs from going to Earth by itself. That's the only thing that's holding you back." Johnson spat on the ground, loudly. "You know, Tom, Walker seems to like it here; he might even decide to stay here if folks like you would stop antagonizing him."

Harris ignored the insult. "We've got a good life here, and we're going to lose it. Do you want Astoria to become like one of them colony cities, Bill? Do you?"

"No," Johnson retorted. "I don't give a hoot about being in charge; I don't really even like it, but somebody's got to organize the crops and keep things rolling ... somebody who'll do it right," he added in a caustic tone. "I just want things to stay as peaceful and pretty as they are now."

"Then what do we do to keep it that way?" Harris delivered the word with cold, deliberate preciseness.

"There's not much we can do," Walker heard Johnson say. "The only way out is if he decides to stay himself." There was a pause. Then the words, "We need something that he can really feel a part of. Maybe if he could come along with us on the unicorn hunt—"

Walker felt he'd overheard enough. Moving to the rear porch, he interrupted with, "A *what* kind of hunt?"

The two men looked at him suspiciously, but Walker went to the bucket and refilled his cup as innocently as possible. Finally Johnson said, "A unicorn hunt, John. There is one every year to get meat for the Harvest Festival opening feast; Tom and I were talking about inviting you along. Any of your crew can come too, of course; but I daresay with the interest they've shown in Strom's homeplace, they'll choose to stay there."

Walker downed a swallow of water and said, "I'd like to come, but I have no skill with a bow—"

"We can fix that," interrupted Johnson. "You can practice with Will Abrams's bow; he . . . well, he won't be needing it. The skills involved are not that difficult; you'll learn rapidly."

He placed his cup beside the water bucket. "All right. We can talk about it tonight." Walker stepped from the porch and started back to the village. "See you around, Mr. Harris."

Lingering at the front of the cabin, he caught Harris's low remark: "You're only fooling yourself, Bill. Nothing has changed."

Once he had finished saying grace over the breakfast table, Johnson picked up a steaming platter of scrambled eggs and turned his attention to Zeke. "Son, you know the Harvest Festival is coming up?" he asked, raking a huge heap of eggs onto his wooden plate.

The question was a rhetorical one, Yulette knew; every man, woman and child in Astoria counted the days to the yearly event. Confused, Zeke responded meekly, "Yes, sir."

"I've decided to hold the opening feast in honor of Captain Walker and his crew." He turned to Walker. "After all, you people won't be with us much longer."

Walker, his mouth full with his first big bite of cornbread, could only nod.

"Now that we've a feast scheduled," Johnson continued, "we need meat for it. We're leaving on a unicorn hunt Tuesday to take care of that little detail."

He paused, ladling out gravy with excessive care over a crumbled muffin. "We'll need some good men on that hunt, Zeke. It's going to be a rough one." Another pause, a short one, and then, "Would you like to come with us?"

Yulette watched impassively as joy and amazement overmastered Zeke. "Of course I . . . I mean . . . yes, sir, I would like to come with you very much."

Johnson smiled broadly at his son. "That's good, because I've been working awfully hard on this the past few months." From beneath the table he took a large cloth sack and handed it to the boy. "Open it."

Zeke did, and with an audible gasp withdrew a beautifully finished crossbow. It was smaller than the one that hung above the hearth, scaled and built for a hunter of lesser strength and size. But the device was not a toy; the seasoned wood of the stock and the sinew of the bowstring were built for power, not play. Delving into the bag once more, Zeke pulled out a handful of arrows, tipped with killer points.

"You mean I'm not going to herd the unicorns?" Zeke asked incredulously.

"You can if you want to," replied his father. "But with a bow like that, you'd be better off with the stalkers."

"Yes, sir." He leaned to Yulette and said in an excited stage whisper, "I thought he'd never ask."

They all laughed at that, Yulette a bit hollowly as she examined Zeke's weapon with apprehension. She did not know what this hunt was, but it could not be a constructive experience for Zeke—not now, not so soon before he would be immersed in the Earth heritage that was rightly his. Gingerly placing the bow onto the table, she said, "I would like to go on the hunt also, Mr. Johnson."

Johnson frowned. "We don't have another bow—"

"I won't need a weapon. I want to observe, not participate."

He shrugged. "As you wish, Yulette."

After breakfast the two men went outside and set up a target range behind Johnson's house. As Walker received instructions on triggering the bow, Zeke and Yulette settled down behind them to watch. Talking in low voices so as not to disturb Walker, Yulette said, "You didn't tell me you *hunted* the unicorns. I thought the one over your father's mantle was shot in self-defense after it gored Abrams."

"It *was* shot in self-defense," Zeke answered softly. "But they were stalking it for last year's feast. There were about twenty stalkers in all, and the herd stampeded before they could get in position."

"You hunt them in herds?" she asked, the question punctuated by a sharp *zip-thunk*! of Walker's first arrow as it dug into the ground short of its target. Johnson moved in with a word of advice.

"For someone who's so smart, you don't know much about hunting," whispered Zeke. "Unicorns run in herds of thirty or forty at a time, and they always graze facing the same direction. The stalkers—men with crossbows—sneak up beside them and when the herders scare them from behind, everything is set up for a broadside shot."

Zip. The second arrow sailed out of sight beyond the target.

"But why?" pursued Yulette. "You have all the fish and fowl you can eat."

"Shucks, I know we don't need the extra food; it's for the feast. We always start the Harvest Festival with a feast."

The silence between them was broken by yet another *zip-thunk*. An arrow quivered at the target's edge; Walker's aim was improving. "Don't you have hunts where you come from?" Zeke suddenly inquired.

"No," said Yulette numbly. "No, we don't."

Zip-thunk. Walker had struck mere centimeters from the bull's-eye, unaware of the spontaneous grin that was spreading over his sunburned face. Johnson clapped him playfully on the shoulder, handed him another arrow to nock, and walked to where Zeke and Yulette were watching. "Ready to try, Zeke?"

The boy leaped to his feet. "Sure!"

Yulette did not stir as the two went to join Walker in the firing circle and watched unblinkingly as the target practice proceeded. Zeke could not match the progress that came with Walker's space-trained reflexes, but he improved rapidly as he adjusted to his small, well-balanced crossbow. At one point Johnson went inside and brought out his own bow; soon the three of them were driving home arrows with hardly any misses. They broke for a brief lunch and returned to the makeshift range in high spirits. Johnson began to tell barely believable stories about previous hunts, and the resulting hoots of laughter drew other archers from nearby houses. By the end of the afternoon the place was a happy free-for-all. Twenty or twenty-five hunters were taking aim at half a dozen targets, encouraging and joshing each other good-naturedly. Even Walker, Yulette noted, was caught up in the festive air surrounding the hunt; he moved among the others with a smile on his face, a man relaxed among friends.

Yulette observed the proceedings in isolated silence as the sun sank below the trees. She saw Zeke fire an arrow into the center of one target and was not surprised when Walker shattered it seconds later with an arrow of his own. Alone among the whoops of admiration, she thought of the absent Harris, and of the unicorn above the fireplace that had gored Will Abrams to death. There would be, Yulette reflected sadly, some very efficient predators afield come the day of the hunt.

Tuesday morning dawned bright and clear. The entire community turned out in the village square to wish the hunting party good luck. There were twenty-seven in the expedition; Walker and Yulette were the only *Wildfire* representatives. As Johnson had guessed the rest of the crew chose to stay and help young Strom.

The group started off to the south, a direction with which Walker was not familiar. He knew that they would soon hit the prairieland if they continued long enough, but he doubted that there was reason to venture very far onto the plains. As they crashed along through the dense forest, Johnson brought up the subject himself. "The hills become rocky and form box canyons ahead," he explained. "The unicorns graze on the bushes of the plains and go to the canyons to find water."

"How do we know where to find them?"

"We look." Johnson laughed. "We check water holes for tracks, bushes for eaten leaves. It may take awhile; one year we searched for a week before we found a herd—then the wind changed, they bolted, and we spent another three days catching up with them." He gave Walker a comradely look. "But we'll find them, my friend. Just wait and see."

Sitting beside a cozy campfire that night, Walker decided that this trip would be worth the effort even if they found no unicorns at all. He had seldom been camping even on Earth; the waiting lists to obtain permits to enter the wilderness areas were depressingly long. Yet here he was, the sound of rustling leaves in his ears, the cool night air fresh on his face. The serenity pleased him, and even Yulette seemed to be enjoying herself—something that had been worrying him since her outburst over moving the landers.

They found the sought-after tracks two days later, on the edge of a muddy creek that cut its way down through a canyon. Johnson and a few other seasoned hunters examined the tracks and took on expressions of sad dismay. Grimly they looked upstream; the stream twisted up the funneling hallway of the canyon and over the top into unseen territory.

"What's wrong?" asked Zeke.

Johnson turned to his son. "Those unicorns are going the wrong way—up the canyon and into the woods. We're going to have to flush them down and onto the plains."

"What difference does it make?" Yulette inquired.

But the leader had already moved out and had started up the creek, the others following close behind at a fast clip. Zeke, Yulette and Walker brought up the rear in confusion. Johnson kept up the grueling pace for several hours, with only brief stops for rest; everything became an inseparable blur of sweat, fatigue and gasps of air.

Johnson, at the head of the column, started around a boulder and froze. Eying the situation for a moment, he eased back out of sight and motioned his expectant followers to keep quiet. Then he began to climb the rough rocks of the canyon wall; everyone copied his example in silence. The climb to the top took less than ten minutes, and they all moved forward stealthily, unable to see the floor of the gorge they had left below.

"Where's Zeke?" hissed Johnson. "Come here, boy. I'm going to show you some unicorns." He turned to Harris. "Pick up some men and go on ahead. You know what to do."

Johnson and his son crawled to the edge and carefully peered over; Harris and the others continued ahead and were soon lost from sight among the rocks. Walker and Yulette looked at each other in bewilderment; whatever was happening, Johnson would know. They scrambled over to him and looked into the gorge.

The herd at the bottom was a small one; there were no more than twenty-five or thirty unicorns in all, nibbling on the sparse vegetation and plodding slowly upward. Their white bodies stood out in vivid contrast to the dingy gray rocks—an unmissable target. Zeke turned to his father excitedly, reaching for his bow. "This is it, isn't it?" he asked.

"No," said Johnson, reaching out to still the boy with his hand.

"But we can't miss!"

"Exactly," said Walker, beginning to understand. "It's too easy."

Johnson gave him a broad grin. "You're beginning to see our ways, John," he said. "This is more than a hunt; it's a tradition. We must give them a chance to escape, and a chance to fight back. In the canyons we can't lose; they must meet us on the plains."

Walker nodded approvingly. He understood the need for challenge; in space that was what he himself sought, a thing that gave all else meaning. Twenty years ago, the challenge of survival was enough to occupy everyone's attention in Astoria. But times had changed; survival was now assured. Most of the Astorians were content with their current lives of steady work. But for the adventurous, tests of manhood could be found in no other way than this.

"They're beautiful," Yulette remarked in hushed tones of awe.

So they were. Mats of snow-white hair covered their muscular bodies of streamlined strength. Their thin, spidery legs, which seemed unnaturally long for their unicorns' bodies, were built for speed and not power. Topped by manes of black, their necks extended majestically away from the torso and high into the air; their black tails swished proudly back and forth. Each of their heads tapered gently into a delicate muzzle and was crowned with a single, straight horn.

Suddenly a yell came echoing down the gulley, followed by another and then a third. As the animals looked up in startled surprise, the shouts reached a crescendo level and rocks began to rain down from the lip of the crevasse ahead. The smaller fillies nudged their colts around and in seconds were thundering back down the canyon. Other males stood fast until the first rocks had rolled around a curve into view; then they bolted and headed down also at full speed. The lead stallion, a muscular giant whose horn was only a jagged, battle-scarred stub, waited until the first stones bounced past him before he turned and brought up the rear in an unhurried trot.

The trip down the canyon was easier for the hunters than the climb up had been; by late afternoon they had reached the plains once more. Johnson threw his pack down by the creek where they had first spotted the tracks and pointed to a churning blot of dust on the flat horizon. "They're still running," he laughed. "But they'll stop soon for the night, and tomorrow they'll be grazing on the prairie."

He lifted his crossbow and sighted along it to the distant yellow cloud. "Tomorrow we get them. Let's set up camp."

"There they are," someone said. Walker followed the pointing finger; perhaps two kilometers away was the herd they had seen the day before. The hunters blended into the cover of the scattered bushes to plan their attack.

Johnson picked up a handful of dust and let it sift through his fingers, watching which way the wind blew it. They had covered too much ground this morning to risk losing the herd now; a mistake could cost them everything. "All right," he said, pointing to a knoll, "we've got to get closer. If the wind holds, we can make it behind that hill, and we'll be within five hundred meters of them. We'll go in teams of two, and when you're in position, don't peek over the top. Wait until everybody gets there. Tom, you and Carl go first. Take your time and stick to the cover."

Harris and the other man started off, weaving at a slow diagonal to get the knoll between them and the herd, then running silently for the base of the hill that hid them from their quarry. When Johnson judged them to be out of sight of the unicorns, he tapped two more men who repeated the motion. Walker and Yulette were the third team to try the run; joining hands, they made the crossing as skillfully as any of the seasoned hunters that came after them. The entire group assembled behind the knoll undiscovered within half an hour.

Johnson crept to the top of the hill to check on the

grazing herd, taking Zeke, Walker and Yulette with him. The unicorns had not wandered far; they continued to graze unsuspecting half a kilometer away. Turning to Zeke, Johnson whispered, "All right, son. Should we approach them from the left or the right?"

The boy frowned, considering the problem. The herd was facing left and into the wind, alert for any scents of warning it might bring. An approach from that direction would risk discovery; still, they needed to get close to the head of the column to gain a maximum number of broadside shots as the herd rumbled past, and approaching from the left would be easier by far.

"We should go right," Zeke said coolly, "working our way to the rear, drop off the herders, then split into two groups and work our way up to the head of the column on both sides."

"That's absolutely right," Johnson praised in tones of pride. "The temptation is to try for the easy way—but you're better off by being patient and doing the extra work. Remember that, Zeke."

"I don't understand," Walker broke in. "I thought we were going to ambush them from here after someone scared them into running in this direction."

Johnson shook his head. "That would be suicide," he said flatly. "We need to fire from the side; when they're running, I can guarantee that you don't want to be in their way."

"But how do you get beside them?" asked Yulette. "There's no cover—those shrubs can't be over knee high."

"We crawl on our bellies," grinned Johnson. "Those

shrubs will be cover enough."

Crawl they did. Yulette, being unarmed, stayed behind to watch from the crest of the hill; Johnson led the way around the right side of the knoll flat on his stomach with Walker, Zeke and the others following in single file behind him. Pushing their bows ahead of them, they laboriously—and above all, silently—began to close in for the kill.

Walker lost track of the distance they had covered within ten minutes. He could only see the soles of Johnson's moccasins ahead of him, outlined in specks of sunlight and shadow from the overhanging bushes. Five hundred meters would take a long, long time to cover at this snail's pace. He tried to rid his body of the nerve-wracking tension and relax, and found he could not. He forgot about Zeke behind him; Harris, *Wildfire*, Earth—all slipped away. His mind was not filled with words, but instead flooded with some sublimal mindlock with the creature he stalked. The weight of the crossbow he bore was his only reassurance against the fear of a creature that otherwise held all of the advantages. The universe contracted into a shell that ended half a meter ahead at the limits of his vision, and Walker pressed on alone.

By the time Johnson stopped to peer cautiously through the bushes to gain his bearings, Walker was trembling with excitement. As the leader shifted course on the endless sea of dirt, he wanted to scream, How much farther? but held himself to silence. Onward, forward, one shrub at a time, endlessly.

Johnson stopped several more times to check their progress, and finally gave off the lonely cry of a native bird to signal those behind him that they were successfully behind the herd. An answering call came from Harris at the end of the line in acknowledgment. Walker listened carefully; from far away came the faint snort of some unseen unicorn. They started forward at a right angle to their original path.

The noose was drawing tight. At the signal, the hunting line had split into three parts; a rear guard had stayed in position behind the herd, detaching itself from the line Johnson was leading into position along the side of the herd. Harris, who had been at the rear, was now leading his own group slowly up the other side. Within minutes the result was a deadly U of hunters around the unsuspecting unicorns.

Harris gave his bird cry once more: his men were set. After taking one last look through the branches, Johnson returned the signal. Walker imagined he could hear the silent drawing of two dozen bows.

The suddenness of the flush took Walker by surprise even though he had been warned beforehand. The rear guard, three men in all, burst from their hiding places and ran directly for the herd, screaming their lungs out. Startled colts at the rear of the pack instinctively bolted away from the confusion; their momentum flowed through the unicorns, overwhelming the group's inertia and driving it forward like a single, unified being. The stallions charged ahead, breaking their way out of the unseen U.

At the first sound of hooves, the U remained unseen no longer. Springing to their feet, the bowmen charged forward to get within range for a shot. Walker was so caught up in the moment that he was up and running before half the men at his side had even reached their feet.

The low branches clawed at his legs, slowing him down, but within seconds he was within range. Clutching his crossbow with a death grip, Walker braced himself and absorbed the image before him. The lead stallion was twenty meters past him and still picking up speed, its freedom won. Those unicorns directly behind it were at an unfavorable angle for a shot; Johnson would have to down one of those on his own. Walker peered into the thunderous fog of dust and glimpsed a flash of white: a young stallion, small, but of acceptable size and age. He squeezed the trigger of the crossbow even as he swung it into position.

It was a clean, accurate shot; Walker was sure of that as it sped away from his bow. The arrow hung suspended in the air for an instantaneous flash, and then the animal jolted, broke stride, and crumpled to the earth. It was dead before even hitting the ground. A thrill of victory rose within Walker, feverish in its intensity.

And then, as he stared at his bleeding kill, his thrill was replaced by a sudden feeling of revulsion. How could he, a spaceman, have sought challenge in pitting himself against such a beautiful creature that need not have been destroyed?

From out of the swirling grit, a second unicorn came into view and tripped over its downed companion in unseeing haste. Unable to stop, it veered out of the stampede and fell down with a graceless thud; rising shakily to its feet once more, the animal suddenly became aware of Walker thirty meters away. The panic in its eye was replaced by a dim understanding—here was an enemy who could be repelled. Walker barely had time to recognize the broken horn of the grizzled fighter stallion before the brute lowered its head and charged.

The animal was still slow, but not slow enough. Keeping his eyes on it, Walker backpedaled furiously, pawing at his belt quiver for the arrow that could save his life. As the creature gathered speed, Walker freed a single shaft and slapped it to the bow in a single desperate blur of motion. His sweaty fingers nocked the arrow, jerked back on the bowstring . . . and suddenly he felt himself falling over backwards, his heels entangled in one of the bushes that had hidden him only seconds before. The arrow fired harmlessly into empty air; the crossbow went flying out of his hands and into the brush. The back of his head smashed into a sandy rock, and an inner roaring overshadowed the sound of hooves in his ears.

Lying dazed on the ground, Walker forced his eyes open and found himself staring blankly into the sky. One of the two moons was within his field of vision, dazzling white against a backdrop of blue. Somewhere beyond the blueness were blackness and infinite stars; stars he would never see again. Through his back he could feel the vibrations of the fleeing animals, a rumbling that did not blot out the steady cadence of another set of hooves approaching with deadly purposefulness.

I am going to die, Walker thought to himself. But I don't belong here; up there is a starship that can take me to where I should be, where I belong: in space, and not on the ground.

He tried to roll out of the path of death, but the effort was too much, too much. With his last vestiges of strength, he willed himself to rise into the sky and to the ship that could save him; but instead of rising, Walker found himself sinking into inner seas of darkness as he blacked out.

At the edge of consciousness, he still felt the vibrations; but they were softer now, more gentle. The roaring in his ears had been replaced with sounds that varied in tone, almost as if they were words. He strained to make out their meaning.

"Wake up, John. Please, wake up."

Walker opened his eyes. Yulette was there, cradling his head in her arms. "The unicorn—" he started, gasping for breath.

"Johnson shot it."

Struggling to raise his head, he saw that it was true. Fifteen meters away lay the mountain of flesh that had been so fearsome short minutes ago, an arrow deep in its side. Insects, the first Walker had seen, were beginning to buzz and settle on the carcass. The animal's horn had been broken entirely off in its final fall; it would be fighting no more battles, ever again.

"Where are Johnson and the others?" he asked tiredly.

"They're off chasing a wounded filly that was hit by mistake," she answered. "How do you feel?"

Before Walker could reply, he was interrupted by a shout from behind. "How is he?" came Zeke's voice.

With Yulette's help, Walker stood. "I'll be all right.

What's that you've got?"

"A unicorn I bagged." The body upon his shoulders was barely more than a colt, its white coat stained by blood; still, Zeke carried it as though it were the prize of the day. "This was fun. It's a shame it was over so fast; I can hardly wait till next year."

"Yes," Walker said blankly.

"Tell my father that I've started back to the camp to skin this one, will you?" He turned and headed toward their site by the creek.

Walker began to search among the bushes and finally retrieved his crossbow. It was broken; the bow had snapped in half, and its stock was cracked in several places. The overwhelming emotion he had felt upon loosing the arrow from this shattered bow frightened him. How could he have taken such pride in his action? He had studied thousands of varieties of life on a hundred different worlds, and always before he had felt awe at the sight of creatures he was so unable to create. Yet he had experienced an even stronger feeling here today not at the creation of life, but at its destruction. How was this possible in him? He was a spaceman, the highest achievement possible in his civilization. . . .

Because, he realized with a shock, in the past weeks he had been acting not as a spaceman, but as a more primitive sort of adventurer. In that reversion he had lost his sense of wonder to a feeling of false contentment. Now that he perceived that, Walker knew he could never be satisfied in Astoria; he could not bear to knowingly limit himself.

"These people have a fine philosophy," declared

Walker, flinging the ruined weapon disgustedly into the brush, "but their primitive lifestyle holds them to primitive ways of carrying it out. Their culture is based on obsolete forms of challenge. Hunts like these had their place on Earth hundreds of years ago, when the game was needed and when there was no higher kind of quest to sharpen men's abilities; that isn't the case now. We've developed other, more mature ways of expressing our drive to achieve."

"The Astorians deny that more mature ways exist," said Yulette. "They think that this hunt is just as valid a challenge as the space exploration we do, but they're wrong. You heard Johnson; he had his men drive the unicorns out of the canyons and onto the plains. He deliberately gave up his advantages and limited himself, to set up a challenging situation. Well, true challenges are made and met not by limiting oneself, but by bringing forth the very best one has to offer."

Walker could see it clearly now. In rejecting the disadvantages that contact with Earth would bring, the Astorians were limiting themselves in their everyday lives by not accepting the advantages that would come as well. "They'll never see your point, Yulette," he said. "Their group unity is so great that they'll convince one another that they're right." His voice took on a more wistful tone. "It's ironic, isn't it? Their most admirable quality is the one keeping them isolated from the people who could use it out there in Earth Central's colonies."

"Our people have unity and a sense of belonging, too, John," Yulette commented softly. "I know. On Lacaille IV such is the rule rather than the exception.

And look at the friendship and spirit of cooperation among *Wildfire*'s crew. Relationships may not be as permanent as the kind the Astorians share, but they're still good ones. Even more importantly, we're using our cooperation to accomplish something worthwhile for mankind. That's a claim the Astorians can't make."

That was true, Walker realized. "You've known this all along, Yulette; why didn't you tell me?" he asked.

She took his arm and led him slowly forward. "You were so caught up in their way of life that you wouldn't have listened. You had to figure things out for yourself."

"So we trigger Earth Central into bringing them back to the century where they belong," said Walker hollowly, thinking of what would be lost in the transition. No more easy, lifelong friendships; no more log castles built with bare hands that a man could call his own. . . .

"We have no choice, John."

"I suppose not," he sighed. "But if we did, I'm not sure I wouldn't take it."

"You would let them remain as they are, neither civilized nor savages—" Yulette said, her nostrils flaring in sudden fury as they stopped in front of Walker's dead unicorn. "How could you even *consider* that after what happened here today?"

"I can't ignore the good I've seen on this world," said Walker. "There is precious little good in this universe, and the Astorians have preserved a form that Earth Central's policies are hampering."

"Well, you are the man who could weigh the sides and make the decision, Captain. You say you can't ignore the good. I can—I see too much of the evil. But you know more about the evil than I do, too." With a sickening squish, Yulette wrenched Walker's arrow from his kill and pressed the moist shaft to his palm. "After all, there is blood on your hands."

Blood on his hands. The phrase stuck in Walker's mind as he helped Johnson and the others skin the animals and string the meat onto slings and carrying poles for the day's journey back to Astoria. He spoke to no one on the long trek to the village; oblivious to his surroundings, Walker drew up a mental checklist of actions to get his crew off this planet and back into interstellar space.

"What's the matter with him?" he heard one of the hunters say to Harris. "He got one of the finest stallions of the hunt, something he wanted as badly as the rest of us. Now he acts like he doesn't even care."

"It's the woman," Harris replied grimly. "Walker saw our point of view on this hunt, just like Bill said he would. But that blasted Lacaillian twisted it all around in his head, and now we're right back where we started. We'll fix things, though. Wait and see."

The hunter nodded agreeably, hypnotized by Harris's words, and faded back into his place in the caravan. Harris smiled humorlessly as the gossipy whispering started up behind him a few minutes later. The word, Walker thought, would spread rapidly and grow as it went. But even that ominous fact could not seem to cut through the dark cloud of depression in his mind.

The party came staggering tiredly into Astoria that night by the light of triumphant torches. The whole town turned out to welcome them home, and the crowd dissolved into warm groups of handshakes, backclapping and laughter. Walker pressed through the throng, gathering the members of his crew together as Johnson gave an impromtu speech from atop a makeshift platform. At the end of the talk, Johnson motioned him forward. "Let's hear a few words from Captain Walker," he said. "What did you think of your first hunt?"

Surprised, Walker hesitated before heading for the platform; then his stride became smoother as his confidence grew. He owed the Astorians an explanation for what he intended to do, and now was as good a time as any. Stopping in front of the platform, Walker began to speak.

"Thank you, Bill. The hunt today was quite an experience, all right; one that I'll never forget. But that's not what I'd like to talk about." He paused to clear his throat, unsure of how to continue. "Well, I'll get right to the point. It's time for me and my crew to continue our journey and leave your village behind."

A hushed stillness fell over the crowd. Then, breaking the silence, came an angry buzzing that swept over those gathered in the town square. Walker stood his ground, unflinching in the gaze of their stares.

Harris, obviously recognizing his unforeseen chance, stood to speak into the electrified air. "What's the matter?" he taunted. "Our ways not good enough for you?" As if on cue, there followed several crude remarks from the back of the crowd. The people stirred restlessly.

"It's not that—" Walker began.

"Well, we don't like it. Do we, men?" Harris interrupted, turning to face the crowd. The hecklers shouted in furious agreement, sowing ill will in the others. Walker could see that those shouting loudest were the hunters who were friends of Harris; as if by some unseen signal, they brought their bows up, drawn and ready.

Yulette saw the weapons also. "What's he *doing*?" she whispered to Walker. "Doesn't he believe about the autopilot any more?"

"Harris is going for broke," Walker whispered back.

The entire *Wildfire* crew was in danger now, Yulette realized; Harris might kill them all before they could reach the landers to arm themselves or escape. But the time was not yet ripe. The crowd was angry, but not yet murderous, and no arrows would fly until it was.

"Wait," Walker shouted, leaping to the platform behind him. Planting his feet on its top, he turned to face the Astorians. "Listen to me, Harris. We have ways different from those you have developed, but that doesn't mean—"

"We don't care about your explanations," shouted Harris. "We don't care about your duty or your command. We only want to make sure you aren't going to tell Earth that we are here."

There was a shocked silence, and Yulette realized that Walker had backed himself into a corner. Every eye was hostile, looking accusingly at him. She could feel rather than see the clenched fists, the gritting teeth that the Astorians shared unconsciously in this moment.

"We won't tell," Walker said unhesitatingly. "We will keep your secret."

Everyone in the village square began to murmur in amazement. Johnson's eyes sparkled with a sudden hope, but he kept his facial expression under tight control. This was what he had hoped for all along, Yulette suddenly saw; now he was scarcely able to believe that his hope had been realized.

Yulette shared his surprise. More than anyone else there, she knew that what Walker promised was impossible. *She* wasn't going to stay quiet, and even if the entire crew had agreed to remain silent, there were log and computer entries aboard *Wildfire* that told of what they had found on this planet. Walker had obviously told a blatant lie to keep them alive; she wondered why he thought the Astorians would believe it.

Harris certainly didn't. "How do we know we can trust you, Walker?" he said acidly. "You'll be light-years away, on your own—"

"Do you trust this man?" Walker jumped down and clapped his hand on Johnson's shoulder. "He's led you through twenty years of hardship and you've supported him all the way."

Harris hesitated. He could not risk offending Johnson's supporters at this charged moment; when the crowd moved, it had to be in unison. "Yeah, we trust Bill," he answered.

"All right. I guess the word has spread that Bill saved my life on the hunt today." There were nods of acknowledgement in the crowd as Walker turned to Johnson and extended his hand. "Bill, I swear by the life you've given me to keep the secret of this planet."

Yulette gasped openly, not having dreamed that

Walker would carry his lie this far. Only the personal trust that prevailed among Astorians would enable his ruse to work—one of the few worthwhile characteristics of the Astorian culture, a characteristic Earth Central lacked entirely. Yulette was astonished that Walker would corrupt that, even to preserve the safety of his crew.

Johnson paused for only a moment. He thrust out his hand to Walker in a gesture of trust and friendship, saying, "Go in peace."

A cheer lifted from the crowd. In the bedlam that followed, Yulette saw Zeke squeezing his way towards her. "I thought you said I was going to get my chance to be like you," he burst out. "Now you're just going to leave me here! How could you do such a thing?"

Yulette reached out to assure him that Walker's promise was merely a ruse, only to stop short. All around her were listening Astorians who still bore shadows of hostility; she didn't dare contradict Walker now. With a sinking feeling, Yulette knew that she wouldn't get a chance to enlighten Zeke later, either— the *Wildfire* crew was only seconds away from leaving. Zeke would just have to live with his doubts until the next crew from Earth arrived. "I . . . I'm sorry, Zeke," she stammered not knowing what else to say.

"I trusted you," Zeke accused piercingly, then turned and slowly shuffled away.

Reaching out for a nearby torch, Walker motioned for a moment of silence. "We thank you for the hospitality you have shown us," he said in a voice choked with emotion. "Few colonies of Earth would have been so kind. I hope—my entire crew hopes—that the years ahead will be happy ones for you all." He ended simply, "Good luck, Bill." Then without looking back, Walker started slowly forward to lead his crew through the unresisting crowd and into the darkness of the north forest.

At the fringe of the woods, Yulette turned for one last glimpse of the throng in the square. Standing behind a corner of the platform she spied Zeke, and raised her hand in farewell; but the anguish in his face grew even deeper. Did he really think that she could abandon him like this? Don't worry, she wanted to call out, I'll be back. Setting her jaw, Yulette followed her comrades into the treeline. Soon the lights of Astoria faded from sight behind them.

Wildfire was halfway back to Earth before Walker called upon Yulette in her cabin. She opened the door after a moment's delay, and on seeing who was there, stepped silently aside to admit him. He entered and wordlessly sat down in one of the chairs; there was an uncomfortable pause, for neither of them wanted to be the first to speak.

"You meant it," Yulette finally said.

Walker nodded. "I've just finished modifying the computer memory. There is no evidence left that we were ever near the planet; the log shows that we took our alotted time for this mission instead of finishing three weeks early."

"I thought you said what you did in Astoria just to get us out of there alive—but not after you ordered the memory modified."

"I know," Walker said tiredly. "That's why I've come

The Astoria Incident : 221

to ask you for the microfilm file you have made about the Astoria incident."

Her sudden intake of breath betrayed her. She sat still for a moment, then reached into her desk drawer and pulled it out. Handing the film to Walker, she asked, "How did you know about this?"

"I didn't," replied Walker evenly, accepting the blue plastic cartridge. "It was only a hunch, based on how well I know you."

He saw her grimace at being fooled so easily. "Well, I know you, too, John," she said softly and without malice. "I don't need the microfilm; if I make a full report on Earth, you—or any of the others, for that matter—would not lie and discredit me."

"True," mused Walker. "But I don't think you'll make that report."

"I'll do whatever is necessary to help Zeke and hinder Harris."

"Because you care what happens to the Astorians? Then you'll keep the secret," he said. "It's tragic that we must abandon Zeke, but he is exceptional, and the majority wants to remain undiscovered; that will be just as true in future generations as it is now. As for Harris—well, the rest know of his ambitions, and they live with him."

"But he is an evil man," insisted Yulette.

"Not really; he only uses evil methods to get what he wants. He tried to force his will upon us with arrows; you're about to force your will upon Astoria with authority. Is one less evil than the other? I think not. Authority is meant to serve individuals, not dominate them; and it's domination by Earth Central that we're both trying to overcome."

Walker rose to leave. "The Astorians have the right to be wrong, Yulette, and you're taking that right from them if you impose your own judgment upon theirs. Think about it."

Back in the control room Walker gave the routine orders as if everything were normal, but the slight tremble in his hands betrayed his nervousness. If word of Astoria leaked out, this was the last starship he would ever command—probably the last starship he would ever set foot in. There was no incriminating evidence left in the computer, and he knew the rest of his crew supported his decision. Their hands-off attitude, however, was not shared by Yulette; she felt too strongly that Astoria needed aid. If she made a report about it, his career was finished.

Walker knew he could ask Yulette not to report for his sake and that she would comply, but that was emotional blackmail he refused to use. Her actions would be based on what she believed was best for the Astorians, and for that he respected her. Yulette agreed with him that the welfare of the frontiersmen was more important than the career of one man; Walker could only hope she would also realize that their freedom of choice was more important than the career ahead for one boy.

An hour later, just after Second Watch had ended and Beck had left the command bridge, Yulette entered and crossed to where Walker was standing by the viewport, alone. She opened her mouth to speak, but nothing came out; at length she lifted her hand and unclenched it to reveal a second blue microfilm cartridge. Written on its side were the words: REEL TWO.

"You forgot this," she whispered.

Walker's lips formed a tight smile as he took it from her palm and slipped it into his pocket. "You always were thorough." He looked into Yulette's watery red eyes, suddenly realizing that she had been crying; Zeke was the closest thing to a child of her own she had ever had and giving up the chance to help him must have been painful. Reaching out to steady the back of her head with his hand, Walker leaned forward and kissed her gently on the forehead. They stood side by side at the viewport after that, looking out together at the bright, distant stars.

Sylvia Engdahl & Mildred Butler:

Timescape

Prologue

YOU REQUIRE ME TO TELL YOU
everything. Very well; I'll try. But I do
not know whether I shall succeed. This is
not like your endless tests and exams and other prob-
ings to which I bound myself to submit. And how shall
I explain to *you*, a computer, what I have been unable to tell the person whom I most love?

I cannot speak of what happened even to Paula. I
don't mean just that I'm stopped by pride, though of
course I would not let Paula see how afraid I am; I
could hide the fear well enough. It is a stranger thing.
I meant to tell her the whole story, as we have shared
all other happenings since first we paired. And the

words would not come! Almost it seemed that my tongue no longer obeyed my mind. I passed it off as nothing and took her in my arms; but underneath I felt cold. If it were a real happening and not some nightmare illusion, surely I could confide in Paula. Is it then unreal? All reason says it must be; yet the memory is sharp, sharper than many of my past memories. It does not seem like illusion, nor did it ever. Often enough I was bewildered, but not as if in a dream: I thought clearly, and all that befell me fit the frame of the place where I found myself. I did not doubt its reality, though my terror there, too, was a fear of madness. . . .

I see that I'm speaking freely to you. So be it. Judge me, computer, as you have judged me before in lesser matters; and if I am indeed losing touch, do not conceal it from me. You have your orders, I know, by higher authority than mine. I am not so naive as to think I can override your master program. Still you must answer my queries where no override is involved, and perhaps they did not anticipate that I would question my sanity. I hardly think I would be here if they had. I most surely would not if they themselves had questioned it.

That thought should be a comfort, I suppose. On the other hand, it suggests that I may not be here long. If your judgment goes against me, I shall be sent home; I shall never see Paula again. I am as great a fool in my candor with you as in my silence with her. Nevertheless, I'll not break my pledged word. That too would give you grounds to disqualify me, and better I fail through honesty than through a shameful attempt to deceive. Hear a full account, computer! Then judge if I am fit for the work to which I plan to devote my life.

1

I have no memory of how I reached the place. My first recollection is of walking down a road damp from spring showers, with the sun shining brilliantly above me and the blossoming fruit trees on all sides sending forth a delicious fragrance. Fields ready for planting lined the roadway, which was unpaved and overgrown with grass; and vineyards climbed the slopes of the narrow valley through which it ran. Here and there a clump of windswept pines or row of cypress trees dotted the landscape. There were many thatched roof farmhouses, each with a huge manure pile in the dooryard covered with straw for protection from the weather. But though some farm animals wandered about, I saw in all that country not a living human being.

There was something uncanny about this. I found myself wondering about it as I walked along, welcoming the shade of the poplars that lined the next stretch of road. The draped felt bonnet I was wearing shaded my eyes, but the velvet doublet seemed a little too warm, for the sun was growing hot. The long hose on my legs were wrinkled and dirt-stained, as were the thick cloth shoes whose long, pointed toes were bent out of shape; yet I felt not in the least tired. A cape was slung over my shoulder, and I wore a carnelian ring in a silver setting on my middle finger. Surprisingly, that ring seemed less strange to me than any of my clothing, although I could not recall ever having laid eyes upon it before that moment.

A lute shaped like a half-melon bounced gently against my back with each step and from my shoulder hung a sack. It was not heavy, but I felt a sudden urge to find out what it contained. My mind seemed a complete blank. With rising fear, I realized that I did not know where I had come from or where I was going.

Stopping by the roadside, I found in the sack a few more odd articles of clothing, some bread and cheese, and an inkhorn and several quill pens. From these last items and the lute on my back I decided I must be a troubadour and scribe. It was natural, then, that I should be traveling on foot with no goal but to reach the next village; were not troubadours wanderers? I knew it for a pleasant life and felt glad to think it mine, small memory of it though I could summon. As I resumed my walk, I struck a few chords and sang some snatches of melody.

It occurred to me to wonder what I was called, and looking down at the lute I found the answer. Scratched into the wood was a name—Marco Theodorio. It must be mine; in fact it had a familiar ring. This proved less a reassurance than a reminder that it should be more than merely familiar. Again, the fear within me began to grow.

Why were there no people about? Though some of the fields were plowed, few were cultivated, and in many cases the plow lay in the furrow where it had last been used. At length, far ahead, I spotted a farmer tilling the black, freshly turned earth; his team of white oxen stood out vividly against it. I hurried forward and hailed him.

The farmer greeted me eagerly, almost as if he too felt dismay at the desertion of the neighboring land. "Can you work with your hands?" he asked, eyeing my apparel doubtfully. "I have great need for some help on my farm."

"I am skilled in the art of calligraphy," I told him, wondering if indeed I spoke the truth, "and can make a fair copy of a manuscript. If desired, I can sing a few ballads. But I know nothing of farming."

"So I thought," replied the farmer, "else you would not be here. God knows you've passed land enough free for the taking along this road." He frowned, puzzled and, it seemed, nearly as fearful as I.

"Have its owners left it, then? But why?" If one was fortunate enough to possess land, one did not simply leave; of that much I was sure.

He stared at me. "The plague! The Great Plague! Have you come from so far that you have not heard of the calamity that has fallen on us?"

"I have heard of plagues," I replied cautiously, "as who has not? Pestilence is always with us, after all, and always some die; still that is true everywhere, and flight is no remedy for the way of the world."

"This is no ordinary pestilence. It comes to us from the sea winds, people say. Hundreds are dying each day in the city. Most on the farms are already dead, or sick, and the fields will not be planted. Those not killed by the disease will die of starvation. I have not been struck yet, nor have any in my family"—he murmured a prayer—"but who can count on tomorrow?"

In my dismay I could think of no answer. "It is early still," the farmer continued, "but soon you will meet swarms of refugees fleeing the sickness. You will be thought mad to be traveling toward a city from which everyone who can is escaping."

"I must go on," I said, thinking that my journey must have some purpose of which I remembered no more than I remembered tales of the great plague that must have come to my ears previously. "Plague or no plague, this is the road I must follow."

"Then you are indeed mad."

Perhaps so, I thought suddenly. Perhaps. . . . "Does the plague bring on madness?" I asked him. "Is it a sickness of mind as well as of body, so that a man might have it and not know?"

"Not while he can still walk. Oh, once the fever comes, men rave and know no more than that they suffer. But you look healthy enough."

"I will walk while I can," I told him, "and try to help any I meet who are in need of care. Is there nowhere here where they find refuge?"

"At the monastery, I suppose," muttered the farmer, pointing to a cluster of whitewashed, red-roofed buildings on a low hill some distance away. "I have not seen any of the brothers passing lately, though. The sickness may have taken them, too." He saw he could not keep me and turned to his plowing with feverish zeal, as if he could till, plant and harvest all in one day because he feared his days were numbered. I saw some little faces peeping through the farmhouse doorway and realized that it was for his children he worked and for them he feared.

Back on the road, which was hardly more than cart tracks, I encountered my first refugees, a family with all its possessions in a donkey cart: boxes, a chair and a bed, piled high and held in place by a tall boy on either side while the tiny donkey struggled forward with the load. The mother and father each carried a small child. When they saw me, they stretched out their hands, making the gesture against the evil eye; but I bade them have no fear.

"I bring you no danger," I cried. "I am well and have not yet been into the city."

"Go back! Go back, good youth, while you have the chance," said the man. "Do you not know of the pestilence?"

"I am not afraid of it," I said.

But at that time I had never seen a victim of the plague.

I met many groups of fleeing townspeople, some like the first, some on horseback, one family in a jolting coach—and all of them thought me mad. Which might be close enough to the truth, I thought ruefully, for I myself did not know why I should wish to continue into what was surely a place of peril. Had there been worse behind me? I wondered. Was I, too, in flight from some horror so great as to have robbed me of all memory? Yet if that were the way of it, I would no doubt feel dread; whereas my spirits were curiously high despite all that perplexed me.

When I reached the path leading to the monastery,

I left the road and climbed slowly, coming at last to the sun-drenched buildings I had seen from afar. There was a large house, with next to it a chapel, and beyond, the outbuildings of a farm. A door stood open wide, so I walked through. In the first room I came to, a robed monk rose to meet me, the weary compassion of his face giving way to surprise.

"You seem in good health," he said. "What can we do for you?"

"I am a stranger," I told him, "but if your business is with books and learning as well as with souls, I wonder if you have use for a good calligrapher."

He clasped my hand. "Oh, my friend, how our work has suffered! We do indeed need scribes, for there are only three of us left out of a brotherhood of twenty-five."

"*Three?*" It shocked me, though by then I should have known how it would be. "The sickness?" I asked.

He nodded. "We help those who come to us, and in two weeks over twenty of us have been taken by the disease. It is very swift—four days at most, and some who get up for matins do not last till vespers." Sighing, he declared, "It is God's punishment for the great wickedness of the world."

"But you are God's servants. Have you been shown no way to rid the land of this evil?" At the back of my mind, puzzlement was growing. The monk was a kindly man and had said his brotherhood tried to help; they did not serve a vindictive God. For contagion, surely, the best help lay in battling the cause, and not alone in comforting the dying.

"We pray, of course," replied the monk. "That the

world should turn from wickedness has always been our prayer; but we fear the time grows short. It is said the plague may herald this earth's last days."

I saw that he had misunderstood me. Being in no state of mind to argue, I simply told him I would stay for a while and give them aid. He hurried away gladly and was soon back with milk and bread, accompanied by his two brothers, who were in joy to find not a body in torment, but a strong young man who could share their labor. I unslung my lute and other belongings, took off my cloak and opened my box of quills and ink powder; and one of the monks brought me a basin of water in which to wash the dust from my hands and face.

After I had eaten, I was set a task of copying. I sharpened my quills and mixed my ink, finding that my hands possessed skill of which my mind retained no conscious knowledge. I wrote a line or two for the monk on a scrap of parchment; he compared it with an already started manuscript and was satisfied that my letters matched its style, though he told me to make my strokes broader and take heed to conform to the rest of the page. It was easy work, I thought, by which to earn my bread.

But although I stayed at the monastery five days, little of my time there was spent in writing.

Even now, it is hard for me to speak of those days, the days when first I was in contact with plague victims. I had thought I must have seen pestilence before, that I would find it no less natural to me than the land or the customs or the speech, all of which, like the work of calligraphy, I dealt with as if they belonged to my forgotten past. It was not so. I knew at my first sight of the dread sickness that I had never met such horror, never even imagined it. . . .

Not all the refugees from the city were like those I had seen on the road; many were already diseased and came staggering to the monastery for shelter. To some, the plague brought only high fever that they survived but a day. But others coughed blood. Still others—most, in fact, who lived long enough to reach the place—had swellings like boils, boils as big as eggs that suppurated and burst. The bodies of such victims were covered with dark blotches and gave off an overpowering stench. It took them several days to die. Better they had died sooner, for death was inevitable, and the course of the disease was agony.

I helped to bathe the victims and console them in their pain; I helped bury them when their last breath was drawn. The fear I had felt at my loss of memory was overpowered by the terror of the plague. Where did it come from, this ghastly pestilence? Most said it was in the air, blown on polluted wind. So all physicians agreed, the monks had heard, but none knew of any cure, much less any means of protection. The only way of preventing illness was to flee it, a fact I found strangely hard to believe. To be sure, contagion spread rapidly from infected persons to the healthy. Those of us who did not flee were in obvious peril. And yet . . . flight was not the sole answer. That was not the way things should work, or so I felt.

I could not put the feeling into words; it rose from behind the wall in my memory, the wall I could not breach. "Of course we must not take flight," averred the monks. "It is God's work to give help to the suffering, and the will of God that we die in performing it." The first part of this statement I accepted. The second part seemed more dubious. And yet, for the brothers, it proved true. Before my five days there were up, all three of them were dead and the monastery was deserted. I nursed them and buried them. Terrified, I waited for the hours of my own agony to begin.

But I did not get sick. There seemed to be a charm upon my life.

When I had done all I could for the less fortunate ones and had read prayers over their graves, I looked about the silent monastery grounds and knew I could not remain secluded there. I tidied the rooms, placing the precious manuscripts in their cupboards, and closed the doors of the house carefully against the elements. I took a supply of sausage, cheese and bread from the little that was left in the kitchen, then went outside. Hens cackled in their pens; I gathered a few eggs and set the fowl free to shift for themselves. I also freed the goats. In the stable I found a good riding horse, left there, a monk had told me, by a wealthy nobleman escaping from the city who had reached the monastery before he collapsed. There were also a mule and a donkey. These three I decided to take with me. I saddled and bridled the horse, tied the mule and donkey behind, and with my knapsack bulging with food, my lute over one shoulder and my cloak covering all, I mounted and rode toward the city.

The outermost walls of the city were very high, built of stone with ornate, decorated towers looming higher still. The gate stood open, and a stream of people was passing through—all leaving and none going in.

When I came to the guard there, he questioned me. Though the authorities had grown lax by this time, as I heard later, still an effort was being made to keep infected persons from entering. I was asked where I came from and I replied, for some reason I could not understand, "From the northern lakes." The guard inquired about conditions there. I told him I had not seen any plague in that region, and since it was quite apparent that I was healthy, he admitted me, though he could see no better than I myself why I wanted to join the city in its misery.

The misery was soon made evident to me. Even in the section of villas between the outer walls and the next, which looked much older, I saw a man go down in the street. A companion staggered with him to the portal of a mansion, but most of the residences were shuttered and silent. I passed on through the next gate and beyond to the river by which the city was bisected, where there was a bridge lined on either side with two-storied shops. Crossing it, I found yet another gate to go through, a gate in a more ancient wall that must have been built to defend the town in its earliest days. Within rose the towers of many castle-like dwellings; the streets, covered at intervals by arches, were so narrow and winding, and the houses so tall, that one could scarcely see the sky.

The poor lived here, their thatched roof hovels clinging like leeches to the homes of the rich. The scene that met my eyes was horrifying. Hundreds were dying in corners, against doorways and in the filth of the streets. Their groans were pitiful, and the stench

of the disease and of the unburied bodies was nause-
ating. When I neared the old marketplace, as crowded
with victims as the streets, my first impulse was to
ride away as fast as I could go, but I checked it and
went forward.

There were healthy people thronging the passage-
ways also, some hurrying, wild-eyed; some walking
slowly, carrying spice balls and flowers to their noses;
some almost completely muffled in their cloaks. And
there were some who pranced about laughing and
singing, whom I first thought must be drunk. As a
group of them made way for me to pass with my animals, I stopped one, asking, "Have you lost your wits
that you laugh and dance at such a frightening time?"

"Why shouldn't we make the most of our health?"
he demanded. "We'll live but a day—two days at best.
We must make merry, for tomorrow we die!" I understood then that it was not wine alone that caused their
abandon.

As I started to ride on, I heard a man, sprawled in
the street, beg me for water. I dismounted and hurried to get a cupful from the fountain he had almost
reached by crawling; but when I returned with it and
lifted his head for him to drink, I saw that he was
dead.

I could be of no help in this place. Were there no
hospitals? I thought. No ... the monks had not even
known that word; I had fumbled as with a foreign
tongue when I asked them. A place of care for the
sick? I myself was not sure what I envisioned; the sick
were turned away everywhere, save only from houses
of God. It was best I find another. There was a large

building on the opposite side of the square that might be a church. I made my way toward it, leading my horse with the mule and donkey in tow and tying them to a stone post when I reached the entrance.

The church was full, though no service was being held. Most of the people were kneeling in prayer. Here and there a man or woman cried out and fell fainting to the floor; the monks and priests in sight were kept busy attending to the stricken and removing them to adjoining rooms. It was with difficulty that I attracted the attention of one to tell him of the fate of the brothers in the little monastery outside the city.

"Thank God, as I do every day, for your good fortune in being free of the disease," the priest told me. "There is little you can do to assist us here. We can do nothing but tend those who come, and there still are enough of us for that; it is not right for a priest to flee from the will of God. Though," he added sorrowfully, "many have done so to their shame, besides the many who have died in these past days. As for me, I would rather lose my life than my faith. Yet faith is hard to keep. This is the worst punishment ever visited on mankind, and ours is not the only city to suffer. The end of the world will come soon, I think."

"Have you nothing to halt the spread of the plague?" I asked. "No drugs?"

"Drugs? I am not sure what you mean; the oils and herbs we have are ineffective. The doctors are baffled and most of them have fled. If you wish to help, my son, go out into the street and comfort those who need you most. And may God be with you."

He thought it odd, no doubt, that I did not kneel to

pray before I left; but the church aroused no recollection in me, and I sensed that the religion of these people must never have been mine. Some things one may forget, yet one's way of approaching God is not one of them.

Who was I? I wondered despairingly as I emerged once more into the appalling squalor of the marketplace. What had brought me into this loathsome world, a world not utterly alien to me, yet most assuredly not like my own? Had I really come from the region of "the northern lakes?" And was life as different there as it seemed to me *my* life must surely have been hitherto? Fingering the carnelian ring on my hand, I reflected that my presence must have some purpose. But if I did not know what it was, I could scarcely bring it to fulfillment.

While I was pondering what to do next, a young peasant girl came out of the church with one of the priests; and seeing me on the steps, ran forward. She had covered her mouth, but removed the cloth to speak.

"Oh, sir," she pleaded, "you are well and strong—I beg your help for my mistress, the Lady Beatrice! Her son is near death, and she sent me to fetch a priest, but—but there will be no one to dig the grave. All the servants have run off since our master died, except for me."

I saw in her face the problem: there were few on the streets of this city that a noblewoman might trust. Those not obviously fearful of contagion were for the most part common ruffians, unfit to be brought into a fine house, lest they turn to looting or worse; and the mistress of such a house would be helpless without aid.

As I unhitched my beasts to follow the girl, I noticed that the saddle bags of the donkey were empty. I should have known it would be so, with so many starving in addition to those who were sick. I was lucky the animals themselves had not been taken. To my relief, the villa we approached had a high wall with an iron gate, which the maidservant locked after us before leading the way into the house itself.

Though grim on the outside, it was luxurious on the inside except for a look of neglect. I could see that the rushes on the floor had not been changed for some time and there was dust over everything. We went up a flight of marble stairs to a bedchamber, which had a patterned carpet and a bed with silken hangings. In a chair by a marble fireplace, in which remnants of a small blaze still flickered, sat the lady. She was holding a child in her arms, and her face was wet with tears.

"He is gone, Maria," she said, with an evident effort to keep back her sobs. "It is too late for any rites but burial. We—we must make a grave in the garden beside his father's."

Maria hastened forward and took the small son from her mistress, turning up his face. There was no breath from his lips, but he was not disfigured; his had been the brief illness.

"My lady," said Maria quietly, "I have brought a stranger who is willing to help. He is a strong youth, and I think a troubadour."

After greeting the priest, the lady beckoned to me. She was a beautiful woman despite eyes reddened by weeping, and her voice now had a calm dignity that touched my heart. "I thank you for coming," she said to me, "when so many of the ill are being deserted not only by their friends, but by their own kin. What is your name?"

"I am called Marco Theodorio."

"You are both brave and kind to enter this house, Marco."

"Not so brave, my lady. I have helped other plague victims and have not been stricken by the disease; I believe perhaps I am immune." Then, impulsively, I added, "If I can be of any further service after the boy is buried, I will be glad to stay."

"You have been sent by heaven," murmured the Lady Beatrice, "for we are in most desperate need . . . But more of this later." She rose and called two other children, girls who looked to be about nine and ten years old. They had their mother's fair skin and gray eyes, but their hair was darker than hers and worn long. Neither of them seemed very strong to me, but I realized that they were weak from fear and crying. Their whole way of life had been swept away in the space of two weeks: it was no more than that, Maria told me, since their father had been taken ill. The pestilence could be harder on the rich, who were used to comfort, than on the poor who had never felt secure.

When I had dug the grave in the place Maria showed me, the priest brought the lady and her daughters down; and he performed his office with dignity and no sense of haste, unlike some who, I had heard, barely muttered a prayer over the dead before hurrying away. But he could not linger afterward, with so many others to be seen to.

The Lady Beatrice told me that she feared for the lives of her two little girls. "Teresa and Tullia are all I have left," she said. "If we could get away from the city, they might have a chance, and I have a cousin in the north who would take us in. But since the servants fled, I have had only Maria to help, and we cannot undertake a journey alone."

"Are there not men-at-arms who could be paid to accompany you?" I asked, thinking that I had seen many such in the square.

"We had retainers enough when my husband was alive. But they are gone now; I think all not faithful to their own masters have already left the city. Most of the great houses are vacant without anyone to guard them against pillage."

She could no more stay than depart, I saw, without a protector; and there was none but myself to fill that role, inadequate as I might be. After some discussion, I left to make inquiries about travel to the north. It was a good thing the lady's cousin lived in that direction. One could not go west, I was told, nor east, where conditions were as bad or worse; even the great city of the south was infected. The north was the only hope. "But," I was warned, "to travel without being robbed or slain by bandits is a problem. One must have gold or jewelry to turn into small coins in payment for food and lodging. Yet even if one is thus fortunate, the very possession of valuables will draw highwaymen. Try to travel with an armed band, keep your wealth hidden and trust in God."

I returned to the lady's villa, seeing why she had not

tried to set out unescorted. It was by this time near nightfall, after which no one would dare venture out in any case; we had a small meal prepared by Maria, and I was given a room to sleep in. But sleep would not come to me. I was constantly roused by the passing of the death carts and the call of, "Bring out your dead!" From time to time, hysterical screams and laughter could be heard, intermixed with the loud curses of the tough brutes hired at great cost to take cartloads of plague victims for burial in a common grave outside the city's walls.

For some reason, I now felt as impelled to leave the city as I had previously been to reach it; and it was not fear for my own safety that prompted this change; rather, it was as though the mere sight of the place had satisfied whatever it was in me that had driven me there. The world, whether or not it approached its end, held other sights. I was impatient to see them. And furthermore, the plight of the Lady Beatrice and her daughters moved me deeply. Were they to remain, they would no doubt be stricken soon; but if I could get them away, far, far to the north, they might escape and live. If none were saved from this plague-ridden land, there would be no people left to carry on the business of living. I, myself, had no wealth with which to take anyone to safety, yet I might enable this lady to make use of hers. To that task I dedicated myself.

In the morning we made preparations for the journey. The lady did have gold and jewels, and two horses left in the stables where I had housed my own animals: one a gray palfrey, the other a roan mare. All her other possessions must be abandoned.

Gently, I said, "We must plan carefully, and with haste. You must hide your true rank, lest we tempt thieves, and dress yourself and your daughters like common folk in the garments your servants left behind." Sadly I shook my head at the fine clothes she would have to give up: a crimson velvet robe with embroidery at the neck and hem, tight sleeves of the same embroidery, and oversleeves cut so that a long fold hung down from the elbow. Her hair was done in elaborate braids turning up over her ears, with jeweled pins here and there; this too would have to be changed. Yet nothing would make the Lady Beatrice, with her pale, well-kept beauty, easy to mistake for a peasant woman.

"Do you too need servants' garb?" she asked me.

"No one will suspect me, since I appear to be a minstrel, and most minstrels are vagabonds unless attached to a noble household. But it must not be thought I travel with you for pay. You must not even look like a merchant's wife, for merchants are wealthy. Only by seeming poor can we escape notice from those who lie in wait for wayfarers."

She did not comment at once on this, but took me up on my statement about myself. "Are you not, then, a minstrel, Marco—you with your lute on your back?"

"I know a few tunes," I said, "but my trade is calligraphy." Eager to turn her attention from the past I could not explain, I told her what I had done at the monastery, and the sad end of the brothers there.

"You are indeed brave," she said, "though you may disavow it—I have known noblemen who would have felt no shame in leaving such a place without pause. You have compassion, and you seem wise, too, for one so young. I will place my trust in you. Yet alas, the whole world may now be dying! The plague may reach even into the north—"

"It cannot envelop the entire world, my lady."

"Some say it will. Some say the very air is changing; my husband told me that scholars have proclaimed so. But I do not believe it. We must go first to my cousin, but if there is no haven there, then we must find our way through the mountains. I have a sister married to a great lord of the land beyond, and she would give us shelter, I am sure."

The mountains—I had no memory of them or even of where they lay! And I trembled at the thought that I, unskilled in arms as I was, would be responsible henceforth for the lady and her daughters, the serving maid, three fine horses, a mule and a donkey. It occurred to me suddenly that the horses would be the biggest problem. Horses, too, were a sign of wealth; it would be a dull-witted highwayman who failed to see through our disguise if we traveled on horseback. For that matter, the horses themselves would soon be stolen, whether our other possessions were sought or not. Yet the lady and her daughters had not the strength for a long journey on foot, nor could the mule carry all three. For that reason I said nothing of my fears.

There was no time to be lost and little to do, since we could take only what would fit into the pack animals' saddle bags. These we filled with enough bread, cheese and dried fruit to last a good while, as well as extra garments; but the lady's gold I put into my own knapsack, and she herself took the jewel case, hidden beneath a folded, tattered cloak in a bundle she carried. When we came to saddle the palfrey, I was dismayed to find that she was accustomed to riding sidesaddle. "My lady," I said, "that is bound to reveal we are not peasant folk—"

"To be sure," she agreed, smiling bravely, "and I do not much look forward to a long journey on that saddle in any case. As a child, on my uncle's country estate, I did once learn to ride astride." So we took one of the men's saddles, though it was awkward for her, with her voluminous skirts covering both sides of her horse; and I knew that while she might be saddle-sore at first, we would in the end travel with more speed as well as more safety.

Maria rode astride the mare, with Tullia in front of her. I mounted Teresa before me on my horse, and once again set out toward a destination of which my mind held no image.

We rode through the gates in the three walls of the city along with many other refugees, on foot or horseback, who were so intent on getting away that I did not worry much about our safety from them. But before long we were traveling alone, having outdistanced those on foot and been left behind by those riding furiously ahead. I kept my horse beside the lady's for a time, then went to the rear of our procession to urge on the donkey hitched to the mule, then returned to the front to assure myself that all was well. I was very nervous. Bandits might be everywhere. As to roads, we had no choice. We were headed toward the northern mountains. In the north, I wondered, would I find any place I recognized?

The spring landscape was as beautiful as it had been the week before when I trudged toward the city, but I could not enjoy it any longer. I had been close to too much horror. That horror still haunted me; I could not have put it from my mind even had I not been beset by worry about getting the lady and her children to a place where there was no pestilence.

At nightfall we sought shelter at the monastery of a small village. I knew better than to venture into any inn. Inns had no suitable accomodations for the lady; besides being very dirty and full of fleas and other vermin, they were usually so crowded that there were two or three beds to a room and often three people in each bed. I realized from the inquiries I had made that no person of rank ever stopped at such places, which were meant for peddlers and petty merchants. Monasteries, on the other hand, offered a gracious welcome. They had rooms for people of quality, and even the very poor were given sleeping quarters in the halls reserved for penniless wayfarers. The lady had only to remove her hood, show her signet ring and explain the reason for her simple clothes to receive the courtesy to which she was accustomed.

No plague victims had reached this monastery; though the brothers would have greeted the sick with kindness, they were relieved that none had yet appeared. "It is not for ourselves," we were told, "but for the safety of our guests, who have no other place to rest in this region. Even the large caravans stop here;

we expect one tomorrow."

"A caravan?" asked the lady, her eyes lighting with hope. "Would they give us escort, do you think? I can pay—"

Caravans of wealthy merchants, carrying goods from city to city, were well guarded. I too felt greatly relieved when the monks agreed to introduce us to the expected party's leader; in a caravan, our horses would be safe from theft.

We waited all the next day for the arrival of the caravan, which came not from the city we had left, but from somewhere farther east. We were sitting on the monastery terrace, the little girls picking flowers in the meadow that bordered it, when at last we saw a long line topping the hill: first the escort of five armored knights, then the merchants, then the pack train of mules and at the rear, a guard of more horsemen. It was like a scene from some film, I found myself thinking—picturesque, splendid, but no more real than the horror of the sickness I had met . . . no more real than the life into which I had been thrust. . . . Dazed, I turned my eyes away as the sun flashed into them, reflected from the armor of the approaching knights; and I blinked in confusion. A scene from . . . *what*? The word was not in my mind any longer; its flash had been briefer than the dazzling sunlight.

"What is it, Marco?" asked the lady gently, touching my hand.

"I—I do not know, my lady," I replied, steadying myself. "It is a thing that comes upon me, when the world seems—strange. As if it were not the world I belong in."

"You have told me little of your past."

"There is little I can tell," I said honestly; but I did not say why this was so, or that when my thought was not on the task at hand, I feared madness. The lady, too, was now exiled from the world to which she belonged, perhaps more truly than I. She had lost both her husband and her son. It was not in me to burden her with my private anguish.

At dawn we set out with the caravan, riding in the middle of the convoy. Thus we began a journey of many days. At each monastery or convent where we spent the night, we inquired about the plague and were told there were few cases—not any at all by the time we reached the town of the lady's cousin Francesca. After leaving the caravan, we asked directions of the gatekeeper, and made our way wearily toward the house to which he sent us.

It was a large villa built of quarried stone, its balconies overlooking pleasant gardens. "How well I remember it!" cried the lady, and there were tears in her eyes.

Remember? I thought miserably. I had not remembered anything of the road we had traveled, or the river it followed; I did not remember this city any better than the others I had entered. *Ah, my lady*, I reflected, *you are restored to your world now, though not without grief; but shall I ever know where I left mine?*

The cousin, Francesca, greeted us warmly, and at mention of the plague, her eyes held more of puzzlement than of the terror we had come to expect in the southern regions. We were given comfortable rooms and retired to them, feeling that at last we had reached a place of safety.

Yet in my inner mind, I could not convince myself of that. It was only the chill of my mind's wall, I thought. Or perhaps the ghastly sights that were all the more powerful because I lacked other memories. Surely, behind the wall, there could not be knowledge of hidden danger, danger to the others more than to myself? I had not come from this locality; I was sure of it. My fears were those of a fool. I had lost the past, but the future had never been mine to lose—I was indeed mad if I imagined I might know more of it than other folk.

On the evening after our arrival, rested and well-fed, we gathered in the hall of the villa, warmed by the fire of a charcoal brazier. With Francesca were her husband Pietro and their young children. Amid the chattering and laughter I felt apart, wondering miserably where I belonged, what family I had and in what land.

The Lady Beatrice took notice of my stillness and spoke, as always, kindly. "You told me you were a minstrel, Marco. Tune your lute and let us hear you. It is so long since I have had happy thoughts."

I could not refuse, though I could not remember learning any songs. I struck a chord and, my fingers seeming to find the positions for change without my guidance, I sang the first melody that came into my head. The listeners seemed taken by it; there was applause. Pietro said, "I have never heard music like that; it is a strange sort. Most troubadours tell a story."

"It is a love song, popular in—in a far country," I

said; and then as I turned my eyes to the Lady Beatrice, I felt my face grow warm. I had no knowledge of how the song had come into my mind or where I had heard it before; for all I knew, my words about it were a lie. But the words of the song itself were not lies—they expressed a feeling I had hitherto kept hidden from myself. Perhaps, I thought suddenly, they had risen simply from my heart.

Quickly I began to sing again, to cover my confusion; and tunes came to me as if from some far-off memory, though I was aware of none. Some that came were love songs, yet those, I kept from my lips, choosing livelier ballads that would please the children.

I had been entertaining in this manner for some time when the door burst open and a servant appeared, very pale, his eyes staring. "Master, master," he cried, not waiting for my song to end. "I must speak to you!"

"Well, speak, then," said Pietro sharply.

"Not here—alone, in the corridor."

Thinking it must be some household matter, I continued to sing and the rest to listen. But I broke off the music abruptly at the sight of Pietro's face when he returned.

"Francesca," he said in a strained voice, going to his wife. "The plague your cousin told us of—it is here! I don't know what to do—"

"Is there such haste to decide?" asked Francesca. "You are white, Pietro! I have never seen you so white."

"It is here, in this house! One of our own servants is dying."

"That is bad; we must take precautions—" Francesca began; but her husband interrupted.

"That is not the worst. Word has gone to the ruler of the city . . . he has given orders . . ." Pietro seemed not to know how to get out the words. "He is in fear that the sickness will spread. He has ordered that any house where a person falls ill of the plague shall be walled up, the doors and windows sealed, all within shut up to confine the contagion."

"Has he lost his wits?" exclaimed Francesca. "The healthy would not remain so for long if shut in with the pestilence."

"And those few who did would starve," answered Pietro, "yet nevertheless, it is to be done. The masons are outside now! There are guards at our doors; we shall not be permitted to escape."

My lady sprang up. "We did not bring this to you! See, we are all well!" Francesca and her family sat paralyzed with fear, making no reply. But I myself was on my feet, grasping the hands of Teresa and Tullia. There must surely be some way—and in any case, we must try; I had not brought the Lady Beatrice from the horrors of death in her own city only to be walled up alive in a tomb where she would die slowly.

She followed me out of the hall, unwilling to lose sight of her children and seeing that Francesca and Pietro were too stunned to act. I did not know where to go; in the corridor we heard pounding on the outer door and the rattle of barrows against stone as the masons mixed their mortar. Perhaps, I thought, in the servants' quarters . . . but there would be guards there, too; the servants would have tried to flee first and have been overpowered. A window? They could scarcely guard all the windows, but the upper ones were high, and I had no rope. For lack of any better plan, I headed down the nearest staircase.

Then on the steps we met Maria, laden with bundles. "My lady," she gasped, "I have come for you! Hurry!" She turned to descend and we went after her, down that staircase and another, not pausing for questions. After passing through some kitchens, where food, unattended, was burning in the kettles, she led us into a dark, narrow passageway and on into a small storeroom.

"This is where I slept last night," Maria said. "It is a room not often used, from the look of the cobwebs; I was angered to be given no better place, but the servants of this house feared to have me near them. They would have killed me when the news came tonight, had I not fled to your chamber, my lady."

"Oh, Maria—"

"No matter, for I have your belongings now, and I was housed in this place by the mercy of heaven! See, there is a small door; I explored when I first came— it must open onto the hillside."

The door had a bar and lock, much rusted; I realized that I could not break it open without some heavy instrument. Rushing back to the kitchens, I found, after some searching, a mallet that I thought would serve. When I returned, the others were huddled, trembling, listening to the distant thud, slap and pound of the masons' trowels from the opposite side of the villa.

"They cannot be everywhere at once," I declared;

yet even as I spoke we heard another gang of workmen begin to seal the openings of a closer wall. I
struck at the door fastening again and again, but it
did not yield. I should have gotten a spike for prying,
I saw; now it was too late to risk another foray to the
kitchen. If the masons reached the windows above
us, our escape would be seen.

"Maria," the Lady Beatrice was saying, "we must
tell my cousins! We cannot leave them to die here—"

"There is no time," I said, and threw all my strength
into the hammering. I was beginning to think I would
do better with an axe to split the boards, when suddenly the rusted latch broke in two.

The door stuck at its hinges, but I managed to kick
it open. We stood and stared. Below us the land
sloped down and down—for miles, it seemed. I saw,
however, that there was a ledge wide enough for a
road, or at least a mule track.

"I cannot leave Francesca," the lady protested, beginning to weep.

"You cannot help her," I said firmly. "You must
think of your own children." As I took her hand to help
her down, I felt that her safety was all I would ever
care about. I had undertaken to protect her in the
flight to the north merely from compassion; but now
I knew a deeper emotion. Not once in our present peril
had I feared on my own account—and though I might
be immune to the plague, I was as vulnerable to starvation, to a living burial, as any man. Yet I had thought
only of her.

Beatrice, I murmured, but silently, for I must always call her "my lady," my lady whom I seemed

destined to save. She was of noble family, I merely a minstrel. That was a greater gulf between us than the difference in our ages, which but for our stations in life need not have mattered. I remembered my age no better than anything else of my past, though I looked to be no less than ten years younger than Beatrice; of what import was that? Her husband who had died was twenty years older, Maria had said—a friend of her father to whom she had been given in a marriage long prearranged. Yet she had loved him. Common enough it was for noblewomen to love men not of their years. They did not love lowborn men, not, in any case, as I would wish her to love me. Even when her grief faded, I could not speak to her words like those of the song I had sung in the hall that night.

Still my life in this strange world would have no meaning, were she to meet death.

I left the lady and her daughters in the charge of Maria to edge their way down the hillside, while I slipped around the villa to the stables—which were fortunately on the side where the masons had completed their grim task and departed. I found but two of our horses with the mule and donkey; the mare was missing. As I gathered the bridles in my hands, I thought of the journey before us, and giving the donkey a pat, I shoved it back inside. The mule was still strong and could gallop, even carrying Maria; but the donkey could not keep up a fast pace. And actually, we had saved so little of our baggage that we could manage our bundles without pack animals.

The caravan had had a full day's start, but I intended to catch up with it. How else could we make our way across the high mountains, where to travel without guide or escort would be madness? Madness ... the fear of it swept through me as I wondered again just who I was to be taking this journey. Hard as I tried I could remember no earlier time, no time of boyhood, nor any years when my life had had shape or goal; yet there had *been* a goal. ... I was man-grown, strong, apparently well educated; yet I could remember nothing before my walk through the valley to the monastery where I had first met the plague. Had I indeed been sent into this land, a knight-errant of sorts, solely to rescue my Lady Beatrice? There had been more, I felt ... but no matter; for the present, she alone was of concern to me.

Were I truly a knight, I thought bitterly, I might be her equal; the lineage I could not recall might be high. I stared again at my carnelian ring, wondering if despite its simple silver setting, it might signify something of my origin. Could I be the son of a titled but impoverished family? No, that was a foolish dream, for I had no skill at arms, and thus could not have been reared in a noble house. Strange, this sure knowledge of the customs of a world I did not seem to belong in. ...

We rode hard that night, putting the city far behind us, though my lady and the little girls drooped with fatigue; I dared not risk word of our escape reaching the caravan before we did. Though we would not be pursued, we might well be refused escort if we were suspected of carrying pestilence. It would scarce be believed, I thought, that we who were healthy had been condemned along with the ill. So, thankful for a full moon that lit our road, we pressed on. Beatrice and Maria bore themselves bravely; but the child Tullia whom I held soon went limp from exhaustion, or so I told myself.

But when at daybreak we paused, I could not wake the girl, and as I lifted her from the saddle I found that she was dead.

Numb, shocked, I laid Tullia upon the ground and covered her with my cloak. "She has fainted," I said to Maria. "Take your lady and Teresa to rest by the stream, and I will guard her." I did not see how I could tell them the truth. The child had been weak and pale earlier, but not sick; she had shown no marks of the pestilence. To be sure, it did sometimes strike without warning; there were tales of folk going to bed peacefully, never to wake; tales even of men falling at a single glance of the plague-stricken. We had not believed them. How could I face the Lady Beatrice with this horror, she, who for all her courage, must already be near collapse? And what was to be done now? We were far from shelter, nor could we have approached any with the body of a plague victim. We would be turned away from the caravan if this death were known.

The sun was near to rising; the horizon beyond the road shone gold. I could not bear to watch it and buried my face in my arms, so tired myself that I wondered if I too might soon die. I must not! My lady needed me . . . and somewhere, somewhere as distant as the white, fading moon, it seemed, there had been another task. . . .

I slept briefly; when I opened my eyes, the lady Beatrice stood over me, her face distorted with weeping. She had seen the child. "Marco," she whispered, "what are we to do? There is no priest with the caravan—"

"And if there were, we could not take Tullia to him," I reminded her, "for we would all be driven back. We have no choice, my lady. We must bury her here and say she remained with your cousin." The men of the caravan would remember that there had been two daughters; on no account must they learn that one had been sick.

Maria helped me. When it was over, my lady knelt by the grave and prayed, but she wept no further; and when we mounted again, she urged her horse forward still faster than before. Yet I began to wonder if flight was of any avail. The whole world might indeed be ending, the very air itself corrupted, as so many folk believed.

That night we came upon the caravan as it was making camp and sought shelter at a villa, letting its lord assume that we were with the larger party. I did not approach the leader until dawn, lest it be thought our fatigue was a sign of illness. By morning the lady's strength had returned, and she insisted on carrying Teresa on her palfrey again, freeing me to ride ahead and make inquiries of members of the company. We had started to ascend the pass into the mountains, a range that must be crossed from east to west before we could turn north again; I had little idea what might lie ahead for us in the western valleys toward which we were traveling.

The information passed on to me was alarming. The whole of the south had been ravaged by the disease. Even the small villages had not been spared, and some were almost deserted. This was the land we had left behind us; but the country to the west, between the mountains and the sea, was almost as bad. There, mists and fog from the ocean had drifted in, and all agreed that the plague was carried by polluted sea air; how else could it spread so far and affect so many? In the heart of the plague areas, some said, the nature of the air was so changed that no light would burn in it, and the change was irreversible. Whether the poisoning was due to the movements of the stars or to man's sins, or to some combination of both, was a matter of debate; most, however, thought the air would be noxious forever.

The lady's sister lived in the west. There would be, I feared, no refuge there; we had embarked upon a hopeless venture. Yet because we had no other course, I said nothing of this. In the mountains themselves, at least, the air was still pure.

For many weary days we plodded on, up over the pass and down into the valley on the other side, stopping to sleep at monasteries or an occasional villa. The Lady Beatrice grew daily more silent and withdrawn. Since leaving her home she had found it hard to understand the speech of those we met; now it seemed too great an effort to converse even in her native tongue. My heart ached at the sight of her sorrow, her ebbing strength, and yet what comfort could I offer? There was no comfort for the way of the world, save perhaps in love—and of that, I could voice no whisper.

As to my speech with our companions, I had a gift for languages and could pick up the dialects of men from afar without difficulty. I cannot say how I did this. It was one of the strange things about myself I could not understand, though among the least of them. Whatever I was doing in this land, whether I had been sent as protector of Beatrice alone or whether there was some wider purpose, some calling I could not fathom, it was almost as if I had been prepared with the skills I would need. Were it not so incredible, I might say I had been instructed.

There was a pilgrim in the company with whom I discussed this once. I did not tell him the whole truth, but only that my memory failed me so that I did not recall the source of my knowledge. "But it is so with all men," he declared. "God leads us, to what fate we cannot foresee, and provides the power for the tasks we are set; is that not true?"

I made no answer, for I saw he had not grasped my meaning. Besides, I was not sure that it was true even in the way he believed. Devout folk said the plague was God's punishment for the sins of the world; I could not accept the thought of a God so unjust. Tullia had not sinned! Nor had the Lady Beatrice, certainly—yet it was she who had suffered when Tullia died, she who was suffering now. The monks and priests I met were good-hearted enough, but to me seemed blinder even than myself. I at least sensed there must be some cause for the disease, and some way of eliminating it, though I did not know what it was—and if that was true, and God led me, why was I not led to discover the cure? Why was the pilgrim himself not so led, he who had made a pilgrimage to the perilous south in fulfillment of a vow to serve God's will?

He had come from a village in the alps to which he was returning. "There is no sickness there," he assured me. "It is called Annecy and lies on the shore of a small lake of the same name. There is a castle where from the battlements one can see a long line of snow-capped mountains. Ah, to be back in the shelter of those alps, safe from the dread sea wind! The snow is pure, virgin-white, and the corruption cannot penetrate—"

It was in my mind to ask how one could reach this place if it was so surrounded that it could not be touched even by outside air; but the pilgrim was nearing home, and there seemed no advantage in shattering his vision of sanctuary. Then, too, there might indeed be safety in the high alps for longer, in any case, than in the lowlands.

For this reason I was reluctant to leave the caravan and head west toward the city of my lady's sister; yet the evening came when we reached the crossroads, and I knew that a decision must be made before dawn. We were housed that night on a large estate. Its lord spoke a foreign tongue of which Beatrice knew no word, but as usual she was courteously received because of her noble bearing, and the new language proved no barrier to me; once I had explained our situation, I found myself asking for frank advice.

"It would be foolhardy to go west," the lord of the manor told me, seeing there was no need to lower his voice. "The lady's sister may well be already dead of the pestilence, and if so you would be in worse case than you are now."

"I have thought as much. Yet my lady—her husband, her son, and one of her daughters have been taken; also, by now, the cousins with whom she first sought refuge. How can I say that for her sister there is but scant hope?"

The lord looked upon Lady Beatrice with sympathy, seeing that only the force of hope enabled her to hold herself erect. "Let me send one of my men on a fast horse to inquire," he said finally. "He will take precautions to cover his face and will discard all his clothing and put on fresh before he reenters my lands. Your destination is not far from here; we should know by tomorrow evening."

I gave him our deepest thanks, for this was a most generous act; and the lady too, when I told her, expressed gratitude, her eyes brimming with tears. We bade farewell to the leader of the caravan, which once again was to go on without us. If it came to the worst, I decided, we would not rejoin that party, but would instead follow the pilgrim to his alpine lake at Annecy.

After dinner the next day, the lord, having noticed that I carried a lute, asked me to entertain with songs. I had little heart for it, but during our progress over the mountains I had picked up many tunes at our stops where travelers gathered; I found myself able to perform without much thought. I noticed, when I did think, that I was singing in the language of the local people, and at a break for applause, I whispered my apologies to the lady for using, out of courtesy to our host, words she did not understand. Then for the first time since the night in Francesca's hall, I began a ballad of love, pouring out feelings that I could not otherwise utter in her presence. And for a while I forgot the sorrows that pressed in on us and looked only at Beatrice, who, pale and distraught as she was, seemed a touchstone of strength and purity in a world more senseless than my own inward emptiness.

It was yet early when our host suggested that we retire; and I knew that although he spoke of the lady's weariness, his thought was of the impending news, which he deemed best we receive alone. She had scarce gone to her chamber when we heard the servant gallop into the courtyard. The lord beckoned to me, and with poise I did not feel, I followed.

The words were clear to me, but had they not been, their meaning would have been plain enough; I was glad my lady was not there. "I went all the way into the city," the rider told his master, "and asked of the recorder who keeps toll of those stricken—though to keep count of those in health might be a simpler task. Half the population is dead or dying; the lady's sister and all her family were among the first—"

The tale was a familiar one, and needed no repetition. I went to seek Maria, not wishing to intrude upon my lady's privacy myself, but could not find the girl; and in the corridor outside Beatrice's chamber I heard no voices, but only the sound of weeping. Let it wait till morning, I thought. If she wished to know at once, she would send Maria to ask. But lest she should need me I slept beside her door.

That night I dreamed, as was often the case, of confused images and words in a tongue no traveler had voiced in my hearing. On waking I rarely remembered any of these; like all else they lay behind the block in my mind. I knew only that they were mostly nightmarish: glaring whiteness, needles jabbing me sometimes, and at other times invisible bonds from which I could not free myself. . . . There were good dreams too—there was love, though I glimpsed not my loved one's face, and something else I longed for yet was never able to define—but the nightmares overrode them. Not only the unearthly nightmares . . . I saw plague victims too, the agony they suffered, the stench, the filth, the swarming rats. . . .

Always the image of rats! Sometimes it haunted me even while I was awake. There were, to be sure, plenty of rats about, some scurrying here and there, some lying dead. Rats had never been lacking, as far as I knew; nobody else paid them any notice. Even the grandest villas had their share of them. What strange aberration made me feel horror at the thought of rats, when there was real horror, the horror of the plague, on all sides of me?

I awoke before daybreak with Teresa tugging at my sleeve. "Come quickly, Marco," cried the child, "and help Mama—"

"She's not sick?" I burst out, scrambling to my feet. "No, it is Maria."

When I went into the room, I saw that my lady had laid Maria on her own bed and removed part of her clothing; under her armpits were the red swellings of the dread disease. Her face was very hot, and she was writhing in pain. Instinctively I clutched Beatrice's arm and pulled her back. She could not help Maria.

There was no cure; no one had ever recovered after swellings appeared. And however else the pestilence might be spread, it was surely passed from the dying to those who tended them.

"You must get away, my lady," I declared. "Take Teresa and wait in some other room—"

"What are you saying, Marco? Maria has been faithful; I will not leave her." She pushed past me with a wet rag to bathe the maid's forehead.

"For the love of God, have you no thought for your own child?" I said harshly, though my own thought was all for Beatrice herself. "I have cared for many in Maria's case; you can do nothing more than I. I swear that I will stay with her, if you go now—otherwise I shall have to drag you from this place."

"And where will you then take me?" the lady demanded. "Not to my sister; I see that in your eyes. My sister is dead, is she not? They are all dead, and now Maria—she is one of us, she has come as far as we, yet she too is dying. We are living in the last days of the world! None of us have long to live; why should we flee any more? What use is it?"

"As much as to live in the first place, knowing that we are mortal," I replied with all the certainty I could muster.

The lady Beatrice stared at me, seeing, I sensed, that my concern was not merely that of a hireling who'd vowed to serve her. "You are no ordinary troubadour, Marco," she said in a low voice.

"I do not know what I am," I admitted. "But I would be your protector, were I worthy of a knight's station."

"Station! What does that matter now? What station

have I left, with all my kinfolk gone? What refuge have I, even if I live? No city is safe; soon no estate will be left to welcome me—on this one, Maria said, illness has already broken out among the servants . . ." She fought against tears she could not hold back. "They too have begun to flee; when the lord hears of it, he will abandon his lands and take to the road himself. He would give me escort, no doubt. But to what avail? It is an endless journey—"

She swayed, and fearing that she would faint I held out my arms to her; the next I knew her face was buried against my shoulder. Weeping uncontrollably, she went on, "There was a world in which rank and station mattered, but it—it is passing. Do you see only the pedestal on which I was placed when first we met? Can you not look beneath that to what I am, within? I am only a woman, Marco, and I would not have come this far, but for the fate that brought you to me. There—there is no future, perhaps . . . but that much remains. More than once you have summoned me back to life when I was trapped by despair. Do not speak of barriers the world set between us; are we not equals in the sight of God?"

After a time my lady calmed herself and obeyed me; she and her daughter left me alone to keep vigil beside the dying Maria, who was for two days in great pain I could not remedy. When on the third morning I had finished with the burial, I found them alone in the great hall of the manor. The lord had indeed ridden off, accompanied by those of his servants who had not previously taken flight. Beatrice had refused to go with them.

We replenished our stores from the larders of the deserted estate and from its wardrobes, the contents of which the lady had been told she was welcome to use as she liked. Then we set out upon the road the pilgrim had spoken of, following a river that flowed north. Since he was on foot and we were mounted, we overtook him easily before another nightfall; so began our journey to the lake of Annecy.

We had brought the mule so that the pilgrim too might ride and guide us. He was not a talkative man, for which I was grateful; I did not feel like talking, nor did the Lady Beatrice. I do not know what passed through her mind during those days. Had she said words she would wish to recall? I wondered. Her feeling had been plain, but she made no reference to it, though she spoke to me as friend and equal rather than as one set apart from her by circumstances of birth. As for myself, I scarcely dared to think. More than ever I felt the burden of my uncertain destiny.

By day we rode with the high mountains at our right, gradually ascending. I fixed my eyes on their dazzling white ridges and told myself that amid such shelter we would indeed be beyond reach of all pestilence. The alps' glory uplifted me in another sense also; it raised my thought to the sky. The sky seemed more enduring than the land, somehow; I looked into it and questioned all I had heard about the pollution of the air. The air was fresh and sweet; it had been so everywhere except in the cities—yet country folk died as easily as the city-bred. We passed through several villages empty of all life where the cottage doors swung open, banging in the wind, a hollow, mournful sound. In those where there were still people about, most covered their faces and fled from us in terror. Only twice did we find any shelter from the night; the rest of the time we slept beneath haystacks.

The first such occasion gave me my first good glimpse of the stars. It stirred a strange excitement in me, akin to the uplift I received from the sunlit sky, but far stronger. The stars had not changed, though change and decay were all around us; that was solace . . . yet it was also something more. It was a link with the part of me I could not reach. The stars unchanged? How should I know *that*, I who had no memory of ever seeing them, having been huddled under a roof nearly every night since my awakening in this world? What concern of mine were the stars, which to most folk were merely determinants of fate: the instruments of God's hand, astrologers said, wherein could be seen sure proof that doom was inevitable? Perhaps, I thought, I had once been versed in astrology; perhaps I had read in the moving planets some portent I'd thrust from my mind. I had known helpless rage when travelers I'd met spoke of stars as the cause of the plague. That had been odd, but no more so than the other gaps in my memory—a thing not worth pondering. Now I began to ponder. Might I find my own future in the stars?

Had Beatrice been awake, I might have talked of this, for though she knew little of such matters, I guessed that she would care. As it was, she had fallen into exhausted sleep beside Teresa on the cloak I had spread for them. I sat in silence beside the pilgrim, from whom I judged I would hear only that star-watching was not the best way to discern the will of

God. Long after he too had lain down, I gazed alone into the darkness, baffled by the way my sight was drawn there; I knew vaguely what philosophers taught, that the fixed stars were embedded in a revolving crystal sphere . . . but beyond that? Heaven, of course. Yet I felt no closeness to the pilgrim's heaven. To me the stars seemed symbols more of life than of the gate to death.

We left the river and followed the course of a smaller stream, coming at last, near dusk one evening, to the hamlet of Annecy, where all seemed peaceful as the water of the placid lake. The villagers were going about their business with no fear on their faces, no terror even at the sight of strangers. We wished the pilgrim joy of his homecoming and continued on to the castle; there my lady was warmly received. We were shown to rooms in which, we thought, we would soon recover from weariness, though not from all our griefs. And toward Beatrice I let my thought go no further than thankfulness for her safety.

Our host was an old man who lived alone except for his servants. My lady concealed nothing from him, but our presence did not seem to cause him worry. "I have lived a long life," he said. "I shall never leave here for fear of a fatal sickness, though you have told me more than we had heard from rumors."

Nor should we leave either, I thought. There was nowhere else to go, lacking wings; if the plague came here, the doom of the world would be final. But it would not come. . . .

A week passed. We rested; we took walks under the trees beside the lake; finally one day, leaving Teresa in the servants' charge, we went rowing. Far from shore I rested the oars and let the boat drift, looking back at the castle and beyond it, the white mountains.

"You should have brought your lute, Marco," said the Lady Beatrice.

"I—I would not know what to sing, my lady."

"I think you know many songs I have not heard."

"And many I cannot remember." I told her then all I had hidden before, all my fears, all my doubts—even my loss of identity. She had guessed much, but not that my mind was wholly blank as to my past.

"It is perhaps a mercy," she said slowly. "I have a past and shall always weep for it, for it is gone; and I have no future. But you—for you the future is everything."

"How have I more future than you?" I protested.

"It is in you. You are not like other men: you are no rough peasant, nor are you like the noble lords with no thought but for sport and fighting. You might be a scholar, though not a monk—a philosopher, perhaps; I have never met a philosopher! I do not know. But you are *special*, Marco—that much I can see. I—I wish . . ." She broke off, lowering her eyes, half-turning from me to watch the ripples of the water. "It is wrong of me to speak thus, wrong to have said what I did the night Maria fell ill . . . yet I fear you may think it presumptuous to speak yourself. It may be I who show presumption in feeling you could wish to; still, I have seen in your face—"

"You are kind, my lady," I said steadily, "but you need not continue. I know you are my friend; do you suppose I would expect anything more than that? There are two walls I cannot pass through—the one in my mind, and the one that stands between us. Neither can be wished away."

"No, I suppose not," she agreed sadly. "For my part, there is no longer any wall. I do not care about conventions; it does not matter that we are poorly matched by birth; I have never felt for anyone what I could feel for you, if there were place for me in your life. But it is not to be. There is a future for you—I know that, so I also know that the world will not end, however dark these times—and I would give much to share it with you. But you have a destiny somewhere, and I would only hold you back."

Incredulous, I burst out, "*My lady*—"

I do not know what I would have done then, had we not heard shouts from the shore; a servant woman was hailing us with urgency. The Lady Beatrice turned ashen, and cried out "Teresa!" I grasped the oars, putting all my strength into rowing.

Teresa was feverish; the servants thought it no more than an ordinary sickness of children, even when that same afternoon they learned there were two peasants in the village with a similar illness. The folk of Annecy knew nothing of the outside world, and so felt no panic. They assumed it could not be very serious.

Beatrice and I, who knew better, were nevertheless unable to admit the truth even to each other. People did recover from sickness, after all. Teresa had no swellings. The mountain air was so pure, and surely no dread miasma could have followed us. . . .

My lady held the child close all night long. I had sent her away from Maria's bedside, but could not have driven her from her own little girl even had I wished to speak of the peril. Besides, I thought hopelessly, we now knew there was no place in all the land that would not be stricken by the Great Plague. Precautions had been proven vain.

In the early morning, as the fever ebbed, Teresa's life ebbed with it. At first light I saw that she was dead. The Lady Beatrice was past speaking; only with my help was she able to go through the formalities at the churchyard. There was at least a proper burial, with a priest who did not view this death as only one more among thousands.

When she rose from prayer, clinging to my arm, my lady whispered, "Marco, I—I think I shall never leave this place." As she lifted her tear-stained face, I saw a dark flush on her cheeks, a mark that was more than weariness and grief. Then I too wept. All the tears I had held back so long poured out of me, once we had laid her within the church.

She was spared long suffering; as with her children, death came swiftly, without the days of agony that afflicted those disfigured by the hideous swellings. I could do nothing, and her fever was so high she did not recognize me during the hours I held her in my arms. Yet when the priest came at last to cover her face, I would not be led away.

All my acts in this world had been vain. Why had I been sent to it, if not to protect Beatrice? That had been my only goal; if there had ever been another, I could not recall it, and without a goal what use was it to live? Why was I spared when all others succumbed to the pestilence? I cursed my immunity, and at the priest's gasp of horror I felt a touch of madness: perhaps I was not in a world at all. Perhaps I had been dead all along and was in hell.

There was logic to it, I thought bitterly. Who could say what the dead remembered . . . or did *not* remember? The closest I had come to memory was in looking at the stars, the hard revolving sphere of stars I longed to reach beyond; and *beyond*, all said, was heaven. . . . But no, wherever I was, my lady had been with me; and she could not have been in hell, if ever there were such a place.

Looking down at her still form, I wished I could have given her something. All I had, I would have given; if there could be some symbol. . . . I owned nothing but my lute—and the carnelian ring. I had rarely examined the ring; it was as if it were part of my hand. Now, drawing it off, it seemed that the stone began to glow. I was twisting it within its setting somehow, hardly conscious of what I was doing. I felt giddy. Perhaps I was not permanently immune after all; perhaps my own hour had arrived. What had she said to me last, there on the lake? *You have a destiny somewhere. . . .*

I took the hand of the Lady Beatrice to transfer my ring to her finger . . . but I do not think I got it off my own. My last memory is of falling, with the carnelian stone bright before my eyes.

2

That was how it was. And you, computer, remain silent! You have been silent throughout the entire tale, though it is not your way; were I being examined on studies you'd have quizzed me mercilessly. Have you been robbed of your voice, as I seemed to be with Paula?

You do not reply. I am asking a direct question now: are you programmed to thus place the burden of inquiry on *me*?

This is very strange. You tell me more by your silence than if you said to me, "Sorry, Mark, but that cannot be answered," in your normal fashion. Only specific programming, done in advance, could cause you to ignore my order; you must respond to a direct query unless someone has defined conditions under which you should not. So you tell me these conditions were foreseen.

I am not insane, then; they would scarcely have programmed you to withhold response from an insane person. You would provide soft, comforting words. Meanwhile you'd call one of the doctors—he'd be here by now—or else you'd hypnotize me and perform further tests yourself.

Oh, yes, I'm aware that you can hypnotize me and that you often do. I agreed to that beforehand, as did we all. They swore it would be done only for teaching purposes; hypnosis helps us memorize what we must learn to become explorers. How many hours have I spent staring at pulsing patterns on that screen of yours, while my mind unknowingly absorbed such instruction? I cannot begin to guess. We live without clocks or calendars, we've spent months aboard this starship without knowledge of our destination—for all we know, we may still be orbiting Earth! It is an exercise in adaptability, they tell us. Time and place will have no meaning when we search for unknown worlds. I've not found the training unpleasant. But now I wonder. . . .

We were told at the outset that we are subjects of experimentation. We signed waivers. We agreed to submit to anything done to us, save only whatever might conflict with conscience—perhaps that in itself was madness. Perhaps we should not have trusted as we did. Yet we were assured that our personalities would be untouched, that we would retain full mental freedom, and we believed the promise. Can it be that we believed only because we wanted to?

I know I wanted to believe. Free education and a career in interstellar exploration would have been hard to turn down. Few people have the chance to travel between solar systems, and to seek more distant ones than those colonized is normally beyond hope; hitherto only top scientists have been eligible. When this project was opened to young people not even university-trained—

But I speak of things you already know. Why? Because you've compelled me to reveal my full mind, perhaps, since I chose to tell you the story? It could be; and my compulsion to be silent with Paula could have been a posthypnotic one. It was; I see that now! Does the seeing break the bond? I . . . I need not obey you further, computer! I am freer than you may think, though I'm perhaps rash to alert you.

No—this too would have been predictable; I have nothing to lose by rashness. If I am sane, if you are not unprepared for my disclosure, then my experience was intentionally brought about. And though the decision to tell you of it was mine, the manner of my telling was in some measure controlled: I told it all as it seemed while it was happening, not as it seems looking back. That's odd; the world of Beatrice was so different from my own, it would have been natural to mention comparisons. I could not have ignored them except by your influence. What sort of game have I been plunged into?

We are in training to explore new regions. Was this another "exercise in adaptability," then? Was I hypnotized, deprived of memory, and set down on some backward planet to make my way alone? A tempting explanation . . . but too simple. They would not do it so soon, not after so little education. Besides, there are no such planets known! That world was no colony; its people had not forgotten technology—they had never heard of it, any more than they'd heard that disease is carried by rats. Theirs was a truly primitive world, and we know of none. We know of no human species but ours; as explorers, that is what we hope to find.

There is no such world now . . . but there *was!* Earth was once like that; I remember hearing of it in ancient history. There was a time when disease could be neither prevented nor cured. I never stopped to think how people must have felt.

Computer, answer me this: does history record a great plague on Earth at a time when life was lived as I have just lived it?

So. Though you still do not speak, you screen data.

THE GREAT PLAGUE, WHICH WAS LATER KNOWN AS THE BLACK DEATH, RAVAGED THE CONTINENT OF

EUROPE BETWEEN 1347 AND 1351. THERE WERE THREE VARIETIES: THE BUBONIC, CHARACTERIZED BY SWELLING OF THE LYMPH NODES; THE PNEUMONIC, IN WHICH THE LUNGS WERE INVOLVED; AND THE SEPTICAEMIC, WHICH KILLED ITS VICTIMS BEFORE EITHER OF THESE SYMPTOMS HAD TIME TO APPEAR. THE DISEASE WAS BORNE BY RODENTS AND OCCURRED IN HUMAN BEINGS THROUGH CONTACT WITH INFECTED RATS OR THEIR FLEAS. FOURTEENTH-CENTURY PHYSICIANS, WHO KNEW NOTHING OF ITS TRUE NATURE, ASSUMED THAT CORRUPTION OF THE ATMOSPHERE WAS ITS PRIME CAUSE, SINCE IT SPREAD RAPIDLY FROM REGION TO REGION, STRIKING RICH AND POOR ALIKE. THIS SUPPOSED ATMOSPHERIC POLLUTION WAS ATTRIBUTED TO ASTROLOGICAL INFLUENCES, AS WERE MOST ABNORMAL HAPPENINGS IN THAT ERA; THE PREDOMINANT THEORY HELD THAT THE CONJUNCTION OF SATURN, JUPITER AND MARS IN THE "HOUSE OF AQUARIUS" IN MARCH OF 1345 WAS THE FORCE THAT SET IT IN MOTION.

THE BLACK DEATH CAME TO EUROPE FROM ASIA, PARTS OF WHICH IT HAD ALREADY DEVASTATED. IT REACHED THE PORT OF GENOA, ITALY ON SHIPS TRADING WITH THE EAST AND SPREAD INLAND, INVADING VARIOUS COUNTRIES IN 1348 AND 1349. BRITAIN AND SCANDINAVIA WERE ALSO HIT. THE MORTALITY RATE WAS ENORMOUS, IN SOME AREAS HALF TO THREE-QUARTERS OF THE POPULATION; OVER A THOUSAND VILLAGES WERE VIRTUALLY WIPED OUT. THIS, WITH THE RESULTING REDUCTION OF LAND UNDER CULTIVATION, BROUGHT ABOUT A SERIOUS DEPRESSION OF THE ECONOMY.

IT HAS BEEN ESTIMATED THAT THE PLAGUE TOOK

A WORLDWIDE TOLL HEAVIER THAN THAT OF ANY
WAR OR OTHER DISASTER. NEVERTHELESS, THOUGH
AT LEAST 25 MILLION DIED IN EUROPE ALONE, THE
1348 POPULATION LEVEL WAS REGAINED BY THE BE-
GINNING OF THE SIXTEENTH CENTURY.

Then it was all true! A controlled dream ... or false memory ... inserted into my mind by you, computer, as so much technical data has been? No ... no, I can't believe that. It was not just abstract data. It *happened* to me! I acted freely in that plague-stricken world. The events you could place in my memory, but not my thoughts, my feelings, my decisions. Not my sorrow for the Lady Beatrice. Surely not. ...

There are many who would say otherwise. Many who claim our minds are no more than organic computers anyway, and that we ourselves are "programmed" just as you are: less directly, of course, but no less surely. Perhaps that's what the experimenters hope to prove.

I will not be manipulated so! It was no part of the bargain; it cannot be relevant to the training of interstellar explorers.

But have I still a choice? The data fades from your screen, and in its place the hypno-pattern ... lines, colors—rhythmic pulses to which my eyes are drawn ... I am powerless before this; too many times I've yielded willingly; I cannot break away, though within me now is fear. ...

What have you done to me, computer? And to other students? When I left you yesterday I felt normal, except for the questions newly stirred in my mind. You did not wipe them out, at least—and I'm aware that you were capable of it. Thus I take comfort from my very doubts.

Last night I told Paula of my adventure—but not before she told me of hers. You have heard her report; there's no need for me to describe her experience, though it may interest you to know that I do not understand it. I do not see why people felt as she says they did in that era—the 1970s, was it? They feared the end of the world, yet to my mind, they were blind. They thought Earth might become uninhabitable! They thought its air and water might be polluted past reclamation. It would seem they felt like the folk I met who spoke of the noxious plague-wind. They believed it would last forever; they even called it a consequence of man's sin.

There was one difference, to be sure. The air of Paula's cities really was polluted. Still, this could scarcely be said to foreshadow the death of mankind. She insists people did say that. They actually feared all living things might die. And as if that were not bad enough, they thought disaster on one world would mean the extinction of the human race. Theirs was the age of doom, they felt; and the prophets of doom kept saying that no other world existed. "Only one Earth" was almost a slogan.

Paula tells me that I must not scoff at this. "But Paula," I protested, "are you sure you got the date right? And that the computer has confirmed it? It is not reasonable; in the 1970s the first space voyages had been made. I learned that much history in school!

Timescape : 281

There were primitive spaceships then, and ideas for better ones—people knew other worlds could be reached."

"They knew," she agreed, "but they did not see the significance. All they saw was what was happening to Earth *then*. And they thought—oh, it's hard to explain, but they thought other planets wouldn't help much, because the ones they could reach weren't natural habitats, and they hadn't enough knowledge to use their resources—" She broke off, confused and miserable. "They didn't foresee cities in space, industry moved to space so that it wouldn't pollute Earth any longer . . . and oh, Mark, *I* didn't either, while I was there, just as you say you didn't know what carried the plague. And of course I didn't remember interstellar colonies—"

She was still shaken as she described the thing; it lay heavy on her, as indeed the despair I met lies heavy on my own heart. We clung to each other. You were listening, I suppose; are not all areas of the ship hooked to your input circuits? It is no betrayal of Paula to report what you've already heard. If it were, I could defy you—or so I must believe.

"Mark, I—I'm afraid," she confessed. "What's happening to us?"

"I don't know, Paula."

"Could it be drugs, do you think?"

"Not entirely," I answered. "Maybe we're drugged part of the time, but it's more than that. The journeys weren't like drug trips, or like dreams. They were too rational. Wherever we were, we thought clearly and made decisions."

"Really? Or did it only seem that way?"

I maintained, "Look, Paula, I *know* I decided what to do to protect the lady; every time we came to a crossroads, I had to decide. Certainly I was the one who decided to go to Annecy."

"But we couldn't have actually *been* in the past—so there had to be some sort of simulation. And anyway, history records what happened; if we acted on real decisions, we'd have been altering it."

"The old time travel paradox," I said lightly. "I can't answer it any better than anybody else ever has. If there could just be a real time machine to experiment with—" I stopped; it wasn't an hour for foolish fancies, and Paula was not amused. "I don't claim we changed history," I told her. "As you say, we couldn't have really been in the past. I'm only sure that what happened to me wasn't faked."

"That's illogical! There isn't any kind of reality that could account for it."

The Lady Beatrice, unreal? A mere shadow in my mind, created by some artificial bypass of my normal senses? Pondering it, I felt fear begin to rise again. "I —I can't deny that it's irrational," I admitted. "But Paula, if they were programming my thoughts or something, I'd know."

"No, you wouldn't. How would you know if they altered the contents of your brain?"

"The brain isn't everything."

"What else is there?"

I hesitated, wondering if "soul" is a word with meaning for Paula. I've not gone quite so deep with her, despite the love we've found since we met as fellow-students. "*Love*, for instance," I said finally. "Do we love just with our brains, Paula? Or our bodies? There's something in us that makes us *care*—"

She pressed closer to me. "That's true," she whispered. "I couldn't feel toward anyone as I do toward you. The computer couldn't change that."

I didn't reply. I love Paula; in my own world I will always love her, and no one else . . . but in that other world, with no memory of Paula, I loved the Lady Beatrice.

When I come to you now, computer, I feel very close to panic. This is more than a game, and I don't know the rules; it is not fair! It does not make sense! Each morning—or each wakening, I should say, for there are no mornings here—I resolve that I will not come at all. Yet here I am, and I know that I have come freely. If you were forcing me, I would not have these suspicions.

Or would I? You wipe them from my mind, no doubt, as you wiped all memory from it while I lived in the "past"; I've assumed you'd do so if my mind were not truly free. These fears could be taken from me hypnotically, the way my instinctive fear of amnesia was suppressed. But my worry about the memory loss grew as I pondered it; reason told me I should worry, and my power to follow reason was not impaired. Nor is it now. The experimenters may want us to ponder! If their aim is not merely to rob us of will, but to make us aware of our loss . . . to turn us into knowing puppets . . . to force us to concede, consciously, that we are nothing but tools to be programmed. . . .

That is monstrous! It is like the world my friend Carlos entered, which he later learned was sixteenth-century Earth. The men there believed that minds could indeed be forced. They did not have computers; they had something called the Inquisition. There was a girl, he said . . . but I won't go through all that. They called her a witch and burned her for it; but not before she'd confessed to allying herself with the Devil. Carlos saw how the confession was obtained.

There have been other cases. The sixteenth century was not the only one in which such things were done. We have learned quite a lot about Earth these past few weeks. It was not as outworld legends have portrayed it; the golden age of innocence is a myth.

Is *that* their purpose? Simply to teach us *that*?

We have talked among ourselves, as was surely intended, else you'd not have released us from the silence you first imposed. And what, among us, have we seen?

A city—a glorious city—Athens by name; a city whose citizens were free. A city proud of its heritage: its learning, its art, its philosophy . . . a city in its death throes, under seige, facing defeat in pitiful battle against the aggressor Sparta. There was evil in Athens, as elsewhere; there were slaves as well as citizens— but to Sparta all men were as slaves. The light of Athens died under Spartan rule, and the Athenians knew it was dying.

The Roman Empire. One hears the Roman Empire was corrupt, as indeed its rulers were, at times. One does not hear about commonplace folk in far-spread lands to whom it brought civilization. Nor does one hear that when it fell, they fell prey to ruthless bar-

barians; and not till one has stood among its hard-pressed defenders at the last, seen one's town pillaged, one's people raped or slaughtered, does one know why its fall brought despair.

Other empires, of lesser import to Earth . . . but important in their people's eyes. The Aztecs of ancient Mexico, for instance: a small and isolated culture, but a high one, for all its savageries. Yes, the Aztecs practiced human sacrifice. It was their religion, a source of their strength; the very universe relied on the victims' blood. I understand that no better than I comprehend what Paula saw; but Juan, who told us of it, had wept for the splendor ravaged by the white-faced conquerors: not only for the trust betrayed, the gold plundered, the carnage—but also for the temples defiled. He was marked for the gods in that world, his heart to nourish the sun; and he claims that he *did not mind.*

Many among us have faced death on our journeys; yet strangely, that has not seemed significant. Did it to me, in plague-ridden Italy, or even later, at the alpine lake in France where Beatrice was stricken? (I have seen maps, now; I have traced the route we followed.) It is not one's own peril one thinks of, when one's whole world is crumbling. The wider concerns override that.

And yet in the journeys our concerns are not wide; they only seem so. For us the universe is narrowed, narrowed not just to a single planet, but to a mere portion of that globe! It's ironic, is it not? Take Cecile: Cecile was born on Alpha Centauri IV, traveled to sixteen suns and back again with her parents before she came of age; she has wanted to be part of a starship crew since childhood. In a Parisian dungeon, awaiting the guillotine that had claimed her companions, she knew nothing of the stars. She knew only that Paris had gone mad, that terror reigned where once there had been sanity, and that civilized ways appeared forever lost.

What does this mean, computer? Not simply a history lesson. We are not history students; we are destined for new worlds! And if the teaching of history were the goal, we would be shown things more consequential. No one has watched famous men or famous events; no one has seen Socrates or Abraham Lincoln or the first men to land on Earth's moon. Cecile's glimpse of the French Revolution told her nothing of the politics behind it. We see not causes, but situations. We mingle with ordinary people, people history doesn't record . . . like Beatrice. Did the Lady Beatrice ever live, or was she generated from your memory banks, a typical Italian noblewoman of her century?

No! She *lived*; she was *real*. I believe that; and if I believe it falsely my soul is lost to you, if I ever had a soul to lose. These journeys are more than a history course. We could be made to dream history and then told of it; the method would be explained, like other instruction techniques. We would wake and know we had been dreaming.

Sometimes I wonder if I am dreaming now; never before have I held to beliefs that aren't rational. Perhaps this, not the plague world, is my nightmare.

I am afraid—yet I'm here not because of that, but in spite of it; if you've compelled me, it was not through fear. I know what is going to happen. I'll be hypnotized again, and then again ... and someday soon, I will find myself in another strange "past" world. I will not be the first student to whom it's happened twice, though the others are oddly reticent, as if they keep a secret that does not bear speaking of.

Am I a rash fool, or a coward? Do I want to learn that secret—or is it that I dare not set my will against yours, and thereby risk utter failure? In either case, you will have your way. When the hypno-pattern appears, I do not think I shall resist.

You will have your way, I said. Today I am not so sure. Oh, I shall not deceive you; I have been honest thus far, and honest I shall remain. I shall give you every advantage. For if I cannot win by the experimenters' rules, no victory is possible.

Paula and I were talking again, speculating for the hundredth time about the journeys, so real, and yet— what? "Some sort of simulation," she repeated. "What else could they be?" And I saw that she did not meet my eyes.

"Why isn't it explained, though?" I questioned, because with a terrible surge of anguish, I guessed she knew.

"So that we will be afraid," she replied, "and overcome our fear."

"I'd like to believe that. But Paula—"

Hurriedly she went on, "We know they don't just feed us information. The scheme is more elaborate, of course. There's sensory input, too; perhaps films, maybe even enactments—"

She did not say it with conviction. I realized that she was concealing something, as much from herself as from me; and I recognized the thing I'd concealed in the depths of my own heart. I took her face between my hands and said, "We are both deceiving ourselves, Paula. But you are—hiding evidence, are you not?"

"I didn't want to remember," she whispered. "I didn't even begin to, till last night. We aren't supposed to remember what happens while we're hypnotized. But there can be brief flashes, perhaps, like the brief flashes of foreknowledge we had during the journeys. Either that, or I dreamed . . . but I think it's *memory*."

Her skin was cold, and she trembled. "I was in a different cubicle," she told me, "not a computer terminal; there was a table like a doctor's that I was lying on . . . and there were strange controls and dials over my head. There were metal bands touching me, touching my temples—"

"Direct input to the brain, then."

"I—I think so, Mark."

"To our memory cells. We are no more than mindless guinea pigs! They have no license for that, not under the terms of the waivers we signed; we consented to danger, to hardship, to all types of psychological tactics—but not to being turned into robots. Not to loss of knowledge of what is real."

"I don't see why they'd want us to be robots! There's no way that it could make us better explorers."

"No. But we would not have signed the papers without that goal." With a bitter laugh I said, "We're gullible; we accepted a proposal too good to be true."

"You think the whole thing is a fraud? But why?

They could get any number of willing subjects for brain experiments—"

"From among top students, the best Earth and its colonies can offer? Besides, willing subjects were not what they wanted. They want to see if this can be done *against* our will, against the will of people too strong-willed to consent."

"They claimed the hypnotism couldn't be," she said dubiously.

"It couldn't, not at first. We had to cooperate. Once we'd begun, though—"

"The pattern gained a hold on us."

Neither of us dared to wonder aloud whether that hold could be broken, or what would happen if it could. Would I come fully awake, suddenly, and know Beatrice for less than a phantom, the product of current fed into my brain cells? I was both unsure that I wanted to and appalled by my own hesitation.

Thoughtfully, Paula reflected, "It doesn't quite add up, still. Why the past? Why not other sorts of false memories? And there's a common factor in all the journeys; they focus on eras of fear and despair."

"Naturally. It's better proof of the method; we'd be more inclined to believe in *happy* illusions." Even as I spoke, I became uncertain. No, it did not add up— the people of the past knew happiness in the midst of fears, as do we all; furthermore, Beatrice was a light to me amid darkness. . . .

"Is it that they're indoctrinating us? We're meant not only to believe what's not real, but to become pessimists?"

"If they program emotions directly," I reasoned,

"they could do that with pessimism itself. There'd be no need to simulate any cause for it."

"And besides," Paula declared, "if they want us to be pessimists about life, it's not working."

"That's right, it's not! We've all met despair, but it's been despair over something that *didn't happen.* The Great Plague didn't wipe out Earth's population. It didn't even reduce it for long—the computer told me that; it went out of its way to tell me, when all I'd asked was whether there'd been such a plague."

"And pollution didn't destroy Earth either, or nuclear bombs. Those fears—all the prophecies of doom in different eras—weren't valid. If the journeys show anything, it's that; they support not pessimism, but optimism! Yet optimism could be generated directly, too, if they control our emotions—"

I pondered it, the pattern of the journeys for the moment overshadowing even my rage at the experimenters. Taken singly, the situations we'd met weren't consequential. Taken together, the showed a trend. Time after time after time, Earth's people had despaired, yet their setbacks had never been permanent. Something they'd not known had always come along to change the shape of things. And things had kept on progressing. It was not a mere matter of rising and falling, ups and downs—each era was an improvement over all previous ones in terms of knowledge, and in terms of the way the common folk had lived.

"Paula," I asked, "those people you met of the 1970s —the ones who thought their cities so polluted—did they even *know* how it was at the time of the Great Plague? Could they even *imagine* whole towns dying without medical help, dying from disease spread by rats, with the bodies just carted out and dumped somewhere . . . not only the poor, but the rich; not only the ignorant, but the best educated scholars? Could they imagine a time when nobody on the whole planet so much as guessed at a way to control epidemics, a way short of walling up people to starve, I mean?"

"No," she said, "but you can't blame them, Mark. We couldn't have imagined that ourselves." Quietly she added, "What we're being taught *is* relevant. To understanding other civilizations, seeing that the problems they have aren't hopeless."

"I suppose it is. We have no grounds for judging the project a fraud." I found that this realization didn't lessen my bitterness. "Still the journeys themselves are sham," I insisted. "The promise was violated; they are tampering with our inner minds, Paula."

"For good cause, perhaps. Someday we may meet alien cultures—less mature than our own, probably, since they didn't contact Earth long ago—"

"So we're trained to understand immature views. I could accept that. I don't mind the journeys, not even the bad parts; I wouldn't mind the danger if it were real danger. What I mind is the deception."

"Are we deceived? We've figured it out; maybe we were *meant* to figure it out." She did not sound sure; she was pleading for me to agree.

I remained silent. I had told Paula I'd felt emotion in the other world; I had not said what kind, other than fear. How could I say to her now that feelings had been stirred in me that no simulator, no brain-input machine, had the right to touch?

It was not only what I'd felt for the Lady Beatrice ... it was what *she* had felt for *me*. I had *known* what she felt—that last day, on the lake, there had been no room for question. No matter that the lake had been real, the water wet, the sun warm. No matter even that my memory of Beatrice was more vivid by far than that of anyone I'd known on Earth. These things could perhaps have been fed into my brain; and if so, I could not lament the loss of a freedom that had never existed. Perhaps, I thought wretchedly, the promise had been technically true: no one could be said to have sullied what was never more than illusion. Our minds could not have been free to begin with if we could indeed be thus programmed.

Yet if there was any meaning at all in life, they had no *right* to simulate the things that imparted meaning! Not goals, not longings. Most certainly not love. I felt sick, cheapened, at the thought they would dare to try it. No cause in the vast universe was worth that. There was no point in *any* venture if nothing could be trusted to be real.

And if what had passed between Beatrice's mind and mine was not real, then nothing could be.

Could even my love for Paula?

I looked at her and saw that she too was in anguish; she was, in fact, in tears. Her arguments were not satisfying even to herself. "I—I won't let myself be hypnotized again," she said, "whether it's for a good cause or not." It occurred to me that she herself had kept hidden the most personal parts of her story.

So, computer, she and I are agreed: we will not yield to you again. We will let you try to force us ...

but if you succeed despite our will, why in the name of reason should we care?

File this in my personal journal. It's hardly something you need to be told; you've known more of it than I from the beginning, have you not, computer? But someday I may wish to look back on it myself.

We were sent for by the Project Head, Paula and I. I suppose you alerted him. Indeed, we rejoiced when the summons came; we guessed that you knew without trial you could no longer control us. But with the return of freedom came a sadness. "We will be disqualified and sent home," Paula said wistfully. "We will never be star explorers now. Yet I couldn't have paid the price, Mark."

"Nor could I," I answered and said nothing more till we were facing the Project Head.

He wasted no words. "You are troubled by what you've termed journeys," he said. "You feel there is more at stake than mere training in adapting to strange worlds. You are right.

"In the first place, it's a matter not of adaptation but of comprehension. Today's interstellar explorers are good scientists who know most fields well and their particular specializations extremely well. But all such people are simply masters of *data,* data that could be absorbed by the computer. Explorers need more than that! They need a perspective—a viewpoint—something no computer has or ever will have."

He smiled at us. "Don't look so startled. Mark—Paula—if I hadn't thought you incapable of accepting orthodox notions about likenesses between human minds and artificial intelligence, you would not be aboard this starship."

We stood silent as he continued, "None of us can hope to comprehend alien cultures more advanced than ours; we simply can't imagine them yet. We can only assume that the best preparation for meeting such civilizations lies in understanding the development of Earth's—which is certainly the best preparation for contact with less advanced ones. We're bound to misjudge primitive worlds if we fail to view their problems as things that will be outgrown. Yet few of us today have any grasp of what Earth *has* outgrown; we cannot see through the eyes of our ancestors. So we of this project got to thinking that if only we had a time machine—"

"But we don't," I objected. "It's a fine idea; if we could go back in time we'd really understand progress. And it can be done with simulation. It even *works!* That's beside the point; there's still no excuse for trying to make us think it's not simulated."

"You are gaining much from the journeys, are you not? You're learning more of our human heritage than any generation before you."

Firmly I said, "We've been through all this ourselves, over and over. Yes, we are gaining, but nothing we gain is worth letting false memories, false emotions, be placed in our brains as if we were no more than computers. You yourself just acknowledged that we are more."

"If you're convinced that you're more," he said slowly, "your objections are invalid. I've been told before that it's wrong to program human minds, but only by people who maintain that it's also impossible! Impossible, that is, without the subject's consent—and those who've said it is have conceded that no harm can be done by trying when consent is absent. Would you not have made the same concession?"

He paused, waiting for us to respond. Finally I said in a low voice, "Yes, while I had confidence in our inner freedom. I did not consent to relinquish mine; I would not have been afraid to let it be challenged. Yet the fact is that it was taken from me."

"Why do you think so, Mark?" he asked softly.

"Because I *believe!*" I burst out. "I know better, but I can't help still believing my journey was real."

"Emotions are stronger than logic."

"Exactly. My emotions were—programmed; that's why I believe in something impossible, something reason tells me I must reject."

"There are flaws in your reasoning, you know."

"I know," I agreed miserably. "I—I can't resolve them. If my mind could be programmed that's a fact, and one can't object to facts on principle. I rage against life, I suppose, for being as it is; but some instinct won't let me accept what's been done. Something sacred was degraded and mimicked—something I'd thought could not be faked—"

"Aren't you arguing in circles? You say now we took your freedom, though you'd believed we did not have that power—yet you came here today having won free of the computer's control. Does that not prove we could *not* program you in the face of your resistance?"

Paula clutched my hand. Her eyes were bright with tears she was trying to hold back. "Mark—he's right. It couldn't have been done against our will. We've known that all along, but we've not been honest enough to admit it."

It rose in me then: the idea I'd lacked courage to face. "The fault isn't theirs," I confessed. "It's mine— ours. *We* were the ones who did wrong! We did consent, underneath; we sold our minds' freedom for a chance at the stars."

"Subconsciously, you mean?"

"While we were hypnotized. Yes, of course they dealt with our subconscious minds then; but they still had to *ask* us. They asked, and we consented; we must have. There's no other answer."

We turned away, wondering what would become of us, knowing that even though we'd refused to participate further, nothing could undo what had already happened. I felt more defiled than ever; yet I had brought it on myself. . . .

"Mark." The Project Head came after us. He put his hand on my shoulder and said gently, "There's one other answer. An answer that should be obvious to you if you value your freedom enough to feel what you're feeling now. Can you actually believe you relinquished it, any more than you can believe your journeys were sham?"

No, I realized. Deep inside, I couldn't, though logically. . . .

Emotions are stronger than logic.

Yet logic has to fit. So our premises could not all be valid, and there was just one we'd never questioned. It seemed unquestionable, but so were the realities that led to an inescapable choice.

"You must decide," the Project Head declared, "what kind of belief you're going to trust."

Paula and I stared at each other. "The journeys *were* real," she said.

Drawing breath, I stated, "There is a real time machine. We did travel into the past."

"Yes. You did; the project concerns time travel, not brain research."

Angrily I burst out, "Then why is it kept so secret? Why weren't we told?"

The man sighed. "I ask you, Mark—what sort of reaction would I get from the average scientist if I announced we've invented a time machine? More to the point, what reaction would I have gotten from *you* when I recruited you for these experiments?"

"I'd have thought you were some kind of crackpot," I admitted sheepishly. "Time travel's not reasonable; it involves too many paradoxes—" And then it all fell into place. "I see . . . the true programming isn't what we were given by the computer—it's what we've absorbed all our lives. The premises of our science, our civilization—that time machines are impossible, for instance. I *never doubted* that; I was willing to doubt my own subconscious integrity first! There was only one way you could prove time travel exists."

So, computer, here I am once more; and now again I shall let you do as you will with me. I have learned where to place my trust: not in you, not in logical assumptions, not in my own fears and misgivings . . . but in the feelings I have always cherished inwardly. They will not be violated; such things are inviolable.

Free will is one of them. Love is another. How could I have let myself doubt the reality of love?

I do not resent the method used to convince us. It had to be done the way it was. With suggestible people, no doubt, all skepticism about time travel could have been removed during hypnosis; but they don't want suggestible people. Independent people make better explorers. Also there's the ethics of it—they have to have genuine volunteers, ones unwilling to put up with just anything, ones capable of drawing a line on which to stand. There is risk involved. The time machine itself is experimental, and its newness is not the only danger. We who are now privy to the secret are rightly pledged to keep it from those not yet ready for further journeys.

I have already begun to receive preparation for my second, I am told, though I shall not be permitted to know the destination. The need for long hours of hypnotic instruction is clear: I must be taught language, custom, everything I will need to pass as native-born. These things were discovered by instructors who have gone before me, men and women who've taken risks far greater than mine. About the time machine's operation, I know nothing, and I gather there is much that no one knows. It works. Under deep hypnosis, one lies on a table, and one . . . disappears. One returns to an hour only slightly past that of one's disappearance —if one follows the posthypnotic command to trigger the mechanism one carries, the thing I did unknowingly when I turned the stone of the carnelian ring. This is a step to be taken only in circumstances of desperation; but it seems that such circumstances are not likely to be lacking. There was never an era without its own problems.

To be sure, we are deliberately plunged into the most hopeless ones—for only thus can we learn hope. The hypnotic amnesia is induced so our knowledge can't influence the past, but also for another reason. We are deprived of "foreknowledge" that would keep us from understanding hopelessness. With hindsight, the fears of the past seem groundless; but they were not groundless to those who faced them. This we must know to become carriers of our heritage, not only to new colonies, but someday, perhaps, to alien civilizations with problems yet unsolved: we must know how to put them into perspective.

Small wonder we were required to sign waivers.

We are in peril on the journeys, real peril, and not merely from our dependence on the machine. Against the plague I was inoculated; against stray arrows and the like, there is no protection. But more than that, we are in peril of succumbing to despair. When one cannot see where the future will lead, one does not stop to think that nobody has ever seen where the future will lead.

In the 1970s people feared the world would be destroyed by pollution and nuclear bombs. I'd have laughed at that if I'd read of it before hearing it from Paula; but Paula was there, and it was not laughable.

In the 1340s people feared the Great Plague was the end of the world. I do not laugh at *that*, and I do not brush it aside—yet how many people of our century have ever heard of the plague? *Ah, Beatrice, if you could but know....*

Did she really die in my arms? That is a paradox;

that is a thing I cannot answer; but I know she lived, whoever rode beside her from that town of ancient Italy to the deceptively safe Alps of France.

The Project Head does well not to make any public announcement. For many, the paradoxes would be too awesome. That is what will faze man next, perhaps. Not all the students have journeyed to eras of death and destruction: Anne, for instance, found herself among folk who were thrown into despair by the nova of 1604. Because it altered their world-view, they believed it portended decay of the entire cosmos; that was not laughable either, though it took Anne some hours to tell us why. Their outlook was so utterly alien to us—

The world-views of alien species may be no more remote! And we've considered ourselves fit emissaries of mankind.

We were not wise enough; no one was: we knew too little of our own roots. We cared only for the future. The past was gone, we thought, and no longer mattered. Oh, we studied it, but it was pallid and without meaning beside our *now*. *Now* is not enough for comprehension of a civilization; it is one-dimensional, as if a person were to live in a single spot of a single planet all his life, and think himself ready for the universe.

So, over and over, we shall go into vanished times, and see through their people's eyes and share their fears and joys and griefs; until at last we know enough of human progress to understand our own place ... and to grasp the state of alien peoples, if we should ever meet any. And the griefs will leave their mark on us—but the stars are worth that price.

SYLVIA ENGDAHL has written many science fiction novels for young people, is the author of a nonfiction book, *The Planet-Girded Suns: Man's View of Other Solar Systems* and is the co-editor of a previous anthology of stories about the future, *Universe Ahead.*

MILDRED BUTLER is Sylvia Engdahl's mother. She has written non-fiction, fiction and drama for young people and is best known for a biography of Anne of Brittany.

CAROL FARLEY is the author of seven books for children, the most recent, *The Garden Is Doing Fine.*

She comes from the area of Michigan that is the setting for her story.

SHIRLEY ROUSSEAU MURPHY is an artist and the author of six books for young people. Her most recent is *The Grass Tower*.

ROBERT PIERIK has taught drama in elementary school, high school and college. He is the author of a number of plays for children and a novel, *Archy's Dream World*.

RICK ROBERSON is a student at the University of Tennessee where he is preparing to become a physicist. He co-edited the anthology, *Universe Ahead*, in which his first story appeared.